"Daddy! So... called out.

Nash closed the door behind him and went into the den, where he and Lizzy watched the truck and trailer head down the drive. After parking, a woman stepped out, glanced toward the house, and ran both hands through her hair in a way that was all too familiar.

He closed his eyes as if it would block out the memories. Instead, it trapped them inside, where they fully awakened.

How could something that happened ten years ago get to him now? Jessica McCoy had been one of his students. And students left sometimes, although they usually gave at least a day's notice and a reason why. Especially the ones who were responsible adults within a few years of his age. Even more so, those he considered good friends. In every case, they'd at least say goodbye.

Make that, in every case except Jess's.

Dear Reader,

I suspect many of us have a special someone who "got away" but maintains permanent residence in our heart. In *The Cowboy's Rodeo Redemption*, the heroine does more than live in the hero's heart. She reappears on his doorstep after ten years.

For Nash, Jess didn't "get away." She abandoned their friendship before he could summon the courage to express his true feelings. Now, giving his twins a stable home is his top priority. By contrast, Jess wants her daughter to achieve the height of barrel-racing success—a dream that Jess herself gave up in favor of settling down. Only, she needs her former crush's help. When old and reignited feelings are revealed, they must decide whether to repeat history by hiding and running away...or embrace this opportunity.

In this third book in my Destiny Springs, Wyoming series, Nash and Jess receive a rare second chance to get it right.

I hope you enjoy their story, and that you have all the second chances in life that you want...and deserve!

Warmest wishes,

Susan Breeden

THE COWBOY'S RODEO REDEMPTION

SUSAN BREEDEN

HEARTWARMING

Harlequin
HEARTWARMING™

Recycling programs for this product may not exist in your area.

ISBN-13: 978-1-335-05135-6

The Cowboy's Rodeo Redemption

 Harlequin Enterprises ULC
22 Adelaide St. West, 41st Floor
Toronto, Ontario M5H 4E3, Canada
www.Harlequin.com

Printed in Lithuania

MIX
Paper | Supporting responsible forestry
FSC® C021394

Susan Breeden is a native Texan who currently lives in Houston, where she works as a technical writer/editor for the aerospace industry. In the wee hours of morning and again at night, you will find her playing matchmaker for the heroes and heroines in her novels. She also enjoys walks with her bossy German shepherd, decluttering and organizing her closet, and trying out new chili con queso recipes. For information on Susan's upcoming books, visit susanbreeden.com.

Books by Susan Breeden

Harlequin Heartwarming

Destiny Springs, Wyoming

The Bull Rider's Secret Son
Her Kind of Cowboy

Visit the Author Profile page at Harlequin.com for more titles.

For the Joneses.

CHAPTER ONE

NASH BUCHANAN SHOULD have been stressing out. But all those daisies made it impossible.

He stared at the whiteboard that was leaning against a wall in the breakfast nook. Its designated place. A few hours ago, he'd used the board to write out his daily to-do list—a ritual that was as much a part of his mornings as the two cups of black coffee from his favorite mug. But all that productive thinking had been literally erased. Now, the board was covered in hand-drawn flowers of various colors and sizes instead.

All was not lost. He was reasonably sure that he and his ranch hand, Parker Donnelly, had completed most of the tasks already. The rest, he'd figure out. He didn't even have to ask which of his twins had cultivated this garden.

"Elizabeth Anne? Can you come here for a minute, sweetheart?"

Never one to take a proper nap, Lizzy had been playing in the den while her sister slept in their bedroom. Nash took advantage of the time to catch up on paperwork in the adjacent study, within earshot, which had given his daughter ample opportunity to do her brand of damage.

Then again, both girls had been in and out of the kitchen throughout the morning, pretending to make breakfast on the toy kitchen set that he'd assembled and placed in a corner. He would reserve final judgment until he could ask the necessary questions.

The pattering of little feet paused at the entrance to the kitchen. The fact that Nash used Lizzy's full name rather than her nickname must have tipped her off that she'd crossed a line.

He lifted the board, swiveled and held it up for her to see.

The precious giggle that followed confirmed what he already knew. There was no better sound to Nash's ears, except it tended to let her get away with just about anything. But with school starting in less than a month, he needed to make sure any boundary issues were addressed. The first-grade teachers might not be so understanding about having their lessons erased from the chalkboard and flowers drawn in their place.

"Do you like it, Daddy? I drew it for you 'cause you're sad a lot."

Sad? Preoccupied, perhaps, but he understood why he'd come across that way. Trying to take care of his sprawling Wyoming Buck Stops Ranch with little to no help, and making it a home his children could grow up in and he could grow old in, did that to a person. Now that Parker had three solid months of experience on the ranch, Nash was beginning to feel much better. Although, in all fairness, Lizzy's random crops of hand-drawn daisies deserved some of the credit.

Finally, he had time to focus on being a daddy to his six-year-old twins, even if he couldn't fulfill the role of mommy, as well. The ladies in Destiny Springs were wonderful role models, if not steady or permanent ones. He'd given up on *steady* and *permanent* long ago.

Nash returned the board to its place, pulled out a chair for Lizzy and pointed for her to sit. After she settled in, he took a seat across from her.

"The flowers are beautiful, but do you remember what we talked about? How this is my chore board and it's important? That's why I bought you and Katherine Claire your own to draw on." Nash made it a point to use Kat's formal name, as well, if only to keep things as balanced and equal as possible. Whether that was a rule for raising twins, he wasn't sure, but it felt right in most cases.

Lizzy looked to her bare feet, which were swinging anxiously while dangling from the too-tall chair. "Kat drew on half of it."

Nash studied the board again. The girls were physically identical. Wispy blondish hair, jet-black lashes, soft brown eyes. But they differed in almost every other way, including artistically. Lizzy was creative, whereas Kat was analytical.

"Is that so? Which flowers are hers?" he asked,

giving Lizzy a chance to either take back the accusation or prove it.

She pointed to a couple of stick pony figures in the lower corner. He hadn't even noticed them. Definitely Kat's handiwork, but still…

"Half, huh?"

Lizzy neither denied nor confirmed. Although the little girl struggled with basic mathematical concepts, he was pretty sure she knew better in this instance.

"Stay right there." He stood, walked to the refrigerator and poured two glasses of milk, adding chocolate syrup to hers. After placing both on the table, he retrieved the last giant chocolate chip cookie, compliments of Becca Sayers at the Hideaway—Destiny Spring's local B and B. She'd brought over three yesterday as a bribe. Said she needed a favor. But two of the treats mysteriously disappeared within hours.

He sat back down. As predicted, Lizzy eyed the dessert.

"Want half?" he asked.

She nodded and sat up straighter.

He broke off a tiny piece, placed it on a napkin and slid it in front of her.

She looked crestfallen. And more than a little perturbed. Exactly the response he was going for.

"That's not half!" she said.

He took a big bite out of the cookie and pointed to the board again, hoping she'd get the point he was trying to make.

"But I like to draw more than Kat does."

Nash took an even bigger bite, taking extra time to chew and swallow. "And I like this cookie more than you do. Is there anything you want to clarify?"

Lizzy huffed and looked down. "Okay. She didn't draw *half*."

"And whose idea was it to erase the board and draw in the first place?" he asked.

"Mine. I s'pose."

Nash smiled, then broke off a bigger section from the part he had yet to bite into. He paused before relinquishing it and waited until she looked him in the eye.

"I appreciate you wanting to cheer me up," he said. "But next time, let's find a better place to plant your garden. Agreed?"

At that, Lizzy smiled and accepted the cookie. Hopefully, she accepted the lesson, as well. Time would tell.

While Lizzy proceeded to dip her cookie into her glass of chocolate milk and make an appropriate mess, he tiptoed down the hall. Kat's slow, deep breathing was noticeable beneath the thick pink blanket. That half of the twin equation had no problem with naps. Maybe because her Breyer horses were all lined up on her dresser as if protecting her in ways that her own daddy couldn't.

Which brought him back around to her horse stick figures on the whiteboard and reminded him of the most important bullet point of all. Not that he'd forgotten.

That favor Becca wanted? In Nash's opinion, it was worth more than three cookies. Although, in all honestly, he wouldn't have said no under any circumstances. Folks helped other folks in this close-knit community. One of Becca's guests was transporting a horse and needed a place to board it for two weeks. In fact, the woman should have already arrived, if his estimation was correct. Becca had texted about twenty minutes ago, indicating that the guest was on her way. What she hadn't told him was the woman's name.

At least he'd insisted on one condition: the guest had to take care of the feeding and exercising and grooming herself.

"Daddy! Somebody's here," Lizzy called out. Kat barely stirred.

Nash closed the door behind him and went into the den, where he and Lizzy watched the truck and trailer head down the drive. After parking, a woman stepped out, glanced toward the house and ran both hands through her hair in a way that was all too familiar.

He closed his eyes as if it would block out the memories. Instead, it trapped them inside, where they fully awakened.

How could something that happened ten years ago get to him now? Jessica McCoy had been one of his students. And students left sometimes, although they usually gave at least a day's notice and a reason why. Especially the ones who were responsible adults within a few years of his age. Even more so, those he also considered good friends. In every case, they'd at least say goodbye.

Make that, in every case except Jess's.

Then again, the most important women in his past had never bothered with such formalities. Why should she have been any different?

Nash opened his eyes and considered that perhaps he was wrong. Maybe this woman only resembled Jess from a distance, although eerily so. Same slender frame. Same porcelain skin. Same silky black hair, although it was cut closer to her shoulders instead of grazing her waist.

No. That was Jess, all right. Either that, or she had a twin he never knew about. And, at one time, he knew so much about her. Or so he thought.

At least he could take comfort in the fact that she was more than capable of caring for her horse, and he could stay out of it. When he'd first agreed to this, it crossed his mind that he may have to step in anyway, for the horse's sake.

He was tempted to go outside and help, but his feet felt as though they were nailed to the hardwood floor. Instead, he watched as she walked around to the horse trailer and conversed with its occupant.

"Is that my mommy?" Lizzy asked.

"No. I'm afraid not."

He should have been used to that question, but it tugged at his heart every time. His ex-wife abandoned them all when the twins were born. She'd come back around when they were toddlers, only to leave again. Without saying goodbye either time.

If she ever did return one day, to stay, he wouldn't let her back in.

"She's pretty," Lizzy said.

She sure is. Even more so than he remembered.

He placed a hand over his chest to calm what felt like a palpitation. It was just stress. Yet, it hadn't happened in years.

"Do me a favor, sweetheart. Go to your room and draw me some daisies. Lots of them," he managed to say, even though a quicksand feeling in his stomach tried to tug the words back inside.

"Are you gonna give 'em to the lady?"

It was a logical assumption, but not a chance. They were for him.

"Maybe if you draw enough to share half, I will. Now scoot!" He pivoted her toward the hallway, then gave her a kiss on the back of the head and a loving shove.

Just in time. Jess was making her way up the steps but paused at the door. He was pretty sure she couldn't have seen them watching from the window, so he wasn't in a rush to answer it.

She lingered for quite a while, as well. He could safely assume why. As with Lizzy pausing at the kitchen door, Jess had to have known what she'd done. She could have returned his call with some sort of explanation. At least he'd been able to get ahold of her folks to confirm that she was all right.

Once she knocked, he paused for a few moments before answering, still unsure of what to say. One thing was for certain: maybe Buck Stops was open to board a visitor's horse for a couple of weeks.

But his heart was closed for business.

WHEN THE DOOR eased open and Nash leaned against the door frame, Jess's breath caught in her throat.

At least he didn't slam the door shut. Not that he would do something like that. Odd, but he didn't seem shocked to see her. Maybe Becca had told him her name, even though Jess had indicated she wanted to surprise Nash.

He didn't say a word, and he'd never been shy about speaking his mind. Yet, he didn't really have to. The way he cocked his head and blinked suggested he was waiting for a long-overdue explanation.

She couldn't explain it back then. How could she articulate it now? She never thought she'd land on his doorstep again. Otherwise, she would have made a more graceful exit. But how do you say goodbye to a man you're in love with but who's clearly in love with someone else? A smarter, prettier, more talented someone at that?

Easy. When you're Jessica McCoy, you don't say goodbye. You simply leave.

They stood in silence until she couldn't take it any longer. She stepped forward and embraced him. Even though they'd been in a student-teacher situation, they'd also become friends. Hugs had come naturally. This one, however, was anything but.

He tensed at first, then softened a little.

"It's good to see you again," Jess whispered, before taking a step back.

He didn't return the sentiment, and he'd barely returned the hug, yet his soft brown eyes suggested that perhaps he felt the same. Then, just as swiftly, he straightened his posture and looked past her.

"Becca tells me you need to board your horse for a couple of weeks."

Jess scraped her splattered ego off the ground after that obviously unwelcome display of affection, pulled her shoulders back and looked out to the trailer. "Two weeks. Then we'll head to Montana for the rodeo there in three. And it's Taylor's horse."

"Your husband?"

"Daughter. She's back at the Hideaway. Becca graciously agreed to babysit for me while I came over here."

"Your daughter is in good hands," Nash said without so much as looking at her.

"That's what I hear." His words further confirmed what Jess had already concluded. Even though she'd talked to Becca only a few times over the phone, they shared a mutual acquaintance who couldn't speak highly enough of the B and B and its sweet owner.

After several moments, they settled back into that place of silence. The whole thing was awkward, to say the least, which was the reason she hadn't wanted to bring Taylor with her. That would have really put Nash on the spot with what she was about to ask.

Her talented eight-year-old daughter had hit a plateau and needed help from the best barrel racing teacher Jess could think of. She wasn't going to let a little thing like her pride get in the way of giving Taylor the type of career Jess herself could have had.

Not that she'd trade having Taylor for anything, even with everything else it had entailed. Specifically, giving up that career to be a full-time stay-at-home mom and wife after taking what was supposed to be a brief sabbatical. Being anchored to one place, rather than traveling the country. Then giving *that* up to be a widow who was left without a financial safety net.

Maybe she would've seen it coming if she hadn't trusted a man who was less than transparent. Lesson learned…and ultimately rewarded, with Taylor picking up where her abandoned stirrups left off. And making a lasting impression in the rodeo world. *Their* world.

She couldn't undo her mistakes, but hopefully she could correct the one that was right in front of her. But that would have to wait anyway, because a sweet little voice called out from behind Nash.

"Daddy! Here's your flowers!" The beautiful little girl handed him a board with a colorful drawing, which made Nash himself blossom.

There's that smile I loved.

"So, you have a little one, too," Jess said.

Nash looked up as if he'd momentarily forgotten she was there. "Where are my manners? This is Elizabeth, but she goes by Lizzy these days."

Jess didn't even have to ask. Although Lizzy favored Nash, she was definitely Roxanne's little girl. Which meant that Nash had ended up marrying Jess's main competition after all.

Even though she shouldn't have been surprised, the gut punch caught her off guard. At the same time, she knew Roxanne was now married to someone else and continued to compete.

Speaking of manners, Nash had yet to ask her inside. But with Mischief waiting in the trailer, she didn't want to linger.

"Go wake up Kat, please. Then you two can come join us on the porch."

"Okay, Daddy," Lizzy said, disappearing down the hall.

Nash stepped outside and left the door cracked open behind him.

"Is Kat your wife?" she asked.

"Daughter. Lizzy's twin. Double trouble, but the good kind."

Raising even one child alone was a challenge—albeit also the good kind. But two? Then again, she simply assumed he was raising them by himself. She could be very wrong. Part of her was aching to ask. He wasn't wearing a ring, and she always figured him for the ring-wearing kind of man. Traditional and loyal.

"And double fun, too, I imagine," she said.

That didn't earn her the warm smile she'd hoped for. More of a slow nod.

"Tell me about the horse," he said, switching the topic again as if Jess was getting too personal. That was fine, because she needed to keep her focus on the reason why she was there in the first place.

"Mischief is a quarter horse. Eight years old, like Taylor, and he's her secret weapon in barrel racing. She's been called The One to Watch. Maybe you've heard of her? Taylor Simms?"

"Simms, did you say?"

"Taylor wanted to keep her daddy's last name after he died. I get it. I changed mine back to McCoy."

Jess wanted to add that she felt it impossible to move forward with the life she and Taylor envisioned without changing hers back. But it didn't feel like the appropriate time for that kind of disclosure.

Nash's eyes softened. "I had no idea. I'm sorry for your loss."

She simply nodded. She hadn't meant to even say that much. Time to get the conversation back on track.

"We're doing good, though. Especially Taylor with her barrel racing. She could be even better. You know how stiff the competition is."

Nash blew out a long breath, then straightened his shoulders and looked straight ahead again. "I exited those circles several years ago, and I don't keep up. No desire to get back into it, either. Don't have the time."

Jess gulped. Had this trip been for nothing? "You don't teach anymore?"

"No, ma'am."

There was a resoluteness to his answer. A "this topic is closed" quality about it. Furthermore, their lives had drifted further apart than she'd ever imagined they'd be. That's what ten years could do. Prior to that, they'd had a strong connection. The rodeo was his world.

And he'd been more open back then. No emotional walls like the one she was slamming into today.

The door opened, and the twins joined them outside. Both wearing matching rubber boots but otherwise dressed quite differently. Lizzy was in the same flowered long-sleeved dress as she'd been a few moments ago. Her twin sported tan breeches and a pink puffer jacket. At least their daddy would be able to tell them apart.

"Lizzy and Kat, this is Jess. She'll be keeping her horse on our property for a couple of weeks," Nash said.

Kat looked up at her. "I like the horses more than I like the cows."

"That's an understatement," Nash said. "Let's get Mischief situated, shall we, ladies? Jess, follow that dirt road. We'll meet you there." He pointed to a path that led to the stables in the distance, even though he hadn't needed to. She remembered.

Jess drove solo while the Buchanan clan walked,

with Nash anchored by a twin on each side. All holding hands.

Once they got Mischief situated in his temporary digs, Nash insisted on giving Jess a tour of the property, even though once again, she didn't need one. Not much about it had changed except the arena was so stark. No barrels. Not even any circular scars in the dirt to indicate they'd ever been there.

His horses were out in the field, lingering by a fence. Probably curious about their new stablemate. The girls ran over to pet them while Nash watched the goings-on with that warm, familiar smile again. All of a sudden, it seemed as though no time had passed.

"What did the bartender say to the horse when he sat down at the bar?" Jess asked.

Nash cast her a questioning look. "I have no idea."

"Why the long face?" she answered.

Nash shook his head and laughed under his breath. She waited for him to tell the next joke, like they used to do during their weekly training sessions. Rule was, the one who dropped the thread had to make Juicy Lucy burgers after practice.

He seemed to think about it as he watched his daughters in the distance, but no joke was forthcoming. Perhaps he'd forgotten about the ritual altogether.

"I have a favor to ask, Nash." Might as well come

right out and say it before they got bogged down in an awkward silence again.

At that, he looked at her. "I thought boarding Mischief was the favor."

Nash's response was so swift and pragmatic, it took her breath away.

"One of them, yes. But I also wanted to ask if you could help Taylor. She's hitting a wall, and I suspect she can do more. I'll pay you for however many sessions it takes."

Once again, he looked away. "Sorry, Jess. I don't teach anymore."

"I know. You did say that. I guess I was hoping you would consider making an exception. For an old friend."

She inwardly winced at the last half because it wouldn't add any points in her favor. In fact, a joke even formulated in her mind. *You may be old, but you're no friend...*

But their friendship had meant something to him at one time, hadn't it?

He put his hands on his hips and surveyed his property while seeming to contemplate it. In the distance, a man was exiting the greenhouse. Nash waved, and the man waved back.

"Friends don't usually up and leave without saying a word, do they?" Nash looked straight into her eyes this time, then added a half smile to apparently soften the accusation. Then again, someone had to say it. In that moment, she realized that maybe he hadn't simply been disappointed professionally and as a friend. She'd hurt him on a deeper level.

But that couldn't be. He'd never so much as hinted at such feelings, and she'd been on the lookout for them.

"I halfway agree," she said. "A good friend wouldn't do such a thing. But a bad friend obviously did. And that friend is truly sorry."

That earned her an accepting nod. She'd take anything she could get.

"Truth is, I'll do anything for my daughter. That includes admitting I was wrong and begging for help from the best barrel racing teacher I've ever known. You'd do the same for Lizzy and Kat if you were in my shoes. I'm quite sure of it."

"Best, huh? What's the punch line?" he asked, pulling his hands from his pockets and folding his arms instead.

"It isn't a joke. But the punch line *could* be that you owe this bad friend a Juicy Lucy. Since I'm trying to be a better friend, I'll let it slide this time."

Attempting to joke around at such a serious, soul-bearing moment was a bold and presumptuous approach, but she wasn't getting through otherwise. Desperation was setting in.

"You've made a good argument, Ms. McCoy. But I don't want your money."

"Because a bad friend's cash is no good?"

Nash softly laughed. "Actually, you prepaid for a couple of lessons that you never got around to taking. But I'm afraid the statute of limitations for using those credits or collecting a refund has expired. I'm not saying that to be cruel. It was in the training contract."

She had to think about it, but he was right. She had bailed before taking the last three lessons. "You remember that?"

"I remember a lot of things."

Whatever that meant. There was lots to remember. Clearly, he wasn't going to elaborate. The old Nash would have.

Once again, that strange silence fell between them. In the background, the girls were arguing about something.

In that moment, she began remembering a lot of things, too. Clear signs. Like the admiring looks he'd give his now ex-wife. Or the way he'd allowed Roxanne to interrupt Jess's lesson time with a question or two. Not that Jess could blame any man for being distracted. In fashion terms, the future Mrs. Buchanan had been a ball gown, whereas Jess had been a gingham day dress.

Furthermore, she still was.

Now that she'd experienced a mental refresh and fast-forwarded to the present, it was her turn to look away.

"So you'll consider it?" she asked.

If he did, it certainly wasn't going to be as a favor. She'd been saving up for this. Sewing until her hands were chafed. Not only for Taylor, but for other mommies on the rodeo circuit.

"I insist on paying you," she said, hoping to prompt a commitment.

Nash pivoted and faced her.

"Okay. You can babysit the twins while I'm with Taylor. That's the only form of payment I'll accept. That said, I'll do an evaluation first. In a couple of hours, if that works for you. If I think I can help, we'll decide whether to proceed."

Not the answer she was expecting. She was counting on the extra hours she'd have with Taylor being gone to catch up on outfits that the ladies were expecting in Montana. Word of mouth had elevated her business. It could also bury it if she didn't deliver the goods. If she accepted Nash's offer, not only would she *not* get that work done, she'd need an extra pair of hands and eyes to watch two little girls instead of only one.

It was the worst form of payment he could ask for. Thoroughly inconvenient and stressful. Furthermore, she didn't have to think twice.

"You've got a deal, Mr. Buchanan."

CHAPTER TWO

TURNED OUT, erasing daisies was no easy task.

Not when his rambunctious little Lizzy had put so much love and effort into her bad decision to draw on his board instead of her own. But as difficult as it was for him to wipe the artwork clean, it was nothing compared to what he'd gotten himself into with Jess.

So much for extricating the rodeo from his life completely. After Jess had stopped taking lessons, she disappeared from the circuit. He never imagined she'd be back, full force, as a rodeo mom. She'd caught him totally off guard.

Offering to evaluate and possibly coach Taylor in exchange for Jess babysitting the twins seemed like a reasonable solution in the weakness of the moment. It wouldn't otherwise be possible for him to keep an eye on the girls. And taking Parker off ranch duties to babysit instead would be a business setback he couldn't afford.

Besides, he suspected this whole issue could be put to rest in one session, especially since Taylor was The One to Watch. If that was true, her skill set should be pure enough that any issue would be obvious. With awareness came correction, and she could practice on her own time, with Jess's help. Jess would have been The One to Watch herself, had she not quit. Problem solved.

Yet, even going through with one session would be enough to pique the twins' interest. They'd want to learn barrel racing, as well. Kat especially. They were like little sponges. And when that happened, he'd be forced to use the word that kept eluding him: *no.*

Like he'd said to Jess, rodeo events weren't feasible. Too much travel. What he didn't mention was money was painfully tight, and his only ranch hand was still as green as a head of lettuce. Then there was the bigger issue that was nobody's business: running into Roxanne and all the complications that would involve. His chest tightened at the thought of it.

Why get the twins started only to let them down? Not that he intended to lie about Taylor if they asked. He simply wasn't going to offer up any information.

Nash grabbed his cell phone and took a picture of Lizzy's handiwork so it wouldn't be entirely erased from his life. With a couple of long swipes using a hand towel, the landscape was wiped clean.

On a whim, he grabbed a black marker and belatedly wrote *NO* in the white space. Big letters in all caps. Couldn't hurt to practice for the next time someone wanted a favor he had no business granting.

"I haven't even asked yet," a man said, startling Nash. He looked behind him.

Parker.

"You scared me." The girls often snuck up on him, but their voices were sweet and soothing— even when they were arguing about something, as they were doing in the adjacent den. Nash would eventually acclimate to Parker's deep tone.

"Sorry about that. I finished weeding, but I might have accidentally destroyed a little of whatever it is you're growing," Parker said.

His ranch hand had come a long way, considering he brought zero hands-on experience with him. But he still had miles to go. Thankfully, Nash had narrowed the weed infestation down to one variety for Parker to tackle. Even gave him pictures to refer to.

"No worries. Today is the day for altered landscapes. What is it you wanted to ask?"

"Thought I'd check the board first, then find out which task you wanted to hand off. However…" Parker pointed to the unmistakable word.

Nash picked up the hand towel again and wiped the *NO* away. That said, there was something Parker could do that he wouldn't mess up. The man was a natural with kids, and the girls adored him.

"Do you mind watching the little angels for a short while? I need to take care of something in the arena."

"You know the answer to that. But I'll be happy to take care of the other issue for you instead. Real cowboys, like me, can handle anything you throw our way."

Nash knew the guy was only half joking. A few months ago, the cowboy in front of him sported button-downs and ties and didn't even know the purpose of a hoof pick. Made sense, though. What business consultant in a fancy high-rise office building in Chicago needed such a thing? The transformation had been fun to watch, but his skills had yet to catch up with his confidence. Furthermore, Parker knew it, which made it all the more fun to play along.

"Terrific. I need a cloverleaf in the arena," Nash said, adding a grin. It wasn't nearly enough direction.

Parker rested his hands on his hips. Nash waited for it.

"Why only one? Four leaves are considered good luck."

Once again, Parker didn't disappoint. Such banter had become their shtick. But the laughter was short-lived as he thought of the joke that Jess had told earlier. For a fleeting moment, it had felt as though she'd never left. Joke swaps had been *their* shtick, back in the day. But he wasn't about to let that start up again.

Nash straightened his shoulders and willed himself to return to the issue at hand.

"That's an excellent suggestion. I need all the

luck I can get. The girls are in the den. Don't mention the cloverleaf. I'll explain later." Nash grabbed his Stetson and headed out the back door.

The cool midmorning air felt refreshing. He took deep, cleansing breaths on the way to the shed that he used to store banished items.

Too bad he hadn't given the barrels away years ago when he'd first considered it. That would've provided a built-in excuse to not work with Taylor. Too late now.

Nash fished out his key ring from his jeans pocket and worked the key into the rusty lock until it gave way. With a determined yank, he opened the door. His breath caught in his throat when he spotted the fifty-five-gallon drums sitting in the far corner. They looked so…sad.

"You're back in business, girls, but don't get used to it," he said, remembering he used to think of the barrels as his children.

He cleared the path and retrieved them, one at a time. They each weighed about forty pounds— slightly less than one twin.

The rest was coming back to him, as well. The location of the score line to the first or second barrel, the ninety feet between them and the one hundred and five feet from those barrels to the third. He mentally calculated the stopping room needed and got to work.

Once done, he backed up to the fence and surveyed his work. A crisp breeze rushed over him, and it felt as though a new life had been breathed into this tired arena.

More like, the best—and worst—part of his old life.

Nash tried to shake off the feeling as he headed back to the house. The girls were snacking on peanut butter and banana slices and crackers that Parker must have fixed for them. He was busy filling in the board with a list of remaining chores and doing an admirable job of it.

"I have a nice surprise for you, girls," Nash said.

They looked up but kept eating.

"You're gonna be spending a few hours with Jess today at the Hideaway," he continued. "How does that sound?"

"The pretty lady?" Lizzy asked.

"That's the one."

Parker looked up. "Pretty, huh?"

Nash knew what his ranch hand was implying. The guy recently got hitched to the woman of his dreams and had even given up a six-figure career to muck stalls for Nash and make a life with her here. That was true love. Now, Parker and the rest of the town were itching to matchmake someone else.

Nash was tempted to tell them all to move along. Nothing to see here except a grizzled rancher who wanted nothing more than to take care of his little girls.

"Pretty is as pretty does," Nash said.

The twins nodded. He wasn't sure if that was still a saying, but it resonated. He'd fallen for another pretty face. The person behind it, however, turned out to be anything but.

He wasn't putting Jess in that category. Yet.

Truth was, he admired the lengths she was willing to go to for her daughter, and even her confidence for showing up after all these years. Furthermore, she was still a good, down-to-earth person overall. Otherwise, he wouldn't have agreed to this.

Didn't mean he was about to forget how it had ended before, or let it get to him when she left again. And she was going to leave. At that point, he'd give the barrels away completely.

He stepped over to the kitchen window and discreetly pulled the curtains closed. In retrospect, he should've waited to set them up. Reduce the possibility of the girls noticing and asking to try barrel racing, too. Then again, honesty was always the best policy. Maybe it would be the practice he needed in flexing his "no" muscle.

There was much comfort in that thought. Yet, it did nothing to persuade his heart, which was throwing a tantrum inside his rib cage. It didn't take long for Nash to admit to himself that it had nothing to do with the barrels.

And everything to do with Jess.

WAS IT TOO late to pack up and leave Destiny Springs?

That was Jess's first impulse after she got back to the Hideaway. Although even she—a card-holding confrontation avoider—wasn't going to act on it this time. She'd just taken a successful baby step in approaching Nash, which could have turned confrontational. She'd find some other way to resolve those restless, unresolved feelings she still had for him. The other challenge: taking care of his two precious little girls without getting equally attached.

Best thing to do in both cases, she swiftly decided, was to treat this situation for what it was: a business arrangement. A place where such emotions didn't belong, especially since Nash otherwise wanted no part of her and Taylor's world.

Jess got out of the truck, opened the cab and grabbed the handle of her so-called portable sewing machine case. It was an industrial model but worth its weight. She needed all the bells and whistles it offered.

Before she could so much as lift it off the truck floor, she heard the distinctive sound of boots drawing near.

"Let me help you with that, ma'am," the cowboy said, swooping in and taking over before she could answer.

Jess was starstruck. Never in a million years did she think that Cody Sayers, of all people, would be helping her with such a thing. As husband of the B and B's owner, he'd retired from professional bull riding not so long ago. But he would always be a legend in rodeo circles. She and Taylor had both been big fans. Now, Jess was an even bigger one.

"That's a kind offer. I'm in the Spandex Room," she said.

"I know. Your daughter has been making the rounds with Becca. Taylor's bragging about how her mom makes all her cool clothes."

Jess bit her lip to suppress a gigantic grin.

"Do you happen to make little boys' clothes, as well?" Cody asked. "My six-year-old son, Max, outgrows his as soon as his mom cuts off the tags. We have to drive about twenty miles to buy more."

Jess had never made little boys' clothes, although she was itching to try. But this was impossible timing for a new project, if he was even serious.

"I'd love to meet him," she said in lieu of committing.

"Oh, you will. Can't miss him. He's the little redheaded bundle of energy."

Said like a proud father. Even though his subsequent smile was infectious, Jess had to force one in return. When Taylor lost her daddy two years ago, something about her changed. How could it not? The typical growing pains for a young girl that age further compounded it. As a single mom, Jess did her best to fill the void left behind.

Once Cody had successfully lifted the sewing machine, she grabbed the bag of groceries she'd bought on her way back from Nash's. They needed to have something in the room to snack on. Not only for her and Taylor, but now for the twins.

Cody took the lead up the porch steps, nodding politely at the endless stream of guests exiting. Mostly women, but a couple of men sprinkled in.

It felt as though Jess and Cody were swimming against the tide.

"Is something going on that I should know about?" Jess asked.

Cody led them up the staircase to the second floor, taking the steps as if he were carrying a down-feather pillow rather than a thirty-pound contraption. "A group called the DEBBs are what's going on. They picked Destiny Springs this year for their annual retreat. You and your daughter got the Spandex Room. It was the only one available, and I apologize for it in advance. Becca thought an eighties-themed room was a good idea at the time. We're planning on redecorating it at some point."

Jess had to admit, the concept did seem odd. The bigger question was…

"Who are the DEBBs?"

Cody reached their room and knocked first. When no one answered, he unlocked it.

"To be honest, I can't remember what it stands for exactly. Engineering something or other. How about we set you up over there?" Cody pointed toward an empty desk.

"Perfect." She'd be able to spread out a little, with room left over for her notions.

He positioned the machine squarely in the center. "The plug is on the left. Can I do anything else for you?"

She thought about it. "As a matter of fact, I need some ideas for activities in the area that would interest a couple of six-year-old girls."

Jess never actually lived in Destiny Springs. She'd driven an hour each way from her parents' house in Sweetwater County to take lessons from Nash. But she'd worn blinders the whole time. So focused on barrel racing, and on Nash, that she never got fully acquainted with this town.

Cody's eyes widened. "Not to alarm you, but I've only seen Taylor around. Do you have another daughter or two I should be looking out for?"

Of course, he shouldn't have to look out for her daughter at all, but his concern was comforting. She was still processing the fact that she'd be wrangling twins for a few hours this afternoon. And if everything went as planned, she'd be doing it a few more times over the next two weeks.

"Not mine. Nash Buchanan's. We're doing a kid swap today for a few hours. Long story," she said.

Cody offered up a knowing smile. "Now, *that* sounds interesting. Nash, huh? Nice guy, by the way. Spoils those girls rotten. Pretty much spoils everyone he loves, come to think of it."

"I'll tell you all about it as soon as I find out how it ends," she said, doing her best to discourage any further conversation.

"I'll hold you to that promise. As far as activities, there's Sunrise Stables right down the road. Hailey Goodwin-Donnelly, the owner, offers pony rides and a goat petting zoo. The kids around here can't get enough of it. Not to mention, she's the best babysitter in town. Just ask the twins."

That was good to know, in case Jess got in a serious pinch. She could use some of the cash stash she'd saved up to pay Nash for lessons, now that she was babysitting instead.

"There's also Kavanaugh's Clothing and What-not and other shops in the square," Cody continued. "And a drugstore with a vintage soda fountain bar a few miles farther down. Georgina Goodwin, our part-time employee, can give you the specifics."

"Thank you. Terrific suggestions. I'll find out what the girls would prefer."

Taylor finally returned to the room, escorted by Becca, who collected a hug from the girl as if they'd known each other for years.

Becca turned to Jess. "If you ever need a second set of eyes, promise that you'll let me know. I'm always around."

"I promise," Jess said.

Becca turned to her husband and nodded toward the hallway before disappearing again.

"That's my cue to leave, ladies. Good luck in Montana, Taylor." Cody gave the girl a fist bump before making his exit.

Jess had been gone less than an hour, and Taylor had already made friends and told them all about her upcoming competition. Not that she minded sharing her daughter with others, but she could sure use a hug or fist bump, too. She took comfort in the fact that Taylor had bragged about her mom's sewing, assurance that she was still loved and appreciated, if not embraceable.

What Jess had in her favor was barrel racing.

Their mutual passion for the sport was like superglue, even though it sometimes seemed as though Taylor didn't really want to travel around the country to rodeos. Yet, when Jess had suggested that they take a year off from competing, Taylor was inconsolable. It was as if Jess couldn't say or do anything right at times.

Before she could initiate a conversation about their favorite subject and find out if it was one of those times, Cody reappeared in the doorway.

"Sorry to bother you. Nash is here with the girls," he said.

Jess thanked him and turned to Taylor. "Okay, my dear. Nash is going take you back to his ranch. You can call me at any point, but I will otherwise pick you up at five. I'm babysitting his girls while y'all are working."

Together, they headed downstairs. She spotted Nash and the twins in the parlor. Not hard to do since the downstairs was otherwise empty. Lizzy was running all over the place while her daddy admonished her to stay in the vicinity. By contrast, Kat sat quietly on the sofa, clinging to a Breyer horse.

Nash stood and removed his Stetson as Jess and Taylor approached. He still had that thick, slightly wavy brown hair that had always remained on the verge of needing a trim.

"Taylor, this is your coach. Nash," Jess said.

Nash extended his hand, and Taylor reciprocated.

"Nice to meet you, young lady. I've heard some wonderful things about you."

At that, Taylor beamed.

"What are you gonna coach her, Daddy?" Lizzy asked. The twins had both joined them at some point.

Instead of answering, Nash introduced their respective girls to each other, then shifted from one foot to the other as if uncomfortable about something. She could relate. This whole arrangement had caught her off guard, as well, even though they'd been the ones to negotiate it.

"Your daddy is gonna work with Taylor and her horse. You met Mischief, remember?" Jess directed the questions to the twins.

Lizzy nodded, but Kat kept staring at Taylor as if she wasn't sure what to make of this person who was temporarily replacing her in her daddy's life. How much had Nash told them, if anything? And how much should she say?

"Speaking of mischief, what kind of trouble do you and my girls plan on getting into this afternoon? Not that you've had a lot of time to think about it," Nash said.

"Cody had a few suggestions." *Or, I could let them watch television in the room while I sew.*

Nash leaned in. "Just don't let 'em out of your sight. One, in particular, goes looking for trouble."

No problem with that. She already felt a protective vibe when it came to these little girls. Besides, her sewing commitments felt like the least of her worries, as was the little troublemaker Nash was clearly referring to.

She didn't know Kat that well—more like, not at all—yet she seemed so serious. The familiarity tugged at Jess's heart. Taylor had turned serious at that age, but with an understandable reason.

Then again, maybe that was Kat's personality, but Jess was determined to get at least one smile out of her this afternoon.

"Ready to get started?" Nash asked Taylor, who nodded, turned and was halfway out the door before he finished the sentence.

"I'll take that as a yes," he said to Jess, sealing it with a wink.

Was that an accident? Didn't feel like one.

She gulped. His winks had always tended to do that to her, yet she knew not to read too much into them.

He put on his Stetson and tipped the brim. "Girls, give me a quick hug before I leave. And mind Jess while I'm gone."

The twins descended on him, with Lizzy hogging most of her daddy. He hugged them back with a vengeance, which only reminded her of the lukewarm embrace he'd shared with Jess earlier.

Kat reached up and slipped her little hand into Jess's, which made her totally melt. So much for thinking of this as a business arrangement.

As Nash stepped out the front door to catch up with Taylor, the DEBBs started pouring in. Jess nodded and smiled at a few.

One of the ladies paused, looked at Jess then down to Kat. "You and your daughter should join us in the barn. We're learning how to antique furniture!"

Jess didn't bother to correct her.

Another woman slowed down long enough to concur, then added, "We have lots of workshops lined up. Please, feel free to join us." With that, the ladies rejoined the flow until the area was once again empty and quiet.

"I don't know about you, Kat, but a goat petting zoo sounds like more fun. What do you think?"

The little girl nodded and offered up a modest closed-mouth smile, which suggested Jess was on the right track with the activity suggestion. That made two votes. Yet, she needed a consensus. That was when something beyond awful occurred to her.

She was missing a twin.

CHAPTER THREE

"IS THIS WHAT you're looking for?" Becca asked.

All the pent-up air exited Jess's lungs, and her stiff shoulders surrendered in glorious relief at the sight of Lizzy balanced on the woman's hip.

Her hand remained glued to Kat's. The little girl had been such a good sport. Poor thing, being dragged outside and even upstairs as Jess scoured the B and B for her sister. Jess released her death grip but kept Kat in her periphery.

"Where did you find her?" she asked.

"I didn't. She found Cody and me in the kitchen."

"I'm so sorry." Becca had already offered to be a second set of eyes for Taylor. How many eyes could one person spare?

"Don't blame yourself. Lizzy does this to everyone, don't you?" Becca said, directing the question to the little girl, who simply giggled as if it were all fun and games. "She never goes very far."

Easy for Becca to say.

Unifying their little tribe was now at the top of Jess's priority list, because her heart couldn't take another round. Neither could her agreement with

Nash. Misplacing one of his precious girls was likely a deal breaker. She was more determined than ever to find some activities that they would all enjoy. But first, she needed to lay down the law.

"Lizzy, do you remember what your dad asked of you before he left?"

The little girl stared instead of answering. Jess could practically read her mind. *You're not my mommy. You can't tell me what to do.* Or maybe that was just the way Jess felt about it. But there were certain lines that shouldn't be crossed when it came to reprimanding other people's children. At the same time, she needed to say something.

"Please ask before you go anywhere without me. Okay?" Jess continued.

When Lizzy still didn't answer, Becca set her down but kept hold of her hand. "Jess has a point. Next time, ask her before you go running off. Understood?"

The little girl seemed to give it some thought. "Okay." She wrapped her arms around Becca's legs. The woman gave her a big hug in return.

Seriously? Jess tried to figure out the magic word because Becca had pretty much echoed her plea. She had thought Kat would be the one who would require the most effort to communicate with. Clearly, she'd need to try harder with Lizzy.

"Okay, this is getting ridiculous. You and Cody keep bailing me out. I insist on doing you at least one favor."

As soon as she said it, the regret set in. Favors

were what got her into this predicament in the first place.

"The only favor we require is that you enjoy your stay. In fact, Cody has an idea for an activity you three ladies can do together. He and Georgina are putting on a fun cooking workshop tomorrow for the DEBBs. You and the girls could join in. There's room, and I'm sure the DEBBs wouldn't mind."

She didn't say it, but a couple of the women had already encouraged her to participate in their workshops. And she'd silently declined. If she could find any spare moments over the next two weeks, she'd need to sew, sew, sew. She wouldn't have the luxury of making new friends. Only new clothes.

Yet, the suggestion was not only brilliant, it felt right. Jess and her mom had so much fun together in the kitchen when she was growing up. The twins would hopefully be fully engaged. No temptation to run away. Of course, she'd have to be extra vigilant about keeping their little hands away from sharp knives and hot water and such. But with Cody and Georgina there, along with a room full of other adults, that should be easy enough.

"I wanna cook cupcakes!" Lizzy practically shrieked.

"Sugar pies," Kat countered.

That seemed to ignite a feud that threatened to escalate into a shouting match.

"Cupcakes," Lizzy insisted.

"Sugar pies."

"Ladies, let's try to—" Jess interjected.

"Cuuuupcaaaakes!"

How could a woman who had already survived the sixes with one daughter feel so helpless and ineffective?

"I'm so sorry. I'll sort this out," Jess said. "What does DEBBs stands for, by the way?"

"No apology necessary. DEBBs stands for Domestic Engineering Belles and Beaus, which is a fancy way of saying stay-at-home mommies and daddies."

That was *not* the kind of engineering Jess was expecting. All of a sudden, even one workshop felt like a bad idea. She'd gone to great lengths to avoid reminders of her previous lifestyle. Specifically, the warmth and security she'd felt when she'd been in that role, only to have it all ripped out from underneath her with the unexpected, sudden death of her husband.

Not that she dwelled on the past. If anything, she was always trying to outrun it. The thought of planting roots now felt like ropes around her ankles.

Perhaps those feelings would be manageable if her emotions hadn't been heightened after seeing Nash again. Followed by the drama of misplacing Lizzy.

After all this, Nash could still decide not to help Taylor after his evaluation today. Based on his initial reaction, it seemed highly unlikely that he'd go through with more sessions. For the first time since she'd concocted this whole plan to approach him, she was relieved that it might not go any further.

Ugh. Now she could add guilt to the thick batter of emotions. Shame on her for even thinking such a thing. Yet, she'd gotten herself in over her head, hadn't she? Double trouble.

And not the good kind.

NASH HAD BARELY blinked when Taylor went from being a restless eight-year-old girl who was toying with her colorful friendship bracelets on the way to his ranch, to a self-assured young woman who'd strapped on her helmet and started warming up.

Then it struck him: was this how fast it would happen with the twins? That they all of a sudden would no longer be his little girls?

All the more reason to wrap up this evaluation today. Get back to spending time with his own children, like he'd worked so hard to do.

From what he'd seen so far, Mischief was sound. As was Taylor's form. During her warm-up drills, she worked both sides of the horse without needing instruction. First, with a walk, then a long trot. Once into a slow lope, she set up the horse for his turns and to stretch his muscles. Perfect.

Nash walked around the outskirts of the arena, surveying her moves from several angles. Without thinking, he settled onto his old favorite teaching spot on the fence to observe. He'd tended to avoid that perch in favor of another stretch of fence after walking away from everything rodeo.

Taylor trotted over to him after finishing her warm-up drills, obviously looking for feedback or direction. He'd reserve that for after the important part.

"Whenever you're ready, go have some fun," he said, offering up a smile, because he seemed to be fresh out of them since they'd gotten back to his place.

It had the opposite effect. She dropped her chin. What was that all about? He could venture a guess. She wasn't a grown-up young lady after all, despite the obvious maturity for her age. She was still a child.

"Hey, Taylor. Before you strut your stuff, I have one question," he called out.

"Okay."

"What did the bartender say to the horse when it sat down in the bar?" As soon as he said it, he realized that perhaps a joke set in such an establishment wasn't the best choice for a young girl. Too late now.

"Why the long face?" Taylor forced a smile, then proceeded to her starting point.

Her mama had likely told her that joke already, which would get him off the hook should she repeat it. Her expression tickled his belly and made him laugh. Nothing forced about it.

But that feeling was short-lived when he realized that the joke was on him. As soon as she rounded the first barrel, he knew Jess hadn't been exaggerating. He believed that Taylor was very well The One to Watch, because Nash sure couldn't look away.

Not that he'd ever underestimate an eight-year-old, but this gal had a level of talent and potential he hadn't seen in a long time. If ever. Except perhaps...*Jess*.

The little cowgirl executed the cloverleaf a few more times with near perfection from what he could tell. Either that, or his coaching skills were as rusty as that old lock on the shed. Her turns were solid. Her seat was secure. And the pocket was appropriate on her turns.

Then, something about the way she raced toward the finish caused the muscles in his stomach to seize. Sure, that always happened during those last few seconds that could mean the difference between first place or no place. Just never to this degree.

In this case, Nash could chalk it up to the fact that those muscles hadn't been used in a while, because nothing Taylor was doing stood out as being wrong or problematic.

This would definitely be their only session, because he had nothing to offer as far as advice, aside from a few small adjustments that wouldn't add up to anything consequential. One in particular.

"Start with the left barrel this time. For grins," he said.

He halfway expected her to defend starting with the right one, but she followed his directive. She and Mischief were equally good on both sides, which wasn't unheard of.

"I'm afraid I can't help you," he said out loud, even though Taylor was too far away to hear.

"That's disappointing, because I came all this way," someone said from behind him.

Nash tensed, then turned around. That was the second time today someone had snuck up on him. This time, it was Parker's wife.

"Hope I didn't scare you. I've looked all around for my hubby but can't find him. Is that Kat?" Hailey asked as she hoisted herself up and settled in next to him on the fence railing.

Strange assumption. Kat was quite skilled for her age, but she'd never rounded barrels, thankfully.

"Nope. That's Taylor. My former student's daughter. They're staying at the Hideaway. I'm boarding her quarter horse for a couple of weeks."

"Huh. How old?" Hailey asked.

"The horse or the girl?"

"You're funny. The girl."

"Eight."

"No way. She's phenomenal," Hailey said as she toyed with her long ponytail.

Hailey would know. She had more experience with horses than Nash, and that was saying something. She'd been part of rodeo circles when she was younger. Everything from mutton busting to barrel racing to calf roping. Now, she literally forged new trails, and a few old ones, with her trail riding business at Sunrise Stables.

"Maybe a little too phenomenal. I'm at a loss on how I could coach her."

At that, Hailey looked squarely at him. "Did you

say what I thought you said? And is that a perk when someone boards their horse with you?"

"It's a long story," he said.

"The short version will do. Otherwise, I'll die of curiosity. I thought you were done with all that, even though you've never told me why, and I won't push."

Nash looked out at Taylor again, who was doing some looking out of her own. Specifically, at the Wyoming landscape. He wasn't sure where she and Jess were living at the moment, but it probably didn't have a view like his.

"I'm doing this as a favor. Jess is babysitting the twins in exchange." He looked to Hailey and waited for the inevitable comeback. That was as certain as death and taxes.

She simply raised a brow. "Uh-huh."

"What does that mean?"

"It means I bet that little girl's mom is really pretty."

"So?"

Hailey grinned and looked away. As if he wouldn't help anyone else in the same situation. Yet, would he? He'd been fiercely protective of his time—especially now that he had more of it to spend with Lizzy and Kat before they started school. That was, until Jess walked back into his life.

Speaking of which, she'd probably be heading back over with the twins soon.

Nash jumped down from his perch and made his

way over to Taylor, still unsure of how he intended to handle this.

"Good job. Let's untack Mischief and get him comfortable, then we'll go inside and I'll make some hot chocolate while we wait for your mom. How does that sound?"

"Do you have marshmallows?" she asked.

"Umm…is there such a thing as hot chocolate without 'em?" he asked.

She grinned enthusiastically. So all it took was marshmallows to turn this serious barrel racer into a happy little girl again.

By the time he turned back around, Hailey was nowhere to be seen. Now both Donnellys were roaming free on his property. But he did find one of them inside. Raiding his fridge.

"Did you ever find Parker?" he asked.

Hailey nearly dropped the cheese plate. "Don't sneak up on me like that!"

"You did it first. Taylor, this is Hailey."

Hailey extended her hand. "You were amazing out there."

"Thank you, ma'am." Taylor accepted Hailey's hand and shook it.

Nash laughed under his breath. He'd always thought of Hailey as a little sister. Not a *ma'am*.

Hailey jabbed him softly in the side with her elbow, then stuffed a large square of cheddar cheese into her mouth.

"Feel free to take some to go," he said. Not that he didn't enjoy having her there. He just didn't want her around when Jess returned with the twins. Hailey had already figured out too much regarding his feelings. Or thought she had. He was still figuring that out himself, because this anxiety coursing through his body was the double-strength variety. More than one energy source was fueling it.

"All right, I can take a hint. I'll leave the cheese for you and take a hug instead." She wrapped her arms around him, squeezed tight and whispered, "I'll be back to hear that long story of yours. I'll even bring the popcorn."

Nash would have ordinarily laughed, but the seriousness of what was about to happen was settling in.

Once Hailey left, he whipped up some hot chocolate as Taylor got comfy on the sofa. Before he had a chance to do the same, there was a knock on the door.

On the other side stood Jess, Lizzy and Kat. The twins nearly knocked him down to collect a hug, which caused his hot chocolate to splash. The marshmallows on top formed a shield that helped curb some of the damage.

"Go show Taylor your Breyer horse collection, Kat. And Lizzy, maybe you could draw some flowers for her. On *your* board."

"Okay, Daddy!" the twins said in unison.

With all three girls in the twins' bedroom and out of earshot, it was down to Nash and Jess. And the decision that had to be made.

"I had a wonderful time with the girls," Jess

said. "We took a drive around the square, then we watched a movie in my room. Tomorrow, we're going to help with a cooking workshop."

Tomorrow. A bold assumption.

"I have to be honest, Jess. I'm not sure I can help Taylor improve. She's everything you said she was. And more."

She looked at him but remained quiet, as if he hadn't tried hard enough. Or maybe that was his own conscience prodding him.

In that silence, he did one more run-through of Taylor's performance in his mind. Once again, his stomach seized toward the end. Although, this time, he knew why. It definitely had something to do with the way she was finishing.

Bottom line: Taylor had too much promise to ignore. Furthermore, he was itching to help. That favorite teaching spot on the fence that he'd avoided for so long was tempting him back over, although he had no intention of getting too comfortable there.

"I understand," she finally said, without any discernable emotion.

"I don't think you do," he countered, although he wasn't going to reveal the depth of that statement. Only the layer she needed to hear. He was willing to let his guard down only so far...

"I'll drop off the twins tomorrow and pick Taylor up. Midmorning. After breakfast. She and I have a lot of work to do."

CHAPTER FOUR

JESS WAS LIVING proof that one could survive without coffee for the first few hours of the morning.

Survive being the operative word.

Good thing she could practically pattern little girls' Western barrel racing shirts in her sleep. Of course, she'd preplanned the special embellishments needed to make each top unique. Just like the little equestrians themselves. So far, her vision had set her apart from other seamstresses who did similar designs for the rodeo circuit. The cloned crop top T-shirt she promised to one of the rodeo moms would be even easier to execute than the shirts.

Then there was the Dudley project. *Definitely* a job for caffeine.

Jess tiptoed past Taylor, who remained curled up beneath a pile of blankets less than ten feet away. The little girl's long, dark brown hair draped across the purple spandex pillowcase and down the side. The sunlight seeping through a crack in the spandex curtains revealed the beautiful chocolate tones within the strands. At least she'd removed the ponytail holder, along with her headphones.

Thankfully, Jess had already let Taylor know that if Mommy wasn't in the room when she woke up, she wouldn't have gone far. No farther than downstairs.

And never for too long without checking in. The trip this morning needed to be a record-breaking one.

Otherwise, she wouldn't have even considered the green spandex guest bathrobe, complete with an embroidered patch that spelled out *Hideaway* stitched in cursive and an attached tag that invited guests to take the robe home as a souvenir.

It would be good enough for a quick trip downstairs, but she wasn't going to use up suitcase space to haul it from city to city. Plus, it wasn't like she was going to run into anyone except perhaps Becca and a DEBB or two. Even if that happened, the day could only get better from there.

She slipped on the fuzzy pink house slippers that she'd brought and followed the aroma of fresh coffee to the kitchen. Hopefully, Becca would let her buy a cup.

Except the woman loading dishes onto a cart wasn't Becca, unless she'd traded her red beachy waves for a blond updo. Whoever the woman was, she must have gotten up even earlier than Jess, considering how polished she looked, from the tidy French twist to the fitted powder blue sweatshirt dress, all the way down to her impossibly white tennis shoes.

Jess was suddenly self-conscious about her own

appearance. She didn't have on so much as a flick of mascara. At least her long bob didn't require much fuss. In fact, it always fell into place whenever she rolled out of bed in the mornings. She'd never been into those fancy hairstyles anyway, although they sure did look nice on others.

"Sorry to bother you." Jess tapped on the door frame softly enough as to not startle the woman. "May I buy a cup of coffee?"

The lady turned around, wiped her hands on an apron and offered a warm smile.

"Nonsense! Coffee is on the house." She retrieved a mug from the cabinet, filled it almost to the top and handed it to Jess. "I left a little room for cream and sugar."

Jess took a sip and shook her head. "It's perfect the way it is."

"Why, thank you. Made it myself. I'm Georgina, by the way. Are you one of the DEBBs?" She grabbed a fruit plate from the counter, balanced it on top of the already overburdened cart and slowly released her grip.

Jess held her breath, but the platter didn't so much as teeter.

"I'm about the only one who isn't, it seems. I'm Jess. My daughter, Taylor, and I are passing through on the way to a rodeo in Montana. We're boarding her horse at Buck Stops Ranch."

Georgina tilted her head and put her hands on her hips.

"So *you're* Nash's gal," she said.

Jess's breath hitched, and she nearly choked on the sip of coffee she'd taken. Not because it sounded so wrong, but because it sounded so...*right*. Probably because she'd wanted to wear that label so badly ten years ago.

Her shock must have been obvious to Georgina, who clapped her hands over her mouth.

"Oh, gosh! I didn't mean it *that* way. I'd heard that one of our guests was boarding her horse at his place, and that y'all went way back."

Okay. Much better. Still, her heart got a little jolt that the caffeine couldn't have achieved.

"I used to be one of his barrel racing students."

"My sister Hailey told me he used to teach," Georgina said, adding the final straw—make that strawberries—to the cart.

Jess set her cup down on the nearest counter, lunged forward and stopped the bowl from crashing to the ground. She took the initiative to rearrange a few of the items into a more stable configuration.

"Thanks. You're a lifesaver. Becca usually helps me, but eggs make her nauseous. Cody was in here earlier making his dish, so the kitchen kind of smells eggy if you didn't notice."

"Allergies?" Jess asked.

"Pregnancy. She should be over the morning sickness by now, but hopefully she'll get some relief one of these days. Until then, she can't even think about them without dry heaving. She even foregoes helping with breakfast in the barn."

"That's unfortunate. Eggs would probably help settle her stomach."

"Spoken like someone who's been there," Georgina said.

Becca appeared in the doorway, "I heard that, and I'm not going near any eggs! I'll live with the nausea. Good morning, Jess. You're welcome to my portion of breakfast."

"That's a good idea," Georgina said. "Why don't you go on down and claim a place at the community table before the other group takes over. I'll be down in a jiffy."

"I would—everything looks delicious. But I left Taylor upstairs. She's still asleep."

"I'm done here and can check on her, if you'd like," Becca said.

"That's a sweet offer, but look at me."

They both gave her the onceover.

"That's so funny. I hadn't even noticed what you were wearing. Looks good on you! But I bet you'd look good in a potato sack," Georgina said.

"I concur. Please take your time at breakfast. I'm not going anywhere except to the other room right now before I…" Becca covered her mouth and made a quick retreat toward the parlor.

The women both sounded serious about her looking fine, but Jess knew otherwise.

"I'll fix a couple of plates and take them back to the room. But first, I insist on helping you with this," she said, gesturing to the cart. Her pride could take a minor hit for a good cause.

"You're as sweet as I heard you were," Georgina said.

Jess was tempted to ask who gave her that description. The only person who knew her that well around here was Nash, and she doubted he'd describe her as *sweet*, judging by his reaction to her reappearance in his life.

"Tell you what, Jess. Come down for coffee whenever you want. If there isn't a fresh pot on, feel free to make one. You'll find everything you need in there." Georgina pointed to the cabinet directly above the coffee maker.

That was music to Jess's ears. She'd need the caffeine to get through the early morning sewing hours she had planned.

The two managed to get the overloaded cart out the door, down the trail and over the threshold of the barn without any casualties. The DEBBs were already there and milling about. A little redheaded boy was walking around to each person and offering orange juice. No one was giving Jess a second look. So far, so good.

"Help yourself to the buffet. If you need any assistance carrying breakfast back to your room, just holler at one of us. Or you're welcome to borrow a tray." With that, Georgina shifted into overdrive, placing all the food in its respective warmer or designated spot. They certainly had breakfast running like clockwork, with everyone pitching in.

Cody was stationed at the end, serving up something from one of the warmers along with that mischievous smile he'd been so famous for. Like every other woman Jess had ever known, she'd had a slight celebrity crush on the Rodeo Rascal when he first rose to fame.

But now I'm Nash's gal.

She bit her lip to suppress a giggle, then got in line.

Once it was her turn, Cody gifted her with a warm smile, although she had braced herself for a smirk. He either didn't notice her attire or was too much of a gentleman to show any reaction.

"Is that Max pouring the orange juice?" she asked as he added a dollop of *migas* to her plate.

Cody beamed. "Yes, ma'am."

Jess could understand why the man was so proud. Max obviously already had a strong work ethic. Very much like Taylor when it came to barrel racing.

"Hey, Max," Cody called out.

The little boy froze in his tracks and looked their way.

"Pour a glass for Jess, if you don't mind, sir," Cody continued.

Max practically ran to a table where the glasses were stacked. The orange juice sloshed around inside the giant pitcher.

"Slow down, cowboy!" Cody called out, then turned to Jess. "He gets a little too excited about helping with breakfast. Hope that never changes."

Jess wanted to tell him to give it a couple of years. Max would be wearing headphones all day.

Then again, every child-parent relationship was different.

Jess hoped for a closer relationship with her own daughter and wasn't about to give up just because their little family suffered an unexpected loss.

"Any chance I could have an extra serving of those for Taylor? She's still asleep upstairs. That is, if it won't make you run out of eggs."

"No chance of that. Vern Fraser makes special trips over here in the mornings. You just missed him," Cody explained as he added another generous dollop.

"You have an open-door policy for breakfast?"

"Fraser Ranch provides the eggs for our morning feasts. It's the least we can do for the special folks in our lives. Just ask Nash." Cody added another lopsided smile.

"That'll have to wait until I'm appropriately dressed. I wouldn't want him to see me like this. Considering we have a business arrangement and all," she said. But in trying to clarify, she felt herself digging an even deeper hole.

Besides, she was stating the obvious. The way Cody looked past her confirmed it. She was difficult to look at.

A man cleared his throat behind her, then said, "Save some for the rest of us."

All of a sudden, Jess couldn't breathe. She looked at Cody and mouthed, "Nash?"

Cody leaned in and whispered, "I didn't see him until he was right behind you."

Jess corralled a pathetic amount of confidence, pivoted on the heels of her fluffy house slippers and put on a huge smile.

Nash smiled back, after a quick onceover that lingered on the slippers. At least he wasn't laughing.

"You're early to pick up Taylor," she said. As in *way* too early. "She's still asleep."

"Actually, I'm here to rob the buffet of some scrambled eggs for the girls. Realized I didn't have any at the house."

Jess tugged at the front closure of the robe, wishing she could somehow make it swallow her whole.

"Eggs. Nature's perfect vitamin," she said for lack of a better response.

Nash simply smiled. And stared.

Jess looked for the nearest exit but figured she'd only look sillier if she made a run for it. As if looking any worse was even possible.

"Thank you, again, for agreeing to see Taylor today, Mr. Buchanan," she said in her most professional tone.

"You're welcome, Ms. McCoy. I'll see you again in a few hours."

She was tempted to say, "Not if I see you first," but refrained. Best thing to do was to cut her losses. Although she hadn't dared to dream that this trip might result in some sort of deeper relationship, like the one she'd yearned for ten years ago, this encounter had just ensured that such a thing would never happen.

Jess pulled her shoulders back, nodded and walked around him and out the barn door without looking back.

Her pride now depleted—but with a full plate of food and a glass of orange juice in hand—Jess somehow made it back to the room without spilling anything. She temporarily set the juice on the ground and opened the door as slowly and softly as possible. Taylor was already awake.

"I brought us some breakfast," she announced.

Jess could practically read her mind. *Did you bring pancakes with fresh strawberries and blueberries and raspberries and chocolate-maple syrup and whipped cream?*

Someday, Jess would make Taylor's special dish again. But with their rodeo schedule and lifestyle, there was no telling when that would be. She didn't want to make any promises she couldn't keep.

Taylor lifted the foil on the plate and stabbed one of the strawberries with a fork, then sampled a small bite of the *migas*.

"What do you think?" Jess asked.

Taylor shrugged. "It's okay." Judging from the next huge bite, she must have decided that it was pretty good.

Jess smiled, shook her head and breathed a sigh of relief. With Taylor temporarily occupied, Jess could make progress on one of the Western shirts while the coffee kicked in.

From there, she needed to organize her thoughts for the two-piece suit that Carol Anne Dudley had requested for her daughter, Meghan. Even a mention on *Dudley's Delightful Duds* could help Jess branch out. Western tops and random clone requests were her bread and butter, but it would be tough getting Taylor all the way to nationals on that.

Mrs. Dudley's opinion was the type of advertising that couldn't be bought. Best of all, she'd given Jess creative license for the design. Hence, the black pleated chiffon bell cuffs Jess planned to add to the yellow-and-black tweed jacket sleeves. They had to be executed flawlessly. She had barely enough fabric remaining.

Same went for the tweed itself. Before she did any patterning or cutting, she'd given Mrs. Dudley a sketch for approval to proceed. Jess wasn't sure if it was good or bad news that the woman hadn't texted her back.

Not that she didn't have plenty to do right in front of her. She double-checked the direction of the grain and pinned the Western shirt pattern into place, then cut and trimmed out the individual pieces. She took one of the sleeves to the sewing machine, positioned it, then released the pressure foot. When she pushed the power pedal, the machine growled back a bit.

"Someone's grumpy this morning," she whispered softly enough so that Taylor didn't hear.

She pressed for longer this time, getting one seam done without a hiccup. Full steam ahead.

Nash's gal is on a roll. She grinned and bit her lip again. No, Georgina hadn't meant it *that* way.

Jess took a break to help Taylor finish off the *migas.* Couldn't let it go to waste. Now wide awake and focused, she positioned the second sleeve and put the proverbial pedal to the metal.

Except, this time, she got nothing but quiet in return. Not even a lazy *hmmm.* She tried again to no avail and checked the outlet and all the connections. Everything looked normal.

She pressed down a third time. Nothing. All of a sudden, those eggs weren't going down so easily. Just when she thought having Nash see her in the robe and slippers was the worst thing that could happen.

Something was broken…and her reputation would be, too, if she couldn't get the machine fixed soon.

NASH COULDN'T STOP GRINNING. Those fuzzy house slippers of Jess's had to be the cutest thing ever, next to that awful robe that she somehow managed to rock. Oh, and the way she'd said that they had a business arrangement, then proceeded to address him as Mr. Buchanan. Not that he needed reminding that it was business, but it made him see her in a whole new light.

A flattering one.

With his own smile firmly in place, his number one priority for the day was to put a smile on the faces of three little girls, as well.

Unfortunately, the odds were against him from

the get-go, judging by the way the twins kept herding the *migas* around their plates with their forks.

"Miss Hailey lets us have Pop-Tarts," Lizzy said.

It was a valid point, as it had been the dozen or so times she'd mentioned it. But the answer was still no.

He allowed such sweets while Hailey babysat only because he felt guilty about abandoning them in the first place. But guilt was not going to guide such important decisions anymore.

Nash flipped the hash brown patties to the other side. A pair of crispy black circles stared back at him.

He'd like to blame the unappetizing breakfast on the fact that he barely got a wink of sleep last night. But the feel of his favorite teaching spot, Hailey's thinking it was Kat in the arena, and those old feelings for Jess that he'd thought he'd put to bed for good were now tossing and turning in his mind.

Then there was something about Taylor's sad expression when he told her to go have some fun that niggled at his conscience the entire night.

Maybe whatever she's carrying on her shoulders is weighing her down, lowering her score.

Nash laughed under his breath at the unexpected thought. If only the explanation could be that simple. Any child as young and accomplished as Taylor had to either be an old soul or have a freakishly mature side. He'd never expected his older students to be happy all the time. It wouldn't be fair to expect it of Taylor either.

With the cast-iron skillet in one hand and the spatula in the other, he walked to the breakfast table and slid a hash brown onto each girl's plate.

"How about some ketchup with those?" he asked.

Lizzy poked the patty with her finger but recoiled at the heat. Neither twin looked up.

"What is it?" Kat asked.

Nash knew what she meant, but he couldn't resist.

"Ketchup's that stuff in the fridge, in the red squeeze bottle. It's made out of tomatoes, and we dip our fries in it."

"The bottle is made out of tomatoes?" Lizzy said, then giggled.

Nash shook his head. "No, silly. The ketchup."

Kat furrowed her brow.

He tried to contain himself, but a giggle slipped out anyway. The image of Jess's infectious laugh tickled his stomach. If she were here, she'd appreciate his bad joke, and Lizzy's clever question.

Soon enough, Kat joined Lizzy with her own half-hearted giggle.

Nash waited for them to stop long enough to see his wounded-puppy-dog expression. Instead of earning some sympathy, it made them laugh until they were both practically bubbling out of their chairs.

Mission accomplished. Almost. At least he got a smile out of these two. The day wouldn't be complete until he got at least one out of Taylor, as well.

His smile was so huge right now he no longer

tried to contain it. This was the best time of each day, in his opinion. Just him and his top two reasons for living. A warm, comfortable home that they'd made their own, and the Wyoming sunrise in the distance. Even Parker coming through the back door and adding more tasks to their chore board couldn't spoil the moment.

"Daddy, can I ask you something, if it's okay?" Kat asked.

That half of the twin equation was always so quiet, so this was a very good sign.

"You can ask me anything, darlin'," he said. If his heart had been any fuller, it would have burst right out of his chest.

"What do barrel racers do?"

At that, he felt his smile deflate. He'd dodged the topic before, but this thing with Taylor had brought it as out in the open as the barrels themselves. Kat had seen the beginning of a race at one of the rodeos. Roxanne was first up and started at an impressive speed. Nash didn't act quickly enough to get them all far enough away from the arena. He'd hoped the memory wouldn't stick. But it had, and now the situation promised to get a lot stickier.

"They compete in rodeos, mostly," he said. "It's like a job. Hard work. Not fun, like you and Sugar Pie have here."

Nash barely had time to blink before Kat turned back into his quiet little twin. Probably because he'd already explained that participating in rodeo events wasn't possible because traveling wasn't possible. Even though it hurt him more to say it than for them to hear it, he'd stand by that explanation.

He wouldn't think of burdening them with the fact that there wasn't enough money left at the end of the week for such things. Between the feed and the hay and the veterinary costs, that left him barely able to afford to pay Parker. Much less, their own bills.

And bringing up the topic of their mother was completely off-limits.

It had probably been a mistake to let the twins do mutton busting for a local event once. Neither had shown a serious interest. With the age limit capped at seven for most of the area events, he had a built-in excuse to say no to that without being the bad guy.

But barrel racing? That could go on for decades.

Lizzy seemed neutral when it came to the topic. Although she was crazy about her horse and was a good rider, she wasn't a rodeo gal. By contrast, Kat loved everything about the lifestyle, even though she wasn't old enough to understand the half of it.

At least he'd managed to thwart the topic, for now. Back to having fun.

Nash retrieved the ketchup out of the refrigerator and placed it in the middle of the table, hoping to invoke the giggling once again.

No such luck.

"You don't have to eat 'em if you don't want to, even though it's not good to waste food. But please eat your eggs," he said.

"If we had a dog, the dog could eat the food and it wouldn't be wasted. I'll take care of feeding him and washing his plate and giving him water," Lizzy said.

"Oh, boy," he said under his breath.

That topic again. Talk about "out of the frying pan and into the fire." Lizzy had been asking for a dog, but there was no way he could add another mouth to feed. Plus, he already knew who would end up with doggy duty, and it wasn't the twins.

Parker snorted in the background. Nash had forgotten he was even there, even though he'd babysat while Nash had made a run to the B and B.

Nash was out of fresh ideas as to how he could change the subject and get them laughing again. Something else had been invoked: the guilt. There was only one way to fix it, even though he'd vowed not to resort to it.

He walked over to the cabinet and grabbed a box of Pop-Tarts. Thankfully two remained. One for each of the twins.

"You girls get changed while I fix these for you." Nash waved the box in front of them, which put a smile on Lizzy's face and seemed to wipe away a little sadness from Kat's. They must have inhaled the sugar, because they were out of their chairs and down the hall before he slipped the treats into the toaster.

Parker had apparently sensed the seriousness of certain topics. He didn't even bother to tease. He simply wrote something else on the board, offered up a sympathetic smile and exited out the back door.

Nash looked at what his ranch hand had written. *Hang in there, Dad.*

"I'm tryin'." Nash cleared the barely touched plates of food from the table. He was messing up as badly with the dog topic as he had with the hash browns. Furthermore, he didn't have a clue how to fix either except to remind himself that he was doing the best he could under the circumstances. Then there was the other no-win situation he was navigating.

Those reawakened feelings for Jess.

CHAPTER FIVE

JESS STARED AT the apron that Georgina had handed to each person in the cooking workshop. Staring back: a comical-looking purple bull, nostrils flaring, and one eye noticeably larger than the other.

"These are yours to keep as a souvenir of your stay at the Hideaway and this workshop in particular," Georgina said.

"Aww," one of the ladies said as she held up the apron for everyone to see. As if they hadn't gotten one, as well.

Aprons. Jess used to have a million of them in her past life. In this life, such a thing would stay folded up in her suitcase, which would be a waste. The thought made her feel surprisingly...*sad*.

"The artist is none other than Max Sayers, Cody and Becca's son," Georgina continued. "In case you couldn't guess, his favorite color is purple, and he adores bulls."

Jess was intrigued. "You had the fabric made from a drawing?"

"Sure did. We don't have a fabric store within a hundred miles of Destiny Springs, much less a place that could do something like this. But I'll be happy to jot down my online resource for anyone who is interested."

"Is the little artist helping us cook today?" one of the beaus asked.

"He's resting up for a trail ride this afternoon at Sunrise Stables. If you have some free time, I highly recommend going on one," Cody said.

That earned a few nods of interest and discussion among the DEBBs. But even with the chatter around her, all Jess could hear was the silent treatment that her sewing machine had given her.

What came through loud and clear, however, was a hard tug on her right arm and Lizzy practically shouting, "I wanna crack the eggs!" Those soft brown eyes pleaded with Jess as if she had a say in how the workshop would be conducted.

Thankfully, Cody stepped in.

"That's one of the most important jobs," he said. "In fact, it's a two-person task. If the others don't mind, maybe you and Kat could tackle that together."

Kat shook her head and looked to the floor. Perhaps this cooking workshop wasn't such a good idea after all. Time for some gentle persuasion because it was too late to back out now.

"It sounds like fun. Let's give it a chance," Jess suggested as she pulled Kat in for a side hug, which the little girl reluctantly accepted.

Cody fetched a couple of step stools—probably kept on hand for his own little one.

He demonstrated by tapping an egg gently on the edge of the bowl before handing the task over to the twins. After supervising their first attempt, which Lizzy hijacked and Kat was clearly okay with, Cody wiped his hands on his apron, stepped around the island and filled the void that the girls had left behind.

"Looks like the girls are having fun," he said.

Jess nodded at his generous assessment. She'd missed the target of finding something the twins would equally enjoy.

"You know them better than I do. Kat doesn't seem too interested in cooking. Maybe the next workshop will be more her thing. Any idea what the topic will be?"

"Work-life balance," he said.

They looked at each other, scrunched their noses and shook their heads at the same time.

She looked back in time to see Lizzy dip her hand into the bowl to fish out a piece of eggshell that had escaped her grip. Georgina swooped in with a fork to assist.

"I made them soap up before we got here," Jess said, loudly enough to be overheard. A few DEBBs glanced over and smiled as if to say, *No worries at all*.

Cody whispered, "When Max first started helping with the orange juice, he tried to stir it with his fingers, but I stopped him in the nick of time. You'll be relieved to know that he's a spoon expert now."

Having met Max, she could totally picture it.

"Too bad. That would have made it taste even sweeter." Jess offered up a silly grin.

Cody took a step back. "Well, there it is! I thought you forgot to bring it downstairs."

Jess cocked her head. "Bring what?"

"That smile."

Jess felt it turning back into a frown, against her will.

"Oh, yeah. That. My sewing machine decided to stop working this morning. From what I could tell after doing an internet search, there's only one place around here that might do those kinds of repairs. Hoping to get over there before they close today."

Cody pursed his lips and nodded. "I know the place. Miller Electronics. They're good, but notoriously slow and always backlogged. I have a better source."

And just like that, Cody lifted the weight of the world off her shoulders as easily as he'd carried her sewing machine up those stairs.

"Give me a few minutes." He sprinted out of the kitchen and down the hallway.

A woman tapped Jess on the shoulder. It was the same DEBB who had been the first to approach her.

"I couldn't help but overhear. Do you sew?" she asked.

"I did until this morning." At least there was a possible upside to the machine not working. She now had a built-in excuse, should anyone else want clothing made for their young sons, in case that was why this lady was asking.

"I love to sew and am pretty good at it. Haven't had time lately. Not in years, in fact. I'm hoping I can get some ideas on how to find time for it from the workshop on work-life balance. You should join us."

Rather than risk sounding ungrateful for the invitation, Jess simply nodded.

"I'm Dorothy, by the way. If you get the notion to talk about notions, I'm in the Velvet Room."

"I'm Jess, in Spandex."

"Now *that's* a tricky fabric," Dorothy said. "With spandex, you gotta stretch and hold. If your arms get tired in the middle, you could be in trouble."

"Wow. I didn't know that." Yet, it made complete sense. That was probably the only fabric she'd never handled.

The woman seemed to know her stuff. Couldn't hurt to have a sewing soulmate in the house. Not many people wanted to talk notions or listen to her ramble on about the periodic frustrations. Needles breaking. Thread bunching. Machines up and dying. Taylor would put on her headphones whenever Jess started grumbling to herself while working on a garment that wasn't cooperating.

"Ms. Lawrence, would you mind slicing some avocado?" Georgina asked.

"Not at all." Dorothy turned back to Jess. "I hope we'll have an opportunity to chat more while you're here."

Nice offer, if not doable.

Cody returned with a self-satisfied grin. "You're in luck. The best repairman in Destiny Springs can look at your machine this afternoon. He'll meet you at your room around five thirty, toolbox in hand."

That wouldn't leave much time for her to drop off the twins and pick up Taylor. But as long as she didn't linger at Nash's, they could make it back. In fact, this was a blessing in disguise, because he'd been standing on the edge of her thoughts ever since she laid eyes on him again.

"Does the repairman have a name?" Jess asked.

Cody's eyes were now trained on the DEBBs who had been corralled into volunteering, and on the girls, who literally had their hands in every task. "He sure does. He's also one of the most respected cowboys in this town."

Jess waited for a name, but nothing was forthcoming except for a mischievous smile.

So that's why they called him the Rodeo Rascal. Did she detect some sort of matchmaking going on? Otherwise, why the mystery?

Whatever the case, Jess wasn't a candidate for a relationship right now. Didn't stay in one place long enough and preferred it that way. She was tempted to tell him not to bother if that's what he was up to, but he was having too much fun teasing her. She wasn't going to spoil it for him. Not after everything he'd done.

"I've lost count of how many times you and Becca have helped me. I might as well stop trying and just take full, unapologetic advantage of your generosity," she said.

"*Now* you're catching on." He added a lopsided grin, then walked back around the island to take over the cooking once again. Lizzy insisted on continuing to help, while Kat returned to Jess's side, still stuck in a puddle of gloom.

"What would you like to do after this? We'll still have some time before I take you two back to your daddy," Jess said.

The little girl shrugged.

"Or we could talk. Woman-to-woman." Even to Jess, that sounded silly, but she was running out of ideas. At the same time, Kat looked up and stared, as if making sure the offer was a serious one.

"Can I ask a question, if it's okay?"

"Of course!" Jess said.

"What does Taylor do at the rodeo with the barrels?"

"You've never been to the rodeo?"

"Yes. But not since I was little," Kat said.

That was adorable, but strange on so many levels. Sure, he'd stopped teaching at some point. But how could a little girl whose daddy used to be one of the best teachers in the greater Wyoming area—in the world, as far as Jess was concerned—not even know the basics about barrel racing?

"The rider and her horse race around the barrels as fast and calculated as they can. The one with the best time and form wins a trophy or belt or ribbon. And usually some cash," Jess said.

"Daddy lets me ride Sugar Pie at home. She's mine, and she's a quarter horse like Taylor's. Lizzy's horse is Cupcake, but she isn't as fast as mine."

"Maybe your daddy can teach you some moves."

Kat simply shrugged and looked down at her feet.

As soon as she said it, she remembered how adamant Nash had been about not having time, or interest, in the rodeo anymore. But he didn't seem like the type of father who would deny his daughters anything if they asked.

Maybe Roxanne had hurt him so badly that he'd abandoned that part of his life. Any discussion was a reminder. That might explain his icy reaction to training Taylor. He'd definitely changed.

She wanted to bring up the topic of barrel racing to Nash for Kat's sake but didn't want him to add any more bricks to that emotional wall she'd detected. Not when she and Taylor had come this far and he was willing to help her, albeit reluctantly. Still, she ached to reach the Nash she once knew.

Then again, she wanted a lot of things.

EITHER JESS WAS twenty minutes early bringing back the girls, or Nash's usually impeccable internal clock was off.

Time otherwise felt as though it was standing still when she paused after getting out of the truck and stood there as if contemplating whether to come over at all.

Nash didn't bother dismounting from his perch

on the fence. Lizzy ran over and hugged the bottom half of his legs, nearly pulling him off anyway. Kat, on the other hand, bypassed him altogether to get a closer look at Taylor, who was rounding the third barrel, then heading toward Kat instead of coming back over to him or taking it home.

He managed to tear his eyes away from that unfortunate situation once Jess approached.

"Back so soon?" He tried to hide his frustration behind a cordial smile.

Kat had already been asking about when they could all go to the rodeo again to watch the horses. Having her see Taylor in action wasn't going to help.

The fact that he'd managed to avoid barrel racing events each time, with one sliver of an exception, was partially selfish. He couldn't watch if Roxanne was competing. Not because he had any feelings left for her. He simply didn't want to risk running into her with the twins.

Of course, Jess wouldn't know that crucial fact. It was awful enough to feel like he was a "bad daddy" because of his unwillingness to even consider it, even though deep in his heart he wished he could. He didn't want Jess to reach that conclusion, as well.

"Sorry about that. My sewing machine broke. Cody lined up a gentleman to come over and look at it in an hour, and I need to be there."

Something about the way she said *gentleman* jolted his ego on an unexpected level, which was silly. It wasn't like she was going out on a date. Even if she was, it was none of his business.

Naw. Couldn't be jealousy he was feeling. Well, maybe a little, if he were being honest with himself. Helplessness, definitely. He was handy around the ranch in many ways—repairing or replacing a broken gate hinge, fixing the timing on a baler, replacing a spark plug on the four-wheeler. But he didn't have the first clue about delicate machinery.

Jess joined him on the fence. "The girls are partially to blame. They couldn't wait to get back home and see you. I put them off as long as possible."

She'd told a half-truth, at best. At least one of his girls wanted to see him. The other was more interested in the arena. Kat was practically wiggling out of her skin as Taylor showed off by finishing a figure eight on the first two barrels and was racing toward the third.

Not that he blamed his daughter for being mesmerized. He'd all but forgotten what an edge-of-your-seat sport it was. But to bypass her daddy altogether? That was a first. And hopefully the last.

He wasn't going to address the issue in front of company, however. Breakfast was always the best time with the girls as far as bringing up thoughts and feelings, so he'd let it slide for now and tackle it in the morning. He'd be smart to pick up more Pop-Tarts at the store in case he needed reinforcements.

No luck pinpointing anything today as far as Taylor was concerned. Only a rehash of his suggestions from yesterday. But he wasn't giving up yet. His intuition wouldn't allow it.

"How did you ladies spend your day?" he asked Jess.

"We attended a cooking workshop at the B and B. Lizzy had the best time. You may have an aspiring chef on your hands."

"I can definitely use one of those." Nash looked out to the girls in the distance, because looking into Jess's light hazel eyes was getting to him again.

"Did you know the first french fry wasn't even cooked in France?" she asked.

Nash's thoughts went immediately to images of his new budding chef attempting to make fries at the house. With this new knowledge that cooking was an attraction, he made a mental note to keep extra-close tabs on her. As if he needed one more thing to worry about.

"Really? I didn't know that," he said.

Jess bit her lip and nodded.

"It's true. The first fry was actually cooked in grease."

Nash thought about it for a second, then laughed under his breath.

He wanted to launch into a joke of his own. In fact, one immediately came to mind: *Is it proper to eat a Juicy Lucy with your fingers? No, you should eat your fingers separately.* But he refrained. Those old feelings were bubbling to the surface, more dangerous than hot grease in a cast-iron skillet set on high. Furthermore, it wasn't a joking matter.

"So…any comeback?"

He looked at her now, unsure of what she was getting at.

"Pardon?"

She was the one to look away now. "Seems like you've forgotten about our joke swap. I bet you still have some zingers in you."

"Not at all. It's just that…"

"Our lives have gotten more serious," she said.

She wasn't wrong. But swapping jokes would only lead to someone owing the other a Juicy Lucy. The fewer trips they made down memory lane, the better.

"And sometimes we put up a wall to protect ourselves," she continued.

Now *that* was the Jess he remembered. The woman who wouldn't let him get away with anything. Even though she used *we*, it was clear she was talking about him. She wasn't wrong about that, either.

"I suppose we sometimes do," he said, stopping short of a full admission.

Jess jumped down from the fence. "Well, then, I guess I'd better take care of Mischief and head out. Find out what's wrong with my sewing machine and if it can be fixed. Kat tells me her horse is Sugar Pie and Lizzy's is Cupcake."

"The girls picked out the names."

"I figured that much. Not that you don't have that in you, too," Jess said.

Nash tried to make sense of the statement, although he had little doubt as to what she meant.

"I'll take care of Mischief this time. You get back to the B and B," he said.

"You don't have to do that."

No, he didn't. In fact, the sooner he got Kat back inside the house and away from the arena, the less opportunity she'd have to get even more attached to barrel racing. And the greater the chance of him giving in to those sweet brown eyes of hers. But Jess needed a favor. And he needed for her to leave before he cracked a bad joke.

"Hey, ladies, Jess and Taylor need to skedaddle. Say your goodbyes," Nash called out.

Lizzy ran over first and gave Jess a big hug. "I'm gonna make some *mee-cuz* for breakfast for *all* of us tomorrow. Will you help me?"

"We made Cody's Rascal's Rodeo Scramble in the workshop," Jess explained.

"He's almost as famous for that now as he was for bull riding." Admittedly, this would throw a huge rusty wrench in his plan to spend some one-on-two time with the twins in the morning and talk about...*feelings*.

In all honesty, he used to dream of starting each day in such a way. Except with a wife. Roxanne had her good points, but she didn't have a domestic bone in her body. At least, the best he could tell. She was at out-of-town rodeos more than she was in the kitchen.

"Can we *pleeease*?" Lizzy begged.

"Jess may have plans. We should be asking her," Nash said.

Jess visibly sighed. "If the gentleman can repair my machine, I'll need to catch up on some sewing in the morning instead. I'm sorry."

"And if he can't, you and Taylor will come over?" Lizzy looked at Jess, who obviously wasn't immune to the little girl's charms.

"Sure," she said after an extended pause. Clearly, that wasn't the preferred scenario, judging by her forced smile.

"Promise?" Lizzy asked.

Jess smiled. "Okay. I promise."

It took everything Nash had not to envision Jess and Lizzy cooking breakfast for them all. Especially after seeing how comfortable the twins seemed to be around her. Ever since Jess had appeared on his doorstep for help with Taylor, he'd deferred to the professional side of his intuition, which had been waving a red flag. The personal side, however, was waving a familiar white one.

Not that it had ever fully stopped.

JESS COULDN'T HAVE timed it better. She and Taylor had no sooner settled back into the Spandex Room when there was a knock on the door.

Maybe a good-looking cowboy could provide exactly what she needed: a distraction from her thoughts about Nash. Especially since she'd had the courage to confront the issue of the jokes, and he'd acknowledged remembering. Awful jokes were the hardest to forget and often the funniest. They'd both doled out some doozies.

One thing was for certain: breakfast at his place in the morning wasn't the best idea. The gentleman on the other side of that door was the only one who could save her from having to fulfill her promise to Lizzy, because going back on promises was at the top of her no-no list.

"Coming!" she called out, pausing at a mirror for a quick hair and makeup check. Taylor had put on her headphones and was sitting on the bed, bobbing her head to whatever tunes were filling her ears.

Jess opened the door. The man who stood on the other side was most definitely a cowboy, in a loose-fitting flannel shirt and heavy denim jeans.

He removed his cowboy hat and covered his heart. His hair was as white as his whiskers. Shoulders slumped ever so slightly at the weight of the toolbox he was carrying.

"Vern Fraser, at your service. Cody tells me you're in need of a knight in shining armor. Since a real one wasn't available, he called yours truly." He added the most charming grin she'd ever seen.

"You sure look like one to me. Please come in."

It was true. Perhaps Cody had acted a little coy when she'd asked for the name. But he wouldn't have recommended Vern if the man wasn't able to help.

Vern made a beeline to the machine. "There's the little troublemaker. A Janome, huh? She's a beauty."

His knowledge put her somewhat at ease. Even more so once he began disassembling the thing and talking through the process.

Jess stepped in closer.

"There's the motor. Let's see if we can get that heart of hers beating again." He unscrewed some bolts that held the piece in place, then eased it out. Wires and all.

"Hmm. None of these are frayed. And the sensor and shield plate look clean and are on tight," he continued.

Jess looked at where he was pointing and nodded, as if she'd understood a word he'd said.

Vern started to put everything back in its rightful place but paused as if a problem was on the tip of his tongue.

"Cody tells me that Nash is training your daughter. Is that true?" he asked.

"He's going to try," Jess said.

Vern rethreaded the wires through the machine and screwed the motor back inside. Then he positioned some sort of black belt.

"That's Nash for ya. Always helping people out."

"Seems like everyone in Destiny Springs is that way. Like you, for instance."

After putting the faceplate back on and double-checking all the connections, Vern tried the pedal. No luck. He stood and rested his hands on his hips.

"I have some good news and some bad news, young lady."

"I'll take the bad news first."

"The motor needs to be replaced. Must be an internal wiring failure, is all I can figure."

"And the good news?"

"No chance Miller Electronics carries it. Not for this model."

Jess tried to wrap her mind around how that was good while Vern crossed his arms and tapped his index finger against his lips while staring at the machine.

"Do you happen to have any *great* news?" she asked.

Vern looked at her and shook his head as if he'd been lost in a trance.

"Didn't mean to scare ya. I forgot to finish my thought. I know who likely carries that motor, but they're in Casper. I can pull some strings and get it here pretty fast."

"I don't suppose you could define *fast*." She already felt as though she was being a bad customer. Which begged the question, how much was he going to charge for all this?

Vern let out a cackle that morphed into a dry cough.

"I'm pretty sure we have different definitions for what *fast* looks like. I'm eighty-four, so a turtle could outrun me. Might be able to get it shipped overnight. At this hour, it likely wouldn't go out until tomorrow morning. So a couple of days, soonest."

That was the great-news scenario? She couldn't afford to lose that much time.

"May I ask what this is going to cost?" Besides her reputation and business, which she could barely stand to think about.

Vern put the screwdriver back into his toolbox.

"I can use my senior discount for the motor. The labor is on the house."

"Oh, no. Not a chance. I'm paying you for your work."

Vern patted her on the arm. "I think it was Arnold Toynbee who said, 'The supreme accomplishment is to blur the line between work and play.' If that saying holds water, it means I'm either the most accomplished person in Destiny Springs. Or the blurriest."

It was Jess's turn to cackle. That was usually the attitude she had about sewing. It also seemed to be the way Nash once felt about teaching, which made her heart literally ache now that she thought about what he'd given up. Or walked away from.

She, for one, knew how it felt to walk away from something you love. And someone.

"Do you remember when Nash used to teach?" she asked, daring to open the subject again and secretly hoping Vern would have some answers.

"Sure do. Folks around here thought he shouldn't have quit. But we all make choices that people don't understand because they don't walk in our boots."

"I know what you mean. Do you have any theories?"

"Nothing I'd bet money on. He's never talked about it. 'Course, folks around town think that some gal broke his heart."

Jess nodded. "Roxanne."

"The ex-wife? That's the reasonable conclusion. But supposedly there was another gal involved, which is why it's such a good rumor. Lots of those circulate around here, and a couple have even turned out to be true. Guess we'll never know for sure. Unless Nash ever decides to confess."

Jess was reasonably sure that wasn't going to happen. She knew he didn't quit teaching immediately after she left, so it obviously had nothing to do with her.

Whoever the other woman was, assuming the story was true, provided slight vindication that her main competition both in and out of the arena hadn't been "the one" for Nash after all. Maybe that's why Roxanne left. Maybe she didn't feel truly loved.

Hmm. Whatever the case, it seemed that neither woman was currently in his life.

Vern jotted something down on a notepad that was sitting next to a landline phone. "Here's my number. If you come across anything else that needs fixin', you call me first." He tapped at the piece of paper as if driving the point home.

"That's too kind, really."

At that, he simply waved his hand as if swatting the compliment away. She would figure out a way to repay him, whether he welcomed it or not.

Jess opened the door for him and watched to make sure he got down the stairs safely, then returned to the room. There sure were some men of integrity here in Destiny Springs. She suspected that Nash was still one of them.

She wished she would have asked Vern if he had

any advice for how to fix the other situation she was facing. But this one wasn't as simple as ordering a new part.

Her excuse for skipping making breakfast with the girls at Nash's had officially fallen through. And she'd made a promise to Lizzy, which she'd hate to break.

Maybe a good night's sleep would provide an answer. Not only to how she might bow out of the breakfast, but also why she kind of didn't want to.

CHAPTER SIX

"Nothing like a good night's sleep to help a gal see things more clearly," Jess murmured under her breath so that she wouldn't wake up Taylor.

Or so the saying goes. She personally couldn't prove or disprove it. Hadn't slept through the night in ages. Last night was no exception.

Her daughter, on the other hand, slept like a true champ.

It was one thing to get up early on purpose to work on her garments. It was another to lie awake, ruminating about the past and worrying about the future.

Ultimately, she concluded that this breakfast was a good thing for everyone involved. Then, she and her daughter could return to the B and B. Taylor could retreat back into her headphones, and Jess could continue patterning. Didn't need a sewing machine for that.

Nor did she need any fancy plans to keep the twins entertained after the kid swap later on. Jess could livestream horse shows on her laptop to keep Kat's interest, and tune into one of the food networks on television for Lizzy. Later, she'd take them out for a root beer float at the drugstore.

With the day neatly patterned out in her mind, and with Taylor still fast asleep, Jess headed downstairs. The kitchen was empty, but the coffee maker was already burping. Serving dishes were neatly stacked and ready to be filled with the morning's breakfast options.

Jess poured a cup and was right in the middle of a big, ugly yawn when someone tapped on a glass panel of the door. Her "knight in shining armor" was peering in from the other side. She set the cup down and rushed to open it for him.

The man was nothing short of amazing. How he managed to knock with his hands full was beyond her. The crate he was holding looked quite heavy and bulky. She held her breath and remained on standby as he eased it onto the counter, in case he needed help.

"I s'pose I'm a little early this morning. I was expecting to see Becca, but you're even better. Don't tell her I said so."

"I heard that, Vern," a woman called from the other room.

"Did I say Becca? I meant Georgina." Vern looked at Jess and put his index finger to his lips.

Jess returned the *shhhh* gesture. Without asking, she grabbed a clean mug from the cabinet, filled it with coffee and handed it to him.

"Well, aren't you a mind reader," he said, adding an appreciative smile.

She managed a closed-lip grin in return.

He took a long swig of the piping hot coffee as if it were room-temperature water. "It's a good thing this coffee isn't as weak as that smile of yours."

She tried to force a bigger one for his benefit, but he simply laughed and shook his head.

"I take it back about you being a mind reader. If you knew what I was thinkin', you wouldn't have to try so hard."

Jess perked up. That could only mean one thing. "You got the motor already?"

"No, ma'am, but it might be something just as good." Vern grinned as if savoring a juicy secret.

The suspense was killing her. Jess gripped her coffee mug so tightly she could have cracked the ceramic.

Vern turned and called out, "Becca, if you're still eavesdropping, please meet Jess and me in the parlor."

"Be there in a sec," she answered.

Vern set his cup down and nodded for Jess to follow. Once there, he pointed to a wooden desk. A huge arrangement of fresh daffodils sat smack-dab in the center.

"For me?" she asked, half-teasingly because what else could he be talking about? She didn't want to tell him that even flowers couldn't make her smile right now. And they couldn't begin to compete with a new motor.

"Set down your coffee. You're gonna need both hands," Vern said.

Jess did as instructed. He lifted the arrangement, handed it to her and began fiddling with some sort of latch. The top of the cabinet opened out to the side. He tugged on another flap, which opened to the front.

Becca joined them. "Are you trying to charm one of our guests by giving away our flowers, Mr. Fraser?"

Vern glanced up from his task. "Are you implying I have to try?"

"Excellent point," Becca said. "Then may I ask what you're doing?"

With some effort, he hefted something that was nested inside, and out popped a sewing machine as if rising out of bed. Vern locked it in place and gave it a couple of jiggles to make sure it was secure, then brushed off his hands.

If her jaw could have reached the floor, it would have shattered as surely as the etched Waterford vase she was holding.

"Wow. I totally forgot that converted to a sewing machine. How did you know?" Becca asked.

Vern patted its metal spine. "I've got one just like it at the ranch, but the Singer inside hasn't 'sung' in decades. Tried everything to fix her. Hopefully, this one is in working order. Miss Jess is in dire need of a sewing machine. Hers is on the blink. I hope you don't mind."

Becca stepped over and ran her hand along the machine, as well. "Of course not. You can use this anytime, Jess."

Meanwhile, Jess couldn't find the words to express her gratitude. When she could finally speak, she had to state the obvious. "I do a lot of work before dawn. I wouldn't want to wake up the others."

Vern looked around the back, found the cord and plugged it into the wall. With Becca's help, they got the pedal positioned on the floor and flipped the "on" switch. He pulled out a stool that had been tucked beneath the desk the whole time.

"Have a seat here and rev the motor while I take a listen," Vern said to Jess.

Becca eased the vase from her hands as Vern headed up the stairs.

Jess pressed the pedal, and the thing purred like a kitten. After studying the interface, she realized it wasn't an industrial workhorse like she was used to, but it would help her get some basics done for now.

A few minutes later, Vern came back down. "I doubt you're gonna disturb anyone. Can't hear a thing up there, and my hearing aids are cranked to the max."

Jess stood and gave him a hug without asking permission. She wanted to cry but managed to blink back the tears. This old cowboy really was a knight, albeit one in faded denim overalls.

After releasing her death grip on the poor man, she turned to find Becca handing her the vase. "Would you mind keeping these in your room? I don't know where else I would put them down here."

And there it was. The first time in a very long

time that someone gave her flowers, even though they were technically on loan. That gift was second only to the magical machine in front of her. Plus, she now could bow out from cooking breakfast at Nash's without going back on her word to Lizzy. If she wanted. Yet, her "wants" seemed to be changing by the day.

Either way, she and Taylor still needed to run over and take care of Mischief. But now she could get some real work done before the official kid swap.

Jess returned to the room and gently squeezed Taylor's arm to awaken her.

"Looks like I have access to a sewing machine here, so we don't have to do the whole breakfast thing at Nash's. We'll still need to feed and check on Mischief."

Mentioning Mischief always woke up her daughter better than any alarm.

Taylor sat up in bed and rubbed her eyes.

Jess glanced at the clock. Perfect timing. Nash had always been an early riser. She could deliver the news about the machine in person when they got to his ranch.

"Get dressed, please, and we'll head over there," Jess said.

While Taylor was getting ready, Jess collected the pattern pieces, along with a few notions to take downstairs so that she could get started as soon as they returned.

"Your phone rang while you were gone," Taylor called out from the bathroom.

A quick glance confirmed it was Nash. He'd left a voicemail. Hopefully, he was canceling their breakfast, which would be ideal. She wouldn't have to be the one to do it.

Instead, the message was from Lizzy, saying how excited she was about the whole breakfast thing. Thankfully, Nash hijacked the call, assuring her that there was no pressure to hang around after they dropped by to feed Mischief, and that Lizzy understood that possibility. But then he had to go and add, "Lookin' forward to seeing you."

Her heart felt as though it were about to blossom bigger than the vase stuffed full of daffodils on the bedside table. She and Taylor had to eat breakfast at some point anyway, right? And they didn't have to linger after the meal was over with. As long as the most important person in her life was on board.

"Taylor, I didn't even ask if *you* wanted to have breakfast over there."

The little girl emerged from the bathroom, all dressed except for her boots, and she was nodding.

The decision was made. Jess texted back.

I'll bring the ingredients since I know what we'll need.

After this, however, it was time to stop playing around and socializing, and instead get to work on another kind of interfacing.

The sewing kind.

IF NASH'S BOOTS could reach his backside, he'd give himself a good, swift kick in the pants. What was he thinking, leaving such a message? Especially the last part.

With phone in hand, he walked back into the kitchen, shaking his head.

"Lookin' forward to seeing you?" he muttered more loudly than he intended. Yet, it was true.

Parker glanced up from the board.

"Don't ask," Nash admonished before his ranch hand could think of a wisecrack response. Thankfully, Parker resumed his task instead. But the smirk told Nash that the subject wasn't closed.

He should have let Lizzy ramble on and on. She could have carried the message all by herself and spared him the Freudian slip. Yet, he didn't want Jess to feel obligated. No matter how hard his emotions were trying to scramble his professional common sense, he had to rein them in. No more talk about feelings. Period.

The exception would be the precious little girls who'd stayed on his heels all the way to the kitchen, arguing between themselves about who got to do what for breakfast. He hoped that didn't mean he had two budding chefs on his hands.

"I get to the break the eggs," Lizzy asserted.

"I get to make the chips, and I'm gonna use sugar and not salt," Kat said.

"You *have* to use salt," Lizzy said.

"No, I don't."

"How about we make some with each? Start getting dressed, ladies. Our guests will be arriving soon. I'll feed the horses. They're probably getting hungry by now."

"Can we feed the dogs, too, and bring one home?" Lizzy asked.

The knot that seemed to be a permanent part of Nash's stomach tightened.

"What dogs?" He was pretty sure he hadn't seen any strays near his property, much less a pack.

"The ones on TV. They live in cages, and they look so cold and sad," Lizzy said.

He knew the ones. The background music was equally heartbreaking. Those animal charity commercials sure knew how to tug on the heartstrings. If he had a million bucks, he'd help as many as possible find a home.

"No," Nash said, surprisingly swiftly and easily. He'd be proud of himself except the harshness wiped any hope right off the twins' adorable faces.

"Not today, ladies," he backpedaled. "We're expecting company, remember? Now, go change into something cute but comfortable."

At least he'd succeeded in kicking the topic down the road a little.

Once the girls were out of sight, Nash turned his focus to the task list that his ranch hand had composed. Pretty impressive. At a glance, everything looked good. Feed cows, replenish food supply, check heifers, fill water… But then Parker smirked and jotted down one last item.

Pick out a dog.

Nash grabbed the nearest rag and wiped away the words.

"Very funny. We can't let the girls see this. They already know a few words, and *dog* is one of 'em," he said.

"We can't let them know anything about the barrels, either. Anything you want to talk through? I'm a good listener."

Nash rubbed the sides of his neck and released a long breath.

"Kat's curious about barrel racing."

"Is that a bad thing?" Parker asked.

Nash's first thought was a defensive one. In his mind, there was no better sport. Kat was a natural on a horse, and she would excel. With the right teacher. She could easily become The One to Watch. But rodeo events were pricey, with the possible emotional price for running into Roxanne being more than any of them would ever be able to afford.

Just as he didn't want Kat to ask about the barrels, he didn't want anyone asking about his own feelings. Specifically, about his inadequacy as a father. But keeping a large part of the reason inside was eating away at his soul. Might help to talk it through with someone, and Parker wasn't the worst choice.

"It wouldn't be a bad thing if their daddy could afford it. Time's an issue, too. I can't be away from the ranch for as long as it would take to do it right."

"What? You don't trust me to hold down the fort? And feed the dog?"

"Oh, you'd do fine with the fort. It's a specific number I'd worry about. I'd want the same head of cattle when I returned." It was a not-so-subtle commentary on Parker's herding skills, which were admittedly improving but had miles to go.

"You'd come back to more. Aren't a few of your girl cows about to welcome little ones into the world?" Parker asked.

Heifers. But close enough. Yet another reason he needed to stay right here in Destiny Springs. Calving season, although his had been delayed this year. Even if Parker had been anywhere near ready, Nash would want to see it through.

"Speaking of little ones, Hailey tells me y'all are thinking about adopting sooner rather than later." It was a brilliant change of subject, if Nash did say so himself.

Parker simply stared and nodded.

Maybe he shouldn't have said anything, but Hailey didn't tell him not to. In fact, she could barely contain herself. Nash was getting a very different vibe from Parker.

"Sensitive topic?" he asked.

Parker raised his brows and shook his head. "Not at all. I'm happy to share."

"Then why so serious?"

His ranch hand looked back to the board. "Sorry, I thought of something…" He grabbed the marker as if he were going to jot down another point but paused instead.

That was weird. Then again, the whole day promised to be that way. Nash waited for Parker to elaborate, but no such insight was forthcoming. Maybe his ranch hand didn't want to talk about it after all.

"Since you're not gonna reveal your innermost thoughts and feelings, I'm heading to the stables." Nash couldn't help but snort, if only to add some levity to a potentially heavier conversation than either of them had bargained for.

Parker looked up. "I'll share my feelings if you go first."

With his Freudian slip, Nash thought he'd already gone first. In any case, he'd shared more than enough for one day. He wasn't about to add that sharing his feelings was at the bottom of his mental chore board this morning, because wouldn't that, in fact, constitute even more sharing?

"If you don't mind, please keep the twins occupied while I'm gone." He grabbed his jacket, Stetson and six carrots from the fridge, and headed out the door.

The cool breeze chafed, whipping across his skin like sandpaper against exposed nerves. The whole morning left him feeling vulnerable, and not in a good way. But this? The smell of the stables? The sound of wind through the aspens? The warmth of the sunlight stretching across the horizon and draping over snowcaps in the far distance? He could discuss his feelings about those things all day long.

"Here you go," Nash said as he presented a carrot to an appreciative Daisy, his oldest horse, who was afraid of children. She gave him a loving good-morning whinny in return. His two herding horses, Sassy and Tiger, both greeted him with nickers and accepted his prebreakfast treat without any drama or fuss.

By then, Cupcake had figured out carrots were involved and stretched her neck toward him as he approached, refusing to be passed over. Next door was Sugar Pie, who was waiting patiently for her treat. It was almost as though the latter two horses had picked up the personalities of their respective owners. Sugar Pie, being serious and methodical like Kat. Cupcake, their only Morgan horse, being unapologetically assertive like Lizzy.

Then there was Mischief. Nash had saved the biggest carrot for his guest, partially out of guilt for what he was about to do: feed the others. But that was his and Jess's agreement, and he'd already violated it once.

"So, Mischief, what do you think is holding Taylor back?" Nash asked.

The horse simply stared. Much like Parker had done. A giggle tickled his throat at the comparison.

"We can't help her unless we talk about our innermost thoughts and feelings," he continued.

Again, nothing but big brown eyes stared back. At least the horse seemed to be listening to him.

Instead of a full-on laugh, a chill coursed through his veins that had nothing to do with the cool breeze that had kicked up since he'd stepped outside.

That's it. Had to be. And to think he laughed off the possibility when it first crossed his mind about

Taylor carrying some sort of burden on her shoulders. Maybe his intuition had been screaming at him, and he'd been too stubborn to take it seriously.

Now it was his turn to stare at the prize-winning horse in front of him. If he could help Taylor break through whatever was holding her back, it would be worth all the feelings he could stomach sharing.

The tires of Jess's truck coming down the drive interrupted the moment, but not the feeling of it. If he were to express his innermost thoughts and feelings right now, he'd have to admit that the excitement of possibly not having lost his touch was invigorating.

Most of all, it was terrifying, because his return to teaching and Jess's return to him were guaranteed to be fleeting.

Nash finished feeding Daisy, Cupcake, Sugar Pie, Sassy and Tiger, then straightened his Stetson and headed back to the house. The sooner they got breakfast over with, the sooner he could test this epiphany he had about Taylor.

And the sooner he could put all this *feelings* nonsense behind him.

CHAPTER SEVEN

BEING BACK IN Nash's kitchen again was like going back in time. Same plaid wallpaper and matching dining chair cushions. Same beige curtains. Same wall clock, with the hour and minute hands doubling as the cowboy in the bucking bronc illustration, although the hands had been frozen in time. As if no feminine force had ever been there and left her mark.

The place was so quiet. Taylor abandoned her the moment they got there and ran to the twins' room. Nash must have gone outside, because the back door was left cracked open.

One thing had been updated, however. Nash used to use a blackboard and chalk to list his daily tasks. Now, a whiteboard and dry-erase marker had assumed its corner in the breakfast nook.

Jess set the bags of groceries on the counter. While she began unloading them, her mind composed another list: additional embellishments for the Dudley project. Perhaps a yellow satin lining for both the jacket and the skirt, and a black velvet border around the collar and pockets. She had just enough scrap fabric to accomplish that.

Perfect!

Nash came in, took off his hat and jacket and hung them on the freestanding coatrack. It swayed a bit against the weight, as if its bones were getting tired.

"Taylor's down the hall with the girls. If I can pry her away, we'll feed Mischief. If not, I'll do it myself. In the meantime, Lizzy can get to crackin'."

Nash squinted. "Pardon?"

"Cracking the eggs. That's her favorite part. Make her wash her hands first. Kat can measure the cheese. I'll fry the tortilla chips, but someone will need to cut up the sausage. It's up to you, but I personally wouldn't let any of the girls do that because andouille isn't the softest and requires a sharp knife. We want them to keep all their fingers. And keep them away from the stovetop so they don't get burned."

This time, he raised his brows. "I didn't realize it would be so dangerous. And complicated."

"Oh, sorry! It isn't. I'm being overprotective."

"I appreciate it. But I have a better idea. I'll take care of Mischief while you and the girls get… crackin'. I'll cut up the sausage when I get back," he said.

Before she could answer, he called out down the hall, "Ladies? Is anyone getting hungry?"

That was enough to extract them from the bedroom.

Nash put on his jacket and hat once again and headed out the door.

She watched out the window as he walked to the stables, and the longing that it stirred in her to have someone to help with the day-to-day duties of life both surprised and overwhelmed her. She didn't get that on the road. Or living in the intentionally bland apartment in Rock Springs that she'd moved her and Taylor into after selling the ranch for barely any profit.

The new place was more a home base than an actual home, but it was a way to keep Taylor in the same school district. The teachers there had been overwhelmingly supportive in letting the little barrel-racing phenom do some remote schoolwork.

Nash's place, however… *This* was a home.

By the time she turned back around, the girls had invaded the kitchen. Lizzy had retrieved a large cast-iron skillet, which she gripped with both hands but still couldn't lift to the counter. The bowl that Kat had pulled from a bottom cabinet sported a slight chip on the rim.

We can do better than that.

After a perusal of his cabinets, Jess concluded that the girls had indeed pulled out the fancy stuff. Make that the only stuff, as far as cookware and bowls were concerned.

"Let's all wash our hands before we get started," Jess said, taking the lead and hoping to set an example. The girls followed, although she had to make

Lizzy wash twice. The little girl was much too eager to get to the fun part.

Before Jess could process what was happening, Lizzy had tied an apron around Jess's waist. She had to loosen the ties a little but adored the thought.

Jess cleared a spot on the counter and retrieved a couple of painted crates for them to stand on. Lizzy didn't even wait for an invite.

While the budding chef selected an egg, tapped it on the edge of the bowl and carefully parted the halves, Jess retrieved the last items from the shopping bags and stealthily glanced over her shoulder to supervise. So far, so good. No fingers dipping into the bowl.

She collected the bag of pre-shredded cheese, fished around for a measuring cup in a lower cabinet and handed the items to Kat.

"Will you fill this halfway with Monterey Jack, pretty please? That would be a big help." She added a huge smile because it was obvious that twin wasn't thrilled with the assignment.

"I want to put sugar on the chips," she said.

"Let's make those together. I'll fry, you sprinkle," Jess said.

"Daddy says we have to make some with salt, too," Lizzy added.

"That's an excellent idea," Jess said.

At least Kat was grudgingly participating, which was more than could be said of Taylor. Her own daughter had taken a seat at the breakfast table and was toying with her friendship bracelets.

Jess understood. Taylor missed her friends back home. Although they were able to Zoom, those bracelets were the only physical connection.

Unfortunately—or perhaps fortunately—Jess didn't leave any friends behind. She knew better than to make any new ones here, because she'd have to leave them, too. Although it felt as though she'd already made a few at the B and B.

Kat finished filling the measuring cup and did a good job of hitting the halfway mark. Lizzy was busy fishing an eggshell from her prized mix. Those washed hands came in handy after all.

With the twins' duties reasonably under control, Jess settled into a chair across from Taylor. Only a few years ago, she couldn't tear the little girl away from the kitchen. Taylor had wanted to stir the eggs or flip the bacon or do whatever task she could that involved the stovetop. Jess wouldn't let her, but her daddy would. It was their secret. Until Mommy dearest found out and put an end to it. But this wasn't their family.

And Nash wasn't her daddy.

How could I have been so blind?

Jess took a deep breath, then reached over and stilled Taylor's hands until she looked up.

"Know what all this reminds me of?" Jess asked.

Taylor blinked and stared.

"It reminds me of that time I caught your daddy letting you flip the bacon, then lifting you up and leaning over the pan so you could watch it sizzle."

A hint of a smile crossed Taylor's face. "You were so mad, but Daddy thought it was funny."

Jess could practically feel the emotional weight tugging at the corners of that smile. They hadn't talked nearly enough about him, and she was at fault for that. For not initiating a conversation out of fear that it was "too soon." For not confronting that fear. Instead, leaving it up to a little girl to decide when she was ready. But there was no manual for handling such circumstances.

"If I remember correctly, we all ended up laughing at *me* by the end of it. Especially after he pointed out how I was encouraging you to get on top of a thousand-pound animal and making it gallop as fast as it could. Yet, I was so afraid you'd get burned by the popping grease. But he loved you too much to let that happen," Jess said.

Taylor's eyes were now glossing over. Jess wasn't holding it together much better, but she was determined to.

"Hey. I could use some help with browning the sausage," she said, then whispered the last part. "That's too big of a job for Lizzy and Kat."

That earned her the biggest smile of the morning.

Even though this wasn't their home, something felt so right about being here and cooking breakfast with the girls while Nash fed Mischief. Jess even began putting together a mental list of pots and pans and utensils needed to make this a more functional kitchen. Her imagination sewed colorful new cushion covers for the breakfast table chairs to replace the timeworn beige ones. It added flowers to a vase that otherwise seemed to serve no purpose on the counter other than to collect dust. She'd also get that bronc buster's hands back to work telling time.

The cast-iron skillet, however, would stay. As if any of this was her business. She'd bet it was the same one that she and Nash had used to cook Juicy Lucys dozens of times after practice.

Even though Nash had offered, Jess went ahead and diced the andouille and heated the skillet. He could cut the onion or jalapeno or avocado. In the meantime, her request must have resonated, because Taylor was all of a sudden at her side.

Since Lizzy was through with the eggs and had abandoned her post, Jess moved the step stool in front of the stove for Taylor, even though she was almost tall enough to cook without one. Better to be up too high. Couldn't take a chance on Taylor pulling a hot skillet on top of her.

"Can I stir?" Taylor asked.

Jess looked to the twins, who had moved on to drawing flowers and horses around the edges of the writing on Nash's chore board, so they were safely occupied and she could focus on Taylor's safety.

"I would love that." Jess handed her the spatula but remained poised to dive in at a second's notice. "I'll fry the tortilla strips."

Taylor had just started with the browning process when Nash walked back inside.

"Ladies, I'm home!" he said with what sounded to be exaggerated enthusiasm.

He studied the girls' artwork and looked down his nose at the twins, which made them both giggle.

"That is one funny lookin' horse," he said, pointing to one of the stick figures.

"That's 'cause it's a dog!" Lizzy practically shouted.

For some reason, he didn't look happy about that clarification. Instead, he stuffed his hands in his pockets and wandered Jess's way, stopping to peer over Taylor's shoulder. Behind the little girl's back, he cast Jess the same kind of down-the-nose look as he had done with the twins.

Jess didn't need an explanation for the nonverbal reprimand. She'd gone on and on about the dangers of cooking, and there she was, letting Taylor help with one of the riskiest tasks.

"I'll explain later," she said.

"No need." He proceeded to retrieve a folding chair that had been leaning against a wall and positioned it between two of the others. Tight fit, for sure. The whole process appeared painfully awkward, as if this home had never hosted more than four people at one time.

Once everything was cooked and combined, Jess helped Lizzy do the honors of giving everyone an equal serving of *migas*. Nash got up briefly to help serve the orange juice and milk and coffee, then squeezed back into their tight circle.

"Everything looks and smells amazing," he said. "A man could get used to this."

Jess suddenly craved some fresh air. Instead, she took a bite of *migas*. Then another comforting bite.

"Even better than Pop-Tarts," Lizzy said, right before piling a large bite on her fork and putting the whole thing in her mouth.

"I doubt our breakfast is gonna run off and leave us, but we can always make more. Smaller bites, and a little slower, okay?" Nash admonished.

Lizzy forced a visible gulp, then nodded. Kat and Taylor took a more measured approach.

"Pop-Tarts are good but not as good as pancakes with blueberries and strawberries and raspberries and chocolate-maple syrup and whipped cream," Taylor said.

Although the comment seemed to be directed to Lizzy, Jess felt the not-so-subtle jab. She hadn't made Taylor's favorite breakfast this morning. She'd helped make Lizzy's.

Then again, maybe it was a compliment.

"We'll make pancakes together tomorrow," Lizzy said.

Very diplomatic of the little girl. And quite presumptuous. Nash must have had the same thought as Jess, because they both remained deathly quiet. *Should we do this again?*

"Since y'all were able to join us after all, I take it the *gentleman* wasn't able to fix your sewing machine," Nash said to Jess.

Thankfully, one of them changed the subject,

although his emphasis on a certain word was curious. Almost sounded as though he was jealous.

"Not yet. But he's working on it. He'll be back over in a few days with a new part. He really knows his stuff," Jess said, taking another bite of *migas* while searching Nash's expression for some sort of confirmation of her suspicions.

He focused on the feast in front of him, giving nothing away.

"Excellent. You're lucky to find someone. Mostly cowboys in these parts. Not too many gentlemen who can fix things like that." He looked up and took a big bite.

Jess swallowed the one she'd taken and dabbed her napkin at the corners of her mouth.

"Turns out, he's a cowboy, as well." She added a smile.

Nash didn't even blink. "A jack-of-all-trades, huh?"

"More like a knight in shining armor. And he's quite dashing and polite, as knights are rumored to be."

"Dashing, huh?" He grinned and looked down, then picked a pan-fried tortilla strip off his plate and bit it in half. Judging by his expression, that one had sugar.

"What does 'dashing' mean?" Kat asked.

"It means he runs away from things," Lizzy said.

"I think, in this case, it means the cowboy mechanic was cute," Nash said.

"He wasn't cute," Taylor chimed in.

An amused look crossed Nash's face. She felt an urgent need to defend her knight in faded overalls.

"Young lady, that isn't true," Jess said. In her opinion, Vern was adorable.

"He's old, Mommy," Taylor countered.

"Anyone over thirty is considered *old* to her," Jess said to Nash, which seemed to humble him a little since he had also surpassed that milestone. By a few years, if her memory served.

The conversation quickly returned to small talk until there wasn't a morsel left on anyone's plate. Jess rose to clear the dishes, starting with hers, but Nash eased the plate out of her hands.

"You ladies did all the work. Let me take care of these."

"That's a nice offer, but I insist on helping. The girls can go do their own thing and have some fun. I'm afraid I don't have any exciting plans for them today. Not yet, at least." Might as well fess up in advance. Nash would hear about their day, anyway, how Jess kept them trapped inside the B and B while she sewed.

Without waiting to receive the go-ahead, the girls ran back down the hall. Taylor followed.

Together, she and Nash cleared the plates and placed them beside the sink. He let the water run until it turned hot, then plugged one side while Jess added the dishwashing liquid.

"Alone at last," Nash said as he began washing and rinsing the plates, one at a time.

This was a good thing. She wanted to get a read

on his thoughts about Taylor. He hadn't offered anything so far.

After the dinner plates were clean and placed in the drainer, he soaped the chipped bowl. He did a thorough job with the task, as if he'd done the same thing every morning for years.

Then again, he'd had to do all the day-to-day tasks by himself, as she'd also been having to do. Exactly how long had Roxanne been gone?

Jess picked up a dry cloth, eased the bowl from his hands and proceeded to dry it. No room left in the drainer, but she'd take care of those next.

"I'm sure you want an update on Taylor's progress," he said.

"Mind reader," she said.

Nash collected the forks and rinsed each as thoroughly as he had the dishes.

"You were right about her talent. But I'm questioning mine. I need a little more time to figure out what's holding her back, because I agree with what you said—she's The One to Watch, for sure." He handed her the utensils to dry, then started on the skillet.

"I have no doubt you'll solve the mystery. You're raising two amazing daughters, by the way. For twins, they couldn't be any more different,"

Nash nodded. "We've been through a lot together. Some rough times but mostly good. Kind of like this old thing." He held up the skillet and pivoted it around as if it were a feather.

Her entire body ached at the nostalgic feelings that piece of cast iron evoked.

"Those Juicy Lucys we used to cook would make any skillet happy. Not to mention, any hungry cowboy or cowgirl," she said.

"Yep."

Even though that one word was all he offered, his smile confirmed he remembered their good times, as well. As with the serving bowl, that wall he'd built had some chips in it after all.

The wall she'd tried to create wasn't faring much better.

Feelings were not part of Nash's plan. But there they were. Right on the surface.

Furthermore, he liked it. He missed all this about Jess. Their long talks. The friendship. Their teamwork in washing the dishes after someone lost the joke swap and had to cook Juicy Lucys.

How I feel when she looks at me.

Most of all, he missed her laughter, although he'd yet to hear it this morning. Roxanne not only didn't have a domestic bone in her body, she didn't have a funny bone, either.

Jess's laugh was contagious. It started out as a giggle, then exploded into a full-throated, open-mouthed, face-to-the-ceiling howl after the punch line settled in.

He came close to telling a joke, wanting to hear that laugh again. But he was already treading on dangerous ground.

Having finished with the dishes, they both turned around and leaned against the counter like they used to do.

"No plans for the day, huh?" he asked. Mostly to make small talk. He didn't expect her to have something unique and exciting for the twins to do at all times. Keeping them entertained was practically impossible.

"To be honest, I was hoping to come up with an idea that would keep them within my field of vision while I got some work done."

Of course she had work to do. Unless she'd received some big life insurance policy, she had to support herself and her daughter. It reminded him of how little he really knew about her. The familiar moments tricked him into thinking that no time had passed between them.

"What kind of work do you do, aside from raising a daughter? Being a single parent is the hardest job in the world," he said, angling himself toward her.

She pivoted to face him, as well. "That's the truth. Parenthood is a full-time gig, but it doesn't pay the bills. I sew. My clients, at least right now, are other rodeo mommies."

He resisted the urge to wince. The more he thought about it, the more he realized her rodeo-circuit clientele might include Roxanne. He hadn't heard whether she'd gone on to have other children. Then again, he'd stopped following all barrel racing news. He didn't want to know.

"Seems we both play two roles. Or, at least I assume you don't have a wife out there somewhere who you haven't told me about," she said.

"Just an ex," he responded without naming names. That seemed pointless at this juncture. Jess was much better at math than he'd ever be. She could add two plus two just fine.

"Does she ever...?" Jess began to say.

"See the girls?"

Jess nodded.

Nash shook his head and hoped that was enough of an answer.

"All I can say is that Taylor's lucky to have a mom like you. And one that sews. I hope she knows that."

"That's about the only thing she likes about me these days."

"I doubt that."

"We share a passion for barrel racing. And all the excitement of traveling from city to city. So there is that. It's more than enough for me to live vicariously through her and her successes."

His breath caught in his throat. He remembered those days.

"I can't imagine doing that now. This ranch is our forever home. Until the twins up and marry and move out. In that order, if I have any say."

Jess laughed softly. "Takes time to really know what you want. Trial and error. Get married too early, and..."

"You end up settling down and planting roots when you don't want to," he said.

"And giving up on what you did," she added.

There. That's what he needed to hear, even though he hadn't wanted to. As much as he could get used to all this—waking up in the same home every morning, and sharing breakfast and feelings with family—it didn't appeal to Jess.

Nash had hesitated asking a question that had been on his mind since she left. However, she'd opened the door, and he was walking through.

"Why did you stop, Jess?"

She gulped hard and stared at him for what felt like the longest minute.

"I've asked myself that question," she said. "I needed a sabbatical. Needed to step away from it all for a while, and that's when Lance stepped in. We got married, I got pregnant, then Taylor was born. All I wanted to do was be there to take care of them. And especially her. Still do."

"From what I can see, you're doing a beautiful job. Besides, you could get back into it." His comment wasn't an idle one. Even though he was entertaining the thought of her having breakfast with them every morning, he was under no illusion that she wanted such a life.

She looked down and scratched at a spot on the counter.

"Right now, I'm focusing on making ends meet. I thought Lance had a good life insurance policy, but he'd cashed it out. Needed the money to pay bills for things I didn't even know he'd bought."

"Ouch."

"Never occurred to me to question why he really needed a new tractor, super-duper tires on his truck, or that the cloth upholstery inside had been replaced with leather. He handled all the finances for us. But he was such a loving dad to Taylor, and a terrific husband to me in many ways."

Nash wanted to say the guy had good taste, too, as evidenced by the fact that he married Jess. But now wasn't the time for such things.

"I'm sorry to hear that." Despite the way their relationship had ended, and all the question marks it left in its wake, he'd never stopped wanting the best for her.

Jess offered a soft smile of appreciation. "Thank you. But, hey, what doesn't kill us makes us stronger, right?"

"How has Taylor handled losing her dad?"

Jess folded her arms and looked to the floor. "I guess as well as any child would. Of course, she doesn't know about the money situation. And I would never tell her. I'd rather she remember only good things about her father. She thinks I sew because I love it. Thank goodness she likes what I make for her, because I couldn't begin to afford..."

Nash inched closer and tugged at her arms until they unfolded. He intertwined his fingers with hers and gave them a squeeze.

He almost admitted he'd had similar issues with Roxanne with the spending but stopped short. He'd felt like a failure for barely meeting her lifestyle expectations. He'd been forced to lower those even further and start saying no after he found out they were having twins. That didn't go over well.

But this moment wasn't about him.

She slipped her hands from his loose grip and gave him a big hug instead, which made any residual inadequacies he'd felt dissolve away. Especially when he hugged her even harder in return, and her form seemed to mold to his.

A trio of giggles erupted from the doorway.

Although he was pretty sure the girls hadn't heard any of their conversation, the long, intimate hug could be interpreted in many ways. And the way they seemed to be interpreting it made them all happy, which only confirmed what he already knew.

His wasn't the only heart in peril.

CHAPTER EIGHT

JESS'S EYES FLEW open when the grandfather clock announced it was 5:00 a.m.

She bolted upright and tried to orient herself to her surroundings, because none of it looked familiar.

It was coming back to her now. She'd gotten up at 3:00 a.m. and come down to the parlor to sew. Must have laid her head down around four and fallen asleep, because she remembered those chimes.

She examined the dot paper where her cheek had been. No drool, thankfully. Just a little smudge from the mascara she'd neglected to remove last night. It was in the shape of a perfect heart, no less. What were the odds? Although she'd lost an hour of productive time, it was unlikely that anyone would wander into the parlor so early.

Judging by the clinking bowls, Georgina was in the kitchen, starting preparations for breakfast. Jess could grab a cup of coffee now from the pot she'd made an hour ago and put on a fresh one for her hostess.

She wasn't quick enough. As soon as she stood,

a woman emerged from the kitchen, holding the carafe. Except it wasn't Georgina. Furthermore, the woman wasn't alone. An adorable, sleepy-looking young boy stayed close to her side.

"I thought you could use a refill," she said, adding a warm smile that rivaled her even warmer voice.

Her timing couldn't have been more perfect. This woman was an angel. Sans the wings.

When Jess didn't answer, the woman picked up the cup that Jess had placed on a side table and filled it to the brim, then looked down at the little boy.

"PJ, would you like to offer Jess some cream or sweetener?"

He held up a small carton of milk and some packets of sugar. It had to be the cutest thing Jess had ever seen. She couldn't say no to that face even if she wanted to.

"I'll take some milk. Thank you, PJ."

The little boy took a step forward and offered her both milk and sugar anyway.

"He helped me carry the eggs in this morning, too. Don't think I could manage without him," the woman said, while brushing the almost black hair out of the little boy's eyes.

"I can understand why," Jess said as she tried to piece this pattern into something recognizable. Vern's ranch provided the eggs, but he was usually the one to bring them over. This must be family.

"I'm Vern's granddaughter, Vanessa," the woman

offered before Jess had a chance to confirm her theory. "He wasn't up to the task this morning but told me you were here and what happened with your machine. And that you'd probably be awake and working this morning."

A pang of guilt cut through Jess's conscience at the memory of Vern hauling that heavy toolbox up the stairs. Then struggling with that big crate of eggs. And she'd let him.

"Is he okay?" she asked.

"He'll be fine. He gets down in his back sometimes. Tends to overdo it. I offered to make this delivery run for him. I'll be back this afternoon to lead a workshop. At least, I think it's this afternoon."

Vanessa had that mind-spinning look that Jess recognized all too well in herself. That "I have so many responsibilities to juggle, I don't know where to start" kind of expression. Jess knew from experience that that was when it was best to take a step back and regroup. She was standing at that same precipice.

"Care to join me for a cup of coffee?" Jess asked.

Vanessa looked at the carafe and bit her lip. "I don't want to take you away from what you're working on."

"Oh, please, take me away for a minute." Truth was, she could use some hot coffee to sharpen her focus, and she didn't want to have any kind of beverage near the fabric. Not even water.

A smile broke through Vanessa's visible stress.

"An offer I can't refuse. Okay. I'll grab a mug from the kitchen. PJ, let's get you something to drink while we're in there."

By the time Vanessa and PJ came back, Jess had organized her next steps to finish one of the Western shirts. For now, she settled into an armchair.

PJ was carrying a glass of milk with both hands. Vanessa eased it from his grip and patted the overstuffed sofa as a directive for him to sit, then eased in beside him.

"Is PJ a nickname or your full name?" Jess asked.

"My real name is Perry Jackson Fraser, but there's a girl in my class named Perry, too, so I got this nickname. I like it."

"If you stay in Destiny Springs long enough, you'll get a nickname, too," Vanessa said. "Except in my case, apparently. Not sure whether I should be insulted or relieved. I don't stand still long enough for them to pin one on me."

Jess couldn't resist. "Really? I got one my second day here. Georgina called me Nash's gal."

Vanessa's brows raised, and her mouth formed an O but nothing came out.

"I had the same reaction. Georgina said she didn't mean it *that* way. And why would she? But you can imagine how I felt."

"There are worse things to be called. Nash is a good man. Gave my cousin Parker a job as a ranch hand, even though he didn't even know what a hoof-pick was used for. Thought it was for cleaning the stalls. Parker denies it, of course. That's another thing about Destiny Springs. You'll hear the most outlandish stories, but they *all* end up being true."

"All?" Jess asked. Vanessa's emphasis on the word was interesting. Vern had already warned her about them, but he said only *some* were true.

Even though hiring a ranch hand with zero experience seemed outlandish, it sounded like something Nash would do. Might be a good topic of discussion between the two of them, instead of dredging up their distant past. Or even worse, the recent past. Yesterday had turned way too personal with that extended hug. She could still feel the softness of his flannel shirt and the strength of his heartbeat.

"I'd like a man like that in my life, but I barely have time for this one." Vanessa reached over and wiped away a drop of milk that had settled on PJ's chin.

The relationship between Vanessa and PJ was at a sweet stage. Hopefully, it would stay that way for her sake. Another single mom, up at the crack of dawn to take care of others, which included Jess this morning with the coffee.

"Cody mentioned a work-life balance workshop. Is that the one you're leading?" Jess asked.

"Yes. Sounds appealing, huh? Specifically, caring for young children and older parents. Some folks call us the 'sandwich generation.' But my workshop adds an extra ingredient—pursuing a new career without the support of a spouse. Some

sandwiches have to thrive with only one ingredient and one breadwinner. Themselves."

"I couldn't have said it any better. Are you starting a new career?"

"Sort of. I'm a caregiver. It's the only thing I know.
Been doing it since before I was old enough to legally
work. But I'm opening my own business in Chey-
enne in a few months and will have professionals
do the legwork, which will hopefully free up more
time to spend with this little man."

"Won't that be fun, having your mommy around
more often?" Jess asked PJ.

"Yaaas!" He nodded enthusiastically, then looked
up to his mom with the biggest smile.

"Sounds like a good plan, Vanessa," Jess said,
stopping short of promising to attend the workshop.
She had Lizzy and Kat to think about. Not to mention, her work projects.

"If you ever get tired of sewing everything yourself, you could do something similar. You could
design, and someone else could execute it. Might
give you more time with your daughter."

"I'd love that, but I'm not so sure how she'd
feel," Jess said. "She's at the age where she's test-
ing boundaries and asserting her independence. She
retreats into her headphones, but she still seems to
like having me near."

"Maybe you could use the quiet time to focus
on yourself. Try some meditation or pampering. It
sounds like you've earned it."

Now, there was a concept. Hadn't even occurred to her.

"Well, I think you've earned a nickname, Vanessa. I hereby proclaim you Earth Angel. If there's anything I can do to help *you* while I'm here, please let me know."

Except for sewing clothes for PJ, so please don't ask.

Vanessa's phone buzzed. The woman read the message and unleashed a heavy sigh. Another ball must have been thrown into her work-life balancing act.

"Everything okay?" Jess asked.

"Grandpa's girlfriend, Sylvie, can't look after him this afternoon. She's leading a trail ride. I may have to see if the DEBBs can fill my workshop time with something or someone else. Unless Nash can step in and help. He's over there now, checking on Vern." Vanessa maintained eye contact as if making sure Jess was convinced of Nash's selflessness.

No need. She already knew.

"Sounds like something Nash would do." The last thing he needed was to step in and help take care of Vern again this afternoon.

"Like I said, he's a good man. He could use a good woman in his life after what he went through. But you didn't hear it from me."

It seemed Vanessa knew Nash better than she'd led Jess to believe, with the way she'd been hyping him up. But Jess needed more information.

"I'm thinking out loud here, but I can't believe

Roxanne could walk away from him. Much less her own daughters," she said.

Of course, Jess didn't know who walked away from whom. But Roxanne was alive and thriving on the rodeo circuit. If it were her being away from her child or children, she'd be too distraught to ever compete again.

"Me, neither. But I think it's a good thing that he has full custody of the twins. He loves those girls so much, and they're crazy about him. He's a good dad."

And a good man, in general. Jess came so close to volunteering to help Vern this afternoon herself, but she didn't know anything about nursing an octogenarian with a bad back. Plus, she'd have the twins, and that might be more than she could manage. However, that gave her an idea.

"I don't know anything about balancing, but I'm pretty good at tying up loose threads. If the DEBBs would be interested in an impromptu sewing workshop in place of yours, I'd be willing to make a fool of myself."

The tension in Vanessa's face softened. "That sounds like a wonderful idea to me, but that's a lot to ask."

Jess wouldn't define it as that, but if it helped her Earth Angel and spared Nash from having to step in and help Vern, she would do it. Besides, a sewing workshop might be fun for the girls. She could give them some felt and glue and rhinestones to play with while she constructed a garment for the belles and beaus.

"I do have something I'd like to ask," Jess said. It was a bold question, but since Vanessa seemed to be playing matchmaker... "Do you think Nash would ever get back with Roxanne?"

Vanessa tilted her head. "I doubt he feels anything for her. I'm not convinced he ever really did."

"Because she wasn't the one who broke his heart?" That was the rumor Vern had mentioned, although Jess had a difficult time believing it.

"Exactly," Vanessa said with a confidence that sent a chill racing down Jess's spine. Whether it was the good kind or bad, she wasn't sure.

Vanessa continued. "Problem is, the only person who knows who did is Nash. And he isn't talking."

"HEALTH IS BETTER than wealth," Vern said. He visibly winced when Nash tugged the heating pad out from under him once he'd shifted to his side.

"Sorry. I'm not the best nurse around," Nash said, although he wished he were setting a better example.

The twins looked on with muted curiosity. Even though he'd wanted to spare them from witnessing the inconveniences of aging and the inevitable aches and pains for as long as he could, they needed to learn how to help. And know that people would be there for them, too, if they ever needed it. That's what family and friends were all about.

Ordinarily, Vern would swing by Nash's and drop

off some eggs for his "favorite Destiny Springs bachelor" en route to the B and B. However, Vanessa had called late last night and asked Nash if he wouldn't mind picking up his portion of eggs while she made Fraser Ranch's usual delivery to the B and B. That way, her grandpa wouldn't be left alone for too long, in case he needed help with something.

Nash didn't even have to think twice. It was worth having to rouse the girls out of bed a little early.

He adjusted the heating pad cord, which could present a trip hazard if Vern got a wild hair and decided to get up and walk around. The picture of health, he was not.

"You don't need to baby me," Vern said. "You and the girls go on home."

"We'll leave after you finish what you started to say about health and wealth."

Nash meant it. Although lack of wealth was his main concern these days, that pesky palpitation from a few days ago still haunted him. He'd gotten his heart checked six months ago. The cardiologist ran the requisite tests and informed Nash that he was as healthy as a bull. And Nash believed it.

Then Jess showed up. Ten years had passed, and much more had happened to her than he'd ever imagined.

"Not sure there's much to add," Vern said. "Except that if we can't have both, we should all have at least one or the other."

"If that were the case, you would deserve to be a millionaire today," Nash replied.

"How do you know I'm not?" Vern cackled. "I'm in better shape than I look. It's just that these parts of ours come with limited warranties. All of mine have long expired."

"How'd you strain it this time?" Nash asked. These back issues were becoming a semiregular occurrence with the guy.

"I was trying to impress a lovely young lady by carrying that heavy toolbox upstairs." Vern pointed toward the culprit by the door in the entry. "Her sewing machine broke down, so of course Cody called on me to help. I think you know her. Jess McCoy?"

Nash did a terrible job hiding his huge grin. It came on so fast. She'd led him to believe it was some young cowboy who'd been the gentleman to come to her rescue. *Dashing*, did she say?

"Uh-huh. That's what I thought. You have a crush on that gal," Vern said.

Nash glanced at the twins, who were busy rearranging the knickknacks on one of the side tables and knocking a few to the ground in the process. Thankfully, Vern seemed amused rather than annoyed.

"You *do* know how old I am," Nash said, even though he himself couldn't find a better word to describe how he felt.

"You're never too old to have a crush. I had one on Sylvie for all of one minute before I fell head over heels for her. Couldn't have hidden it if I'd wanted to. But don't worry, your secret is safe with me," Vern said as he gave him the thumbs-up.

"Care to shake on it?" Nash held up his pinkie.

Vern latched on. "Ha! I haven't made a pinkie promise in years."

With his secret safe, Nash covered Vern loosely with a fuzzy blanket, leaving the heating pad exposed. He put another log on the fire and stoked it. Lizzy tried to ease the poker from his hand, but he tightened his grip. This was definitely not a toy.

"Do me a favor, sweetie. Can you and Kat bring Mr. Vern a tall glass of ice water?" He didn't want their input on this topic. Not after they'd witnessed the hug. And later, when he'd tucked them into bed, they'd asked if Jess was his girlfriend. He had to explain that friends sometimes hugged, too, and that it was perfectly fine as long as both people were okay with it.

Yet, there was something much more special about his and Jess's hug. Even the girls picked up on it.

The front door flew open, and PJ ran inside, followed by Vanessa. She helped her son remove his jacket, then took off her own scarf and draped the items over the existing coats and sweaters and hats.

"Were your ears burning?" she asked Nash as she wandered over.

Not that he should have been surprised. People in Destiny Springs enjoyed a little gossip as much as anyone. Single folks and their personal business seemed to be the preferred topic.

"Girls, come over here and feel my ears. Tell me if they're burning."

He leaned over, and they eagerly complied.

"Yes!" they said in unison.

"I guess the question is, why would they be doing that?" He directed the question at Vanessa.

"I had coffee with someone you know who's staying at the B and B."

Why was Jess up this early?

Nash couldn't say he knew Vanessa well, yet she felt like family because Vern was like family. They'd crossed paths as youngsters. A few months ago, she'd come to Destiny Springs to help with Vern alongside Parker. But, unlike her cousin, Vanessa had bigger plans than to settle down here.

For now, whatever this ear-burning nonsense was, it needed to cool down real fast.

"The lady said she's Nash's gal. That's you!" PJ added.

Nash looked to Vanessa. "What?"

"Georgina inadvertently referred to her as 'Nash's gal' before realizing how it sounded. How funny is that?"

"Jess is a sweet *gal*, that's for sure, but she's not mine." In another week and some change, she'd be on her way to Montana with her daughter.

"Mommy has a nickname, too," PJ said.

"How about you and the girls go play upstairs." Vanessa pivoted him toward the stairway and gave him a kiss on the top of his head before he ran away with the girls hot on his heels.

"And what might that nickname be?" Nash asked.

"Earth Angel."

"Like the song?" he asked.

"No. Like, I brought her a cup of coffee while she was working, and she gave me way too much credit."

Vanessa walked over to Vern and readjusted the heating pad that Nash had just positioned. "Can I get you anything, Grandpa?"

"Not a thing, angel. You don't have to fuss over me."

"Speaking of angels, you saved Jess's life, you know," Vanessa said to Vern, who promptly tried to swat the compliment away.

"She gets up two hours early so she can finish all her sewing commitments before she has to leave for Montana," Vanessa continued.

"She mentioned getting up before the crack of dawn," Vern said. "I hope she can find a better solution. Lack of sleep is hard on the body and the mind."

Nash understood that all too well. He hadn't slept through the night since Roxanne left them the first time. The twins were two handfuls as infants, and it wasn't getting easier with age. Now he realized that he'd handed off that responsibility to Jess every day since she got here. Maybe the trade he'd insisted upon wasn't so equal after all.

Sure, he couldn't fix a sewing machine. But there was something he *could* do to help, starting with offering to feed Mischief in the mornings. The extra time it took her to come back and forth to his house for that could be better spent on her own projects before having to juggle twins.

Besides, it was just breakfast for one additional horse, right?

Right. Kind of like *migas* with the girls had been just breakfast—one that led to an extended hug, which had led to thoughts of something else. Something he'd dared to imagine ten years ago but didn't dare act upon.

Kissing her.

CHAPTER NINE

"Do I LOOK as brokenhearted as I feel?" Nash asked in a low tone.

Jess gulped. The conversation she'd had with Vanessa about Nash and the mystery woman was still fresh on her mind.

"Who broke your heart?" she asked.

His eyes shifted toward Kat, who had followed Lizzy to the parlor entry to look at the crowd that had assembled there.

"Someone isn't happy, although I'm not sure why. I suspect it has to do with me coaching Taylor. Anything you could do to cheer her up would be greatly appreciated."

Not the pressure Jess needed today, with this workshop now on her plate and a parlor full of DEBBs waiting for her to start.

The good news was, what had felt like the worst idea to volunteer ended up being nothing short of brilliant. She was going to use this time to make progress on one of the garments she owed.

"Girls, go ahead and find a spot inside," Jess

called out. "I'll be there in a sec, and then we'll get started on some fun stuff."

Jess then turned to Nash. "I was planning to start one of the barrel racing shirts I owe to a rodeo mom as the workshop topic, but I'll distract the girls with felt and rhinestones. Just wanted to let you know, since rodeo stuff is a tender subject."

"I appreciate it. Those shirts look like some she and Lizzy already own, so no concerns. Besides, you're not putting her on a horse or anything."

"No danger of me doing that," she said. He'd been open about his problems, and she wasn't going to add to them.

He softly smiled and nodded for Taylor to follow him.

Once the two were out the door, Jess got situated at the front of the room and looked out at the eager faces of the DEBBs. All she saw was irony.

Those sweet, trusting folks were looking to a self-taught seamstress—one who'd never taken a formal lesson herself, much less presented one—to teach them something.

Lizzy had claimed the big, overstuffed chair nearest the sewing machine. She was a little wiggly but otherwise attentive and ready to help. Jess had a new idea for how to involve her in the process, in a fun way. Even more fun than felt and rhinestones. She'd have Lizzy trace around the sample shirt to make a pattern on the dot paper.

Kat had retreated to a chair in the far back of the parlor. It was almost as if she were stating the obvious: she felt left out. It broke Jess's heart. After all, Lizzy and Jess had bonded over cooking, and Kat's own daddy was bonding with Taylor over barrel racing. Not only that, but the lessons were continuing.

Then a possible solution occurred to her. Jess straightened and served up her most confident smile to the group.

"Does anyone here have a favorite top or skirt or pair of pants that they'd love to duplicate?" she asked.

Nearly all the hands raised.

"I used to have a top like the one I'm wearing. It was my favorite. I paid a little over one hundred dollars, but I made this duplicate I'm wearing for under five. The only difference between the two is that this one doesn't have a fancy label. I'm not sure what material that label was made from, but it couldn't have been worth the extra ninety-five bucks. Especially since no one ever saw it."

That got everyone's attention. Except Kat's. But Jess was just getting started.

"For today's workshop, we'll be duplicating a girl's Western barrel racing shirt from a clone. Lizzy, I'll need your help with drawing the pattern. Dorothy, would you mind helping Lizzy lay it out nice and flat while I make sure my model fits the prototype?"

"I'd love to," Dorothy said.

It wasn't lost on Jess that she'd now owe the lady a favor.

"I need a model," Jess said, although she already knew who she'd pick. "Let's see, it needs to be someone who fits the sample."

Kat sat up a little straighter but didn't volunteer. At least she'd been listening. Jess walked to the back of the room.

"Do you want to model for me?"

Kat nodded so hard Jess was afraid she'd throw out her neck. Talk about a transformation. Now there was no doubt in Jess's mind that the little girl was interested in the sport.

"Good! Let's run upstairs to my room. I want you to try something on."

Kat hopped out of the chair.

Jess took her hand, and they approached Dorothy. "Would you mind talking to the group about sewing while we're gone?"

It was a big ask, but Dorothy seemed more than willing. At this point, Jess was out of viable options.

Together, Jess and Kat went to the Spandex Room, where Jess fished out the folded top from her work stack and handed it to her little model.

Jess turned around to give her some privacy. "Let me know if you need any help."

After a few long minutes, Kat said, "I'm ready."

Other than the sleeves being nearly an inch too long, it looked like the shirt was made for her.

"I *looooove* it." Kat practically ran over to a full-length mirror and twirled around to see all the angles. "Where is the number?"

"That's something they assign the barrel racer before the competition."

Jess's answer deflated Kat's smile. Not completely, but enough. So much for this bright idea.

"How do you feel about pink?" That may be her only saving grace. She remembered Kat had been wearing a pink puffer jacket when they first met.

The little girl confirmed with a nod.

"Good. Change back into your other clothes and we'll get started making this." Even though this shirt design had a scalloped yoke and Jess didn't have enough contrasting fabric to help it stand out, she could use the same pink fabric and add black piping to fancy it up. She was pretty sure she had rhinestone snaps somewhere, as well. The client was going to love it.

Hand in hand, she and Kat returned to the group. Dorothy had taken full command of the workshop, explaining the different patterning paper.

"Then there's my favorite. Dot paper, also known as alphabet paper, which is what Jess is using here. See how it has these blue marks, evenly spaced in a grid? It's a little more expensive but worth it, in my opinion."

"Thank you for helping, Dorothy. If I get any more speaking engagements, can I hire you?" Jess asked.

"I'd be hurt if you didn't." Dorothy smiled and exited the proverbial spotlight.

Now, for the other smile Jess wanted to see.

She explained the first steps to the group. Specifically, how to fold the material and position different parts of the garment to create the pattern pieces. Lizzy had the important task of drawing around all the edges while Kat looked on with a highly contagious enthusiasm.

Jess added a dotted line around all the drawn pieces and then proceeded to cut them out. For time's sake, she talked through the rest of the process of cutting out the material and assembling the garment. While necessary, it ended up being a bad idea. In the background, she picked up on chattering.

"John had a favorite linen shirt that he wore out. Maybe I'll surprise him and make one like it for our twelfth anniversary," one of the ladies said.

The thought of wedding anniversaries poked at Jess's pincushion of a heart. She'd sewn matching cotton shirts for her and Lance to celebrate their second.

"That is a wonderful idea!" another lady said. "I think I'll pattern some new drapes for our bedroom. We both love plaid. Wesley absolutely hates the red, white and blue ones that came with the house."

Jess closed her eyes and tried to refocus on the task at hand. But the warm memories of decorating her own primary suite as a newlywed sprang to mind. Her bedroom these days was whichever hotel room she shared with her daughter on their way to the next rodeo.

Although traveling so much hadn't been the eas-

iest life for either of them, it was still better than
being tied to a so-called home built on a chiffon-thin
foundation. But that was a lifetime ago. She had an
important task right in front of her now.

She resorted to an old trick she used when barrel racing: focusing on what she wanted most, and
pretending as if it were waiting for her at the finish line. In this case, she wanted this workshop to
be over with.

After adding the final snap, Jess turned around
and stood. The chattering stopped.

She raised the shirt high enough for everyone
to see. "Ladies and gents, here is the almost completed project. I wanted to touch on all the steps,
but I need to go back and do some finishing."

That was an understatement. At least she hadn't
lost any of the attendees, even though she'd gone
over the allotted hour.

Jess had finished the top in a decent time frame.

After the DEBBs thanked her and dispersed, she
finished the shirt while the girls pulled everything
out of her notions toolbox as if they'd discovered
some cool new toys. She nudged the pincushion and
needles out of their reach. Lizzy zeroed in on the
tailor's chalk and was trying to draw on a scrap of
dot paper. Kat, on the other hand, seemed to have
reverted to her gloomy self.

"You're a natural at modeling, Kat. Maybe you
could be one when you grow up," Jess said, realizing a little too late that she shouldn't encour-

age that traveling-required profession, either, for Nash's sake.

Kat toyed with some of the bright-colored thimbles. "Do models get to keep the shirts they model?"

Jess knew what Kat was asking. She also knew that this shirt wasn't her best work. Definitely not well-made enough for her client. Yet, it had served the purpose for the workshop, if not making Kat completely happy. But one thing might.

"Today, they do," she said. The words were like a vitamin B infusion for the little girl, who pepped right up.

The good ideas kept coming.

Jess rummaged through a couple of travel cases and found a good-sized square of muslin. She then pulled the velvet square that she'd proposed to use for the Dudley project and held it against her heart, hoping it would give her the right answer, because, as Georgina had said in the cooking workshop, there wasn't a fabric store within a hundred miles of Destiny Springs.

"Lizzy, would you mind handing me some black thread, please?" She then turned to Kat. "What's your favorite number?"

Kat didn't even have think about it. "Eight."

"Any special reason?"

"Taylor is eight, and I want to be eight."

"Well, you're about to get your wish. Lizzy, I'll need your help. Can you draw a big number eight on this pattern paper?" Jess marked some parameters so that the little girl would get the proportions right.

"While you're at it, draw a daisy. A big one, about the size of my hand." Jess could make a pink daisy from the scraps and add something in the center. That way Lizzy wouldn't go home empty-handed.

Jess sewed the flower first, adding some backing between the pink layers and a giant black button in the center.

"For you, my lady," she said as she handed it to Lizzy.

"That's pretty!" Lizzy said, brushing her tiny fingers over the petals.

One down, one to go. Jess cut out a square of the muslin and used a zigzag stitch on the edges so they wouldn't fray. She then cut out the number that Lizzy had drawn and trimmed it out of the black velvet scrap she'd brought down. Her scissors rounded the curves like a barrel racer would.

"Did y'all know that the original barrel racing configuration was a figure eight and not a cloverleaf? And that the women received scores on their horsemanship and outfits?"

They both shook their heads. Kat seemed especially intrigued. Lizzy, not so much.

With some careful positioning, Jess sewed the number onto the muslin, tacked all four corners onto the back of the shirt so that it would be easy to remove, and held it up for Kat to see.

"What do you think?" she asked.

Kat didn't have to answer. Her beautiful smile

was everything in the moment. If this turnaround didn't impress Nash, she wasn't sure what could.

"Can I wear it now?" Kat asked.

"Sure! We need to try it on anyway. Make sure I don't need to alter anything else."

When they all went back upstairs, Kat couldn't change into the shirt fast enough. But when the little girl turned around, Jess not only saw the competitor's number she'd tacked onto the back, she recognized a whole other layer of irony.

In trying to tread softly around a certain subject, she may have intentionally barreled through it.

NASH ASSUMED HIS old teaching spot on the fence railing. Knowingly this time. But this was as far as it was going to go.

He watched Taylor go through the pattern. Positioning was good coming in. Mischief was supple in his rib cage. They powered out of the turns beautifully. One new thing did stand out today: her start was a little shy, and she still wasn't running home as fast as he thought she could.

The question was, why? The trickiest part was rounding the barrels, and she slayed those.

If he thought taking her through what Jess used to call the lazy daisy drill would help, he would gladly add three more barrels and rearrange them in a loose daisy pattern. But that was a lot of trouble and wouldn't be necessary if his intuition was right. In fact, they could wrap this up today, and he could move on with his life. More importantly,

Jess could get back to doing what she needed to do with her work, because the inequality of their trade was now weighing *him* down.

Nash motioned Taylor over. "What do you think about when you're out there?"

She looked away as if searching for an answer. "Um, I don't know. I just try to block out the noise, and I focus on the first barrel."

"Good. Do you give a pep talk to Mischief?"

"Yeah. Sometimes."

"Does he ever give you one back?"

Her brows scrunched. "No. Of course not. Horses can't talk."

Okay, maybe she was a little too mature to fall for that.

"True. But he listens to you, doesn't he? You teach him to focus on what you both want to accomplish through actions. And he answers in his own way."

"I s'pose."

"I want you to try something. Think about how much fun you and Mischief have out there."

That hint of a smile faded, which was exactly the response he'd hoped for.

"Humor me," he said.

"Okay. I'll try," she said.

Once she started, his stopwatch confirmed what was clear to his eyes. Sure enough, this time she was over by an extra five seconds or so. His timing method wasn't too precise, but with that much of a lag, it didn't need to be. That time difference equaled centuries in barrel racing.

Her chin practically touched her chest as she approached him again.

"Sorry," she said.

"No need to apologize. Ever. Let's go inside and get some hot chocolate. With lots of marshmallows."

Taylor gave Mischief a side kick and steered him toward the stables.

"Let him stay out here," Nash called out. "We aren't finished."

No doubt in his mind that her issues had nothing to do with her skill level and everything to do with her emotions. Was Jess pushing, and was this Taylor's way of pushing back? Or was it not fun for her anymore? He was determined to find out.

Taylor sat quietly at the breakfast table while Nash warmed up the milk in a saucepan, added the chocolate mix and poured it into mugs. He topped them both off with an overflowing handful of marshmallows.

From his place across the table, he could easily gauge her reactions. He took a sip and intentionally dipped his upper lip a little too deep before setting the cup down.

"Okay, Miss Simms. Time for a serious talk."

She finished taking her sip, looked up, then started giggling.

"What?"

"You have a mustache!"

"No, ma'am. Not possible. I shaved this morning."

"You do! It's a marshmallow mustache."

He wiped it away. "Better?"

She confirmed with a nod.

His mustache might be gone, but her smile remained.

"We really haven't had a chance to talk," he said. "I'd love to know about your barrel racing journey. When did you discover that you loved it?"

Taylor shrugged. "I don't know. Ever since I was a little girl. Mommy showed me how to do it once, and I liked it and was good at it."

Nash had to blink. Strange, but something about the way she said it reminded him of the first time he put Kat on a horse. She not only liked it, she loved it. Furthermore, she was a natural, too. Little girls and their horses. Such a treasure.

"You're *extremely* good at it. I know it's hard work, but do you also have fun out there?"

Taylor looked away. "Sometimes."

Now he was getting somewhere. Exactly where, he didn't know.

"What happens the other times?"

She shrugged.

"I'm a good listener, if there's anything you want to talk about," he said.

No admissions were forthcoming.

"I have something I'd like to talk about, and I feel like I can trust you with my feelings," he said.

She looked at him. "Okay."

"I'll need a pinkie promise. Do you know what that is?"

"Um, no."

Nash extended his hand across the table, pinkie curled. "It means we're friends and we can talk about whatever is bothering us, without judgment. Hook yours onto mine and we shake."

He suspected that whatever weight she was carrying, he could lift it right off and all would be fine. Jess was a good mom, and Taylor was an otherwise happy and well-adjusted young girl.

She did as instructed. They released and Nash leaned back in his chair.

"Whew! Thank you. I've been wanting to tell someone about this." He wasn't much of an actor, but she seemed to buy it.

Taylor sat up straighter.

"My daddy wanted me to be a bull rider. Started entering me into contests when I was seven. But I hated it so much, I pretended to be sick to get out of doin' it. I was scared of falling to the ground. I have a thing about that, I guess you could say. Have you ever done anything like that to get out of competing?" he asked.

Taylor seemed to think about it. And think…

"No. I was sick once, but it was for real. I threw up and everything. I always want to ride and have fun, but sometimes it makes me sad 'cause Daddy can't have fun anymore because he died."

It was Nash's turn to sit up straighter, propelled upright by the depth of her confession. It didn't have anything to do with Jess pushing her too hard, or the possibility that Taylor didn't enjoy the sport. She self-sabotaged.

He was right about her carrying a weight on her shoulders after all. Yet very wrong about the type and the extent of it. She shouldn't feel such guilt.

"Does your mom know how you feel?"

Taylor looked down and shook her head. "I don't think so. She's so busy, and I don't want to bother her 'cause she has to make lots of clothes."

"Would you like for me to talk with her?"

The little girl shook her head.

He took a few deep breaths while collecting his thoughts. He hadn't prepared for this scenario, so he'd have to speak from the heart.

"Taylor. Look at me and listen very carefully. I'm a father, so I can tell you this with complete authority. No daddy would *ever* want his child to stop having fun just because he wasn't there. In fact, I hope that if something ever happens to me, my girls will have even more fun. I'll be looking down and smiling so big when that happens."

Taylor's eyes started to water. Had he said the wrong thing?

"Really?"

"Yes. I'm totally serious. Your mom would feel the exact same way. Promise you'll talk to her about it whenever you're comfortable. No parent is ever too busy." He took a huge gulp of his now-lukewarm hot chocolate, making sure to get plenty of the marshmallow on his upper lip, then set the cup down.

She nodded in agreement and took a big gulp from her own mug and made sure she got a mustache, as well. Now they both were giggling.

He stood. "I have an idea. Let's go see if Mischief recognizes us."

Together they practically sprinted back to the arena, where the horse greeted them at the fence. Of course, he already knew Mischief wouldn't be fooled, but that wasn't why he'd suggested it. Time for this little girl to have some fun again, and what was more fun than marshmallow mustaches?

Problem was, he was having a little too much fun himself. His intuition was back and ready to compete. Maybe he'd been doing a little self-sabotaging himself the past several years.

The more he thought about it, the more he remembered when he'd stopped having fun. Didn't occur to him to define it that way until now. It was the day he realized Jess had left without so much as saying goodbye. Just when she was reaching her peak as a barrel racer. He'd never felt like more of a failure as an instructor. Took him a while to stop teaching completely. Figured it was nothing more than a temporary slump.

It wasn't.

Not that he couldn't have a comeback, like Jess was having vicariously with Taylor. Unfortunately, if he got back into teaching again, it would take him away from everything else he needed to do.

He'd already started the process of rebuilding Buck Stops into a cattle ranch, which had been his father's and grandfather's legacy. Until he inherited the place and decided to focus on horses instead.

Besides, it wouldn't be fair to Kat. How could he justify teaching others but not her?

He couldn't.

With that impulsive thought put to rest, he focused on Taylor. Her helmet was on, and she looked genuinely excited.

"Okay, here's the plan. Visualize something you really want, but don't tell me what it is. Keep that for yourself only. Imagine the thing you want most is waiting at the finish line. The faster you get there, the sooner it's yours."

She nodded and assumed her starting point outside the arena gate. Her first start was fast, and her finish was even more impressive, confirming that she really did have a breakthrough today. The second try was even better.

When Taylor headed back over, he jumped from his perch and applauded. Her enthusiasm was apparent not only at the start and finish. The middle also improved.

Now for the hard part: telling Jess how the breakthrough happened. Taylor promised to share it with her mom. On her own terms and in her own way. That didn't mean he couldn't assist in making that happen, if possible.

For now, he needed a plan to hand the training

reins over to Jess and get back to spending time with his own girls.

"I'm so proud of you, Taylor. The officials in Montana should go ahead and give you the trophy, because no one else stands a chance." It wasn't an exaggeration.

At that, she beamed.

Our little girl is back in the game.

Nash's breath hitched. Taylor wasn't his. Not even close. But he felt like a father to her in this moment. All the more reason to wrap up this arrangement. Except he still owed Jess a favor for pulling double duty with the twins. She needed a day off to work on her sewing. And to spend time with her daughter and give Taylor an opening to confess what she'd confessed to him about her dad. The little girl had earned a day off, too.

"Guess what? No practice tomorrow unless you want to. You and your mom are welcome to do so anytime."

"Okay," she said.

"But y'all can't leave Destiny Springs without doing at least one fun thing, if your mom catches up on her work. I can make some suggestions."

"Can you and the twins come with us?"

Not the plan he had in mind. His thoughts immediately went to Jess. The proximity did them no favors last time. At least they'd be with the girls, thus reducing the possibility of another extended hug. Or one of those kisses he'd been trying, and failing, not to imagine. Except, how could kissing Jess ever be considered a bad thing?

The excitement on Taylor's face, combined with the tickle he felt in his heart, made it impossible to say no. So he didn't. It was either the greatest decision he'd ever made…

Or the worst.

CHAPTER TEN

"LADIES, STAY WHERE we can see you," Nash called out, even though he didn't want to see what he was seeing. Specifically, the number tacked on the back of the pink Western shirt that Jess had sewn and let Kat keep.

He hadn't noticed the number when she'd come home yesterday. The girls raced off to their room after collecting a hug, and Nash couldn't take his eyes off Jess.

All three girls looked back. Taylor waved. Lizzy grabbed Taylor's and Kat's hands and tugged them toward the children's corral.

How was it that he could manage such a breakthrough with Taylor but not get his daughter to change the shirt that she admitted Jess sewed for her? Considering how wrinkled the thing looked, she must have changed out of her pajama top and back into it after he'd tucked them in for the night.

His whole purpose for suggesting they spend their "together" portion of the day at the local farmers market was to have some fun and avoid certain discussions. With all the goings-on and music, there was less chance they'd have to tread into deep waters. But now, he didn't have a choice.

Today, the music at the farmers market was not only familiar, it offered a neutral subject.

"Recognize this song?" he asked.

Jess squinted as she seemed to mull it over. "Can't think of the title, but didn't Montgomery Legend sing it better?"

Nash had to laugh. The band wasn't the best he'd heard in town. But that was part of the charm of these weekly events, along with the booths of fresh fruits and vegetables, baked goods and handmade crafts.

"I'll tell Monty you said that the next time I see him," Nash said.

"Monty? Are you serious? You actually know him and are on a nickname basis?"

"Is that a big deal?" he asked, remaining intentionally stoic and leaving out the part that Becca's mom was dating the legend himself.

"Only if it's true," Jess said while rolling her eyes. "Sounds like one of those Destiny Springs rumors I've heard about."

"This town has a few of those, that's for sure. One or two of 'em have turned out to be true."

"One or two?" Jess flashed him a look he couldn't quite define.

"What?" he asked.

She looked down to her boots as they walked. "Nothing."

They stopped within several feet of the tent where

the girls had gravitated, directly inside the gate of the children's area. Taylor was seated in a high director's chair while one of the local artists painted a big smiley face on her forehead.

Next was Lizzy, who asked the young man to cover her face in daisies.

Good thing he and Jess wanted to watch and not talk. It was uncomfortable being around her after that hug, to say the least, but in a good way. Not as uncomfortable as seeing Kat take the director's chair and get a number eight painted on her cheek. Now he'd be forced to look at the number coming and going until he could talk her into washing it off.

Even though the face painting was free, Nash pulled a five-dollar bill from his pocket and handed it to the artist as a tip.

"Thank you, sir. What a beautiful family y'all have," the man offered in return.

Nash and Jess looked at each other, but neither corrected him. Jess simply said, "Thank you. We think so."

"We'll keep an eye on your girls if you two want to wander around for a bit." The man pointed to a couple of ladies, who both waved while running herd on a manageable group of kids within the fenced-off area.

Nash knew the women. They'd babysat the twins here a couple of times while he did some produce shopping. Plenty of fun stuff to keep them busy.

"What do you think?" he asked Jess.

"Works for me."

Nash motioned the girls over. He hooked two out of three. "Jess and I will swing back around in a while. Y'all stay here. Let Lizzy know, please."

Kat and Taylor nodded, then ran back inside the corral.

"Good idea. We need to talk privately anyway," Jess said.

His thoughts exactly. As long as the discussion didn't involve Taylor's breakthrough, although that would be much more pleasant than the topic of Kat's shirt.

They wandered past the vegetable tents first. Somewhere between the carrots and the cabbage, Jess asked the dreaded question.

"Any progress with Taylor?"

"As a matter of fact, yes. We had quite a breakthrough yesterday," he said.

"What did the trick?"

Nash inhaled deeply through his nose, then exhaled. Not only for effect, but to relieve the tightness in his chest.

"Breathing the Wyoming air. It can cure whatever ails you," he said.

"There you go again. Another wild Destiny Springs story," Jess said. "Seriously, what happened?"

"It came down to her starts and finishes. Neither were fast enough. She had some hesitation."

"Wow. I never even picked up on that watching her. Very astute of you. How did you help her overcome it?"

"I promised I'd let her tell you."

Jess shook her head. "Then I may never find out."

Nash was tempted to say more, but at least he'd planted the seed that there was something she would care to know.

"Does that mean our training arrangement is over with?" she asked.

Nash paused in his steps. Even though getting back to his own life was important, he'd like to make sure Taylor didn't revert back to her old habits. He was emotionally invested now.

"One more session before y'all leave in a week or so to be certain her improvement wasn't a fluke. In the meantime, the two of you can come over and practice whenever the mood strikes. I'll leave the barrels in place."

Considering Jess's response—or lack thereof—he wasn't sure whether that was a good answer, or a bad one.

"Whatever you think is best. I didn't come all this way to ignore your advice."

It was a subtle reminder that this was, and should stay, a professional arrangement. Since Jess was going to have at least one more afternoon with the twins, there was something he had to get off his chest.

"Follow me. We need to have a chat." Nash led her to the other side of the tents, where some bistro tables were set up and a vendor was making hot beverages.

They took a seat without ordering. She looked

nervous, which was nothing compared to how he felt having to bring this up.

"About the barrel racing shirt," he began to say, although he had trouble formulating the rest of the words without sounding ungrateful.

Jess dropped her chin. "I apologize. You'd mentioned she was down. It was the only thing I could think of to cheer her up. I know you're in a difficult spot with the subject, but I figured that once we're gone, she'll move on to something else."

"I did ask for you to cheer her up. You get an A-plus for that. And I'm afraid I'm getting a failing grade on letting her try." He hadn't planned to wade too deep into more reasons than he'd already provided. But there he was, up to his knees in explanation.

"I understand. Barrel racing is a huge time commitment. You're raising two young girls and manage a ranch. You even quit teaching, after all. And you once loved it."

Boy, that was the truth. Another truth was, he was starting to love it again. But he'd learned the hard way that certain loves weren't destined to last, no matter how much you wanted them to.

"I wish things were different, Jess. I've gone to great lengths to discourage anything involving travel. I can't accommodate that right now. But I'll just come right out and say it. The sport is also cost prohibitive."

It was the truth, if not the whole truth. Difficult

to admit, but not as difficult as bringing up the part about Roxanne.

Jess cocked her head, then looked down. "And then I came along and messed it up. I'm so sorry."

"Not your fault in any way. I certainly don't regret helping Taylor."

Jess looked up. "You mean that?"

"Of course."

"Good. Then no more secrets. Okay?"

That was a tall order in some ways, but not in a very specific one.

"I'd expect nothing less from my *gal*," he said, adding a wink for good measure. He'd been holding on to this secret and waiting for the right moment.

If a tomato booth had been Jess's backdrop, she would have blended right in with the way her face turned red.

"Vanessa told you?" she asked.

"No. PJ let it slip."

Jess shook her head and laughed. "I could never be upset with that adorable little boy. Her, either, for that matter. Besides, I'm the one who told them about Georgina's gaffe. I think we both know how it's so *not* true."

"Not at all," he said.

"Not in the least. I mean, can you imagine?"

Actually, I have been.

"Right. Grizzled cattle rancher, willingly tied to his property, and the glamorous traveling mother of a rising rodeo star."

Jess looked at him with some level of sympathy, then shook her head.

"Nothing glamorous about me. And at least the property you're tied to—as you describe it—is providing a warm, wonderful home for you and the girls."

Except for denying the glamorous part about her, everything she said was true. Furthermore, he detected something in her voice that sounded as though she wouldn't mind a warm, wonderful home for herself and Taylor.

"Destiny Springs is a small town, and not very glamorous, but I highly recommend it. There's always room for two more," he said.

Jess sighed, then looked at him, cocked her head and smiled. "When I finally decide to give up the glamour, this would definitely be my first choice."

When. That sure sounded a lot more promising than *if.*

"You'd bring the glamour with you. But you're here now, so we should capture this moment." He pointed to a photo booth across the way. Another couple had exited and were waiting on their photos to print.

"Gosh, I haven't seen one of these in years," she said.

"The girls always have a great time with it. Mostly making silly faces. Wanna try?"

He stood and extended a hand.

Jess gave him the side-eye, then stood. "Okay to the 'trying it' part. But I do NOT want to look silly."

"Me, neither. Let's not even smile." He put on his best serious look.

At that, she not only smiled, she also let out one of those beautiful laughs. After the other couple retrieved their photo, they stepped inside.

"These booths are a lot smaller than I remember." She was forced to half sit on his lap.

"Ready?" He pressed the button anyway.

"No!" she said, right as the first flash went off.

Nash burst out laughing.

"How long between shots?" she asked.

"A decent pause."

"Does it give you a warning? Like a red light or something? I can't remember..." Jess moved her face closer to the glass. Sure enough, the flash went off again.

"You lied! That was more of an *in*decent pause! I'm gonna look hideous!"

"That's not possible," he said.

She looked directly at him now as if deciding whether to take his observation seriously.

Oh, he was serious. Vern was right: you were never too old to have a crush.

Another flash went off, capturing that thought. That moment. It was no longer a question of *if* he'd kiss her, but *when.* This was the perfect moment to do what he should have done ten years ago but didn't dare.

The crease between her brows softened. As they closed the few inches between their lips and kissed, the camera issued its last flash.

Jess's eyes flew open. He'd never closed his. Yet, she wasn't the one to pull away first.

"See what happens when you let down that wall a little?" she asked.

Felt like more than a little. He'd take a wrecking ball to the whole thing right now if he could talk her into staying.

By the time they exited the booth, a few other couples were waiting their turn.

Nash and Jess guarded the photo output bin as if it were Fort Knox. When it finally spit out the print, he grabbed it and they huddled together and fast-walked toward a vacant spot. Both giggling like teenagers the entire way.

Once safe from wandering eyes, they examined the result together. Jess expressed horror at the first two, and fondness for the third. But he barely noticed those.

Maybe he'd avoided talking about his feelings today, but he was doing a pretty good job of showing them. In fact, he was about to steal another kiss. Right here. Out in the open. His phone pulled him away. When he saw that the message was from Parker, another kind of feeling swept over him.

"What's wrong? You turned pale," Jess said.

He reread the text and willed his heart to settle down. He'd taken it around some serious emotional barrels already today.

"There's an emergency at the ranch."

"Did Parker give any specifics?"

Nash shook his head. He tried to return the call, but his ranch hand didn't answer.

"Let's get you back," she said, easing the photo strip from his hand and tucking it into her purse.

Together, they sprinted to the children's area, where they wrangled the girls.

On the drive back, Nash tried to appear normal. No sense making the twins worry when he didn't even know what was going on himself.

"I'll take the girls for a while, just in case it's something the twins shouldn't be exposed to," Jess whispered.

Even though that made sense, Nash shook his head. "That's too much to ask. It's tough enough to entertain two, never mind three."

"I'll come up with something. And it won't include any type of barrels. I promise. I've been wanting to check out Kavanaugh's ever since Cody mentioned it. They might enjoy a girls' shopping trip, as well."

"That's certainly an option, if you enjoy herding kittens. But if you need to get some sewing done, take their whiteboard with you. That's how I keep 'em busy when I have work to do in the house."

Jess nodded. "I like that idea."

"Anything to help. I'll return the favor, I promise." He didn't tell her what a relief it was to not have to worry about the girls in this moment. As a single mom, she clearly understood such things.

"We'll talk about that later, if at all. Right now, I

want you to take care of your home and ranch. Let me worry about everything else," she said.

That's my gal.

JESS MAY HAVE been trying to digest a mixed bag of feelings, but one thing was for certain: she wasn't going to take Nash up on his kind suggestion that she get some sewing done.

There was another situation that needed mending first.

The moment Jess entered Kavanaugh's Clothing and Whatnot, she knew she'd leave with the sound of a cowbell ringing in her head like a serious earworm. The thing was tied to the door, which she held open for the girls.

It would be worth it as long as she left with a new top for Kat to replace the barrel racing shirt. She wished he would have admitted the money problem sooner. She, of all people, understood budget constraints.

An earworm might also be helpful in coaxing her thoughts out of that photo booth. Away from the tender kiss she kept playing over in her mind.

A young man looked up from straightening some clothing racks in time to secure his stance before the twins nearly plowed him down. Taylor followed but stopped short of giving him a hug, too.

After he extricated himself from the twins' grip, he came over to Jess, who was taking visual inventory of the place.

"I'm Ethan, the owner," he said. "You must be Nash's gal."

A coincidence? Jess wasn't prepared for *that*. She would have otherwise formulated a comeback.

Ethan broke out in a laugh that Jess could only describe as donkey-like. "Georgina and Vanessa were in here yesterday with PJ. Told me you were taking care of Nash's twins. Overheard 'em talking about the whole *Nash's gal* snafu but how the nickname suits you."

Jess forced a smile. "That's embarrassing. It's not true, you know. I'm not his gal."

Although, after that kiss, maybe she was. But that was staying strictly between the two of them.

"Oh, I know that. Don't be too hard on 'em. When people give you a nickname around here, that means they like you."

"What's yours?" she asked.

Ethan looked to the ceiling and shook his head. "Well, I'll be. I guess I don't have one. And I grew up here."

Ouch. Yet again, Jess seemed to have stepped in it.

"What's Nash's nickname?" she asked.

This time, Ethan really looked stumped. "Seems like he used to have one, but for the life of me I can't remember. If I think of it, I'll let you know. Anyhoo, what can I help you with today? Or are you just browsin'?"

"I'd like to find a blouse for Kat, anything with

daisies for Lizzy and a bracelet for my daughter, Taylor."

She could practically feel her wallet getting lighter. Then again, she'd saved money to pay Nash, and he wouldn't accept it. This would be a worthy use of that stockpile.

"The girls are looking at the jewelry right now. We have some writing pens with pretty flowers pasted on the end. One of 'em may even be a daisy, but I'm no expert. They're at the far counter. Unfortunately, we don't carry clothes for little ones."

That confirmed what Jess had deduced at a quick glance.

"In that case, I'll look at your women's tops." If she could find one that Kat liked, fabric-wise, she could either alter it or completely remake a top out of that material.

"Feel free to try on as many as you like. Dressing rooms are over yonder, and there's a full-length communal mirror by the chairs."

"While I'm doing that, would you mind showing Lizzy the flower pens? I'll buy whichever one she wants." No doubt Taylor would find a bracelet she liked, even though the ones she practically lived in were her favorites.

The purchase for Kat would be a little trickier. Jess located a couple of tops that she could work with by the time the girls finished their shopping and joined her. Lizzy flashed a pen with a huge fabric daisy attached to the end. Couldn't have been more perfect. Taylor sported a bracelet with silver intertwined horseshoes.

Then there was Kat, who was wearing the twin to Taylor's bracelet. Although the jewelry looked junior in design, the items were sized for a grown woman's wrist. The girls must have helped each other figure out a way to clasp them so that they wouldn't fall off.

Now Jess had not only sewn Kat a barrel racer shirt, it looked as though she might be buying her a horseshoe bracelet. At least it wasn't specific to barrel racing, and the little girl was an equestrian anyway.

Besides, the fabric of the items Jess picked out couldn't begin to compete with that. Maybe she should give up and they should all go to the drugstore with the old-fashioned soda fountain instead. See if they were expecting Nash's gal there, too. That would make her day complete.

As Jess was in the process of surrendering the tops and skirts and dresses to their racks, Lizzy tugged at one of the garments.

"Don't put this one back. Daddy would like it." The little matchmaker gave Jess the most mischievous grin.

A floral maxi skirt. Jersey, cut on the bias. She'd grabbed it because it had enough fabric to transform into a short dress with long sleeves. The background was black, and the flowers were faded. Subtle. Sophisticated but girly. Paired with some boots and leggings, it would look beyond adorable on Kat.

Jess held up the skirt. "Your daddy would like this, huh? Then we should definitely buy it for him. Do you think this one will fit, or would he need a larger size?"

"Not for him. For you!" Lizzy insisted.

"Daddy would like this one, too. You should try it on." Kat tugged at one of the blouses in Jess's other hand. Meanwhile, Taylor had collected several more tops and sweaters.

This was getting way out of control, in more ways than one.

"I'm limited to three items. Oh, well." Jess shrugged, made a frowny face and pointed at a sign that was clearly posted.

"Just ignore that. I know the owner personally," Ethan called out, then unleashed the donkey again.

Now all three little girls were wearing matching grins.

"Okay. I'll try them on." But that's all she would do. At least it would keep them entertained for a while.

Jess handed her purse to Taylor for safekeeping since there wasn't so much as a chair in the dressing room.

"I'll come out and model the things that I can fit into." For once, she was glad she'd gone up a size. The things they picked out looked quite small.

Jess first tried on the blouse that Lizzy had picked out. Even though there wasn't a mirror in the room, she already knew it wasn't working. Too frilly for her taste, but she drew the curtain back and showed the girls anyway. They all looked at her as if they didn't recognize her.

One down, a dozen to go.

Next, she tried on the floral maxi skirt that Lizzy had picked out. If Kat wasn't interested in the fabric, she would be. It couldn't have been a better fit, that was for sure. She could pair it with her tall black boots. This time, when she opened the curtain, they all smiled and nodded.

"Buy that one, Mommy," Taylor said.

Jess's first thought was, *I could make this for a fraction of the cost.* But since Taylor liked it so much, it was worth whatever the price tag read.

"That skirt is thirty percent off, but I'll give you another ten," Ethan called out.

Sold.

Once she pulled the curtain closed, she realized they may be there for a while if she actually tried everything else on. She had to admit, this was fun, but she, for one, was getting hungry. They had to be starving, as well, even though they were too excited about this little experiment to have noticed.

Then there was Nash, and whatever was happening. She and the girls could get some food to go and eat together at the ranch. Assuming the coast was clear. In the meantime...

"I have some candies in my purse, if you'd each like one," she said. At least, she hoped she still had enough. Butterscotch was her mindless pleasure.

She could polish off half a bag before stopping to breathe. She'd get them something healthy after this, like a good mom would do.

Her own summation threw her a little. She really did think of the twins as hers for a split second, which was crazy. More than that, it was a reminder that the twins didn't have a mother.

Jess shook off that sad thought as quickly as she did the sweater and maxi skirt and contemplated which outfit to try on next. In fact, it was actually quiet enough to think for a change. The girls, who had been chattering nonstop, were now dead silent. Which meant they must have found the candies.

Crisis averted, for now.

A wave of discomfort washed over her as she reached for one of the sweaters that Taylor had picked out.

The photos...

Time felt as though it were standing still, until the giggles from the other side of the curtain turned into shrieks and laughter. Lizzy first, followed by Taylor. Even Kat joined in.

Jess shifted into overdrive, paying zero attention to what she put on, then drew back the curtain.

One look at their faces, and there was no doubt in her mind that they'd seen it.

The kiss.

Judging from their impish smiles, they liked what they saw.

"What else did you find in my purse besides the candies?"

Lizzy let out a giggle. "You kissed Daddy."

It had been easy enough to explain away the hug they'd witnessed. But this required a response from both parents. Bottom line: she needed his help with this one.

Jess extended her hand. "And he kissed me. Grown-ups do that sometimes when they really like each other. May I have my purse back, please."

Taylor relinquished it. Jess reached for her cell phone inside and tried to dial Nash. He hadn't left a message, nor was he answering.

That left her with only one conclusion. As badly as she needed his help right now, he might need hers even more.

CHAPTER ELEVEN

IT TOOK SOME GUESSWORK, since Parker hadn't provided any logistics, but Nash finally spotted his ranch hand outside in the far distance with one of the heifers.

He sprinted past the calving barn and caught up with them.

"I was putting down some fresh hay and got the swinging gates all mixed up. She made a run for it," Parker explained. "What do I do?"

Nash willed his heartbeat to normalize. Unless it was a breach, this wasn't an emergency. His first inclination was to call Jess and let her know everything was okay. But in the blur of panic, he'd left his cell phone inside the house.

"First, we stay calm and get her back into the calving barn," Nash explained while evaluating the heifer. "She's still in stage one. Going on twelve hours now at my best estimate."

"How long does it take?"

"In my experience, anywhere from four to twenty-four."

"What if we can't get her back in the barn?" Parker asked.

Nash was sure that was doable, but Parker obviously needed reassurance. And an education in case something like this happened again when Nash couldn't get back as quickly.

"She'll give birth out here, and we'll get both of 'em back inside."

Better for something like this to happen today rather than in the next couple of days when a rainstorm was predicted to move through the area.

"Should I saddle up Tiger and Sassy?"

"Nah. Not for only one. Helps to have the visibility, but you need to know how to herd on foot."

Nash took the lead, explaining the steps to Parker along the way.

"You gotta be aware of their flight zone. That's the distance that'll cause her to flee. Also, be aware of the balance point, which is where you place yourself. Figure out which side you need to be on to get her to move in the direction you want."

"I'd understand if you fired me," Parker said as they successfully herded the heifer back to the calving barn.

His ranch hand seemed serious. Unfortunately, Nash couldn't muster the energy to tease him at the moment. But he could tuck this incident away in his proverbial pocket to torture the guy with later.

"Let's give her a little privacy. We'll check on her about every thirty minutes," Nash said, once the mommy-to-be was situated inside.

Now that Nash had time to breathe and look around, he was pleasantly surprised. Parker really had spread out fresh hay, and the other heifers were partitioned off in their own bays.

"Perfect," Nash said, until he noticed something about the way sunlight was hitting the ground around the mommy-to-be. As if she were on stage, in a spotlight. "Looks like we have another problem, though."

"Uh-oh. What did I do this time?"

"Nothing. Unless you've been shouting from the rooftops about how much you love Hailey." He pointed skyward.

A few of the shingles had come off. Nothing a ladder and a little time couldn't fix. He'd bet the ranch that he wouldn't be able to get a roofer out before the rain started.

"I'll let you take your pick. You can either go into town and get some roofing materials, or you can stay here and check on our new mama and her baby in thirty. If it ends up being a breach, don't panic. Call me immediately."

"I'm not even going to ask what that is. I'll grab the keys."

"Grab my cell phone when you get back, too. I need to let Jess know what's going on."

"Will do, boss. But before I go, I have something else to tell you," Parker said.

Nash anchored his boots into the dirt. "Go on."

"I met a fella the other day. A retired cattle herder

who needs to burn off some energy. He'll work for you for free, and I could use the help."

Now, there was some possible good news. Too good to be true, in fact. At the same time, it would mean breaking in yet another ranch hand.

"What's his name? Is he from around here?" Nash asked. Maybe he knew the guy.

"Gus something or another. Lived near Jackson Hole for several years but has been staying with some relatives in Destiny Springs until he finds out where he's going to land."

Not so helpful. And not good if this guy had no ambition beyond burning some time. Not to mention, he might not even decide to stick around. Sounded as though he went whichever way the wind blew. At least with a paid employee, he knew that person needed the work and was serious. Then again, once a cowboy, always a cowboy.

Nash's defenses crumbled at the thought.

"All right," Nash said. "I'll talk to him. But no promises."

Parker's huge smile was a bit overenthusiastic. No doubt he would be relieved to have some help on the ranch. Nash would, too. Plus, an experienced cowboy would be able to distinguish between a true emergency and something they simply needed to keep an eye on.

"I bet you won't be able to say no," Parker said.

Funny, that seemed to be Nash's dilemma with Jess. But this Gus fella wouldn't have the same kind of charms, so it should be a breeze to make a good decision.

After Parker made a swift exit, Nash went through the calving barn with a fine-tooth comb, searching for anything else that needed mending. Other than getting his ranch hand comfortable with the gate configuration, he hadn't come across anything that couldn't wait a week or two.

He wandered back to his heifer, who was quickly entering the next stage. Looked like she was ready to get this part of the process over with.

Still, the gal didn't know how good she had it. His grandfather had built this calving barn, and his dad had updated it with superior ventilation. With the gate configuration Nash had put in place, it sported six bays that could hold about twelve calves each. With only four heifers expecting, each had her own private suite, so to speak. At least, for now.

His dad would be none too pleased that the barn had been used to store hay, among other things, for the past fifteen years since Nash inherited the ranch, sold off most of the cattle and focused on horses instead. But he'd certainly be proud that Nash was taking it seriously now.

Before hardly any time had passed, he heard the frantic tires of a truck in the distance. Nash had to laugh. The guy couldn't hightail it out of there fast enough.

If Parker was going to be squeamish at all, he left just in time. The heifer was now full-on stage two, which forced Nash's anxiety into another stage, as well. He braced himself.

One thing Nash didn't have to worry about was keeping the girls entertained or safe at this moment, many thanks to Jess. That was always tricky. They would wander off in an instant. Wasn't easy being responsible for so many lives in a given moment.

Perhaps his hopes were a bit premature regarding Parker because the sound of footsteps quickly approaching set off a new alarm. Except it wasn't Parker who was running into the barn. It was arguably worse.

Jess stopped several feet away, completely out of breath. The girls were nowhere in sight.

After a confusing, terrifying moment, where his mind started wandering down some dark alleys, she broke the silence.

"I'm here to help."

JESS WISHED SHE could take a picture of Nash's expression. His mouth was open but absolutely nothing was coming out. She could only imagine what he must be thinking.

"Don't panic. I handed off the girls to Parker. He's taking them with him to town. Said you needed this." She handed him the cell phone, which he promptly checked, then typed something in.

What she didn't say was that she'd promised Parker she'd make an appearance in his upcoming DEBBs workshop in exchange for babysitting. His idea. The poor guy was afraid no one would show up for *Your Home Is Your Business*, his portion of the dual workshop. She could always bow out of the other portion of the workshop, whatever that was, and get back to sewing.

Jess rolled up her shirtsleeves and walked over to the heifer.

Nash grabbed an extra pair of gloves from a workbench and handed them to her.

"Do we know when the water bag appeared?" she asked.

"About an hour ago. Presentation is normal, thankfully. Last thing we need is a breach."

She exhaled some pent-up tension and took a step back. "Hopefully, we can just monitor her from here. Is that what you're thinking?"

Nash simply stared, but then a smile slowly emerged.

"What?"

"Where did you learn about all this?" he asked.

"It was one of the skills I honed during my marriage."

"Lance was one lucky rancher," he said. "Brains, beauty and calving skills."

Her breath hitched a little, although she tried not to let it show. *You could have been the lucky one.*

They held their gaze for the longest time, until the mommy-to-be let out a serious moan.

"Oh, look! It's happening," Jess said.

They both stood ground to assist, if necessary, but otherwise gave the heifer a bit of room as the miracle unfolded. The birth of...

"A son," Nash said after a quick examination of the calf. "Except the little guy needs help breathing."

Together, they proceeded to clean the fluid from the calf's nose and mouth, then tickled the inside of his nostril with a piece of straw until the calf coughed.

"Finally, a baby boy in the Buchanan family," she said, which made him smile, as if a son was on his wish list.

They finished and took several steps back to observe one of the scariest parts, in her opinion.

"I hope mom doesn't reject her baby," Jess said.

Nash's warm smile cooled instantly. "Some tend to do that."

"You've been through that before, I take it," she said.

"Yeah. On a personal level. Roxanne rejected her babies."

Jess's heart could have stopped in that moment. She hadn't made such a connection when she'd spoken those words, even though she pretty much knew Roxanne had been the one to leave. Just not so heartlessly.

She closed the space between them and gave him a big hug. "I didn't mean to remind you."

Nash returned her embrace for a long moment, then pulled away enough to look at her.

"No reminders necessary. I live with that fact every day."

Her heart ached for him and the girls during

what should have been a very special moment. The cow was rejoicing in her newborn.

She wasn't quite sure how, or even if, she could make things better.

But then he straightened and pointed to the roof. "I'm guessing Parker told you that was the reason he needed to go into town."

She looked up. As if he needed one more emergency to deal with.

"He mentioned a roof problem but not the extent of it. I'll reclaim all the girls as soon as he returns. Give you and him time to fix it without the distractions."

Nash's cell phone dinged. He checked the message and texted something back. Then he smiled a tortured smile.

"I'd texted Hailey to see if she could look after the girls for a while, but she can't. She can babysit tomorrow afternoon and evening, though."

"Good. That will give you a chance to keep an eye on these two," she said, pointing to the cow and her calf.

"Actually, I asked her about babysitting all three of the girls. If you're comfortable with that."

"I don't understand."

"I owe you a Juicy Lucy for helping with this. I'm cooking."

No, she wasn't entirely comfortable, but it had nothing to do with Hailey babysitting Taylor. It had to do with her being alone with Nash because that kiss had temporarily blurred her common sense. She'd meant it about settling down in Destiny Springs if she ever settled down. But that couldn't happen anytime soon. Not with Taylor's career taking off.

She'd wrestle with those feelings tomorrow. The issue at hand was still unresolved.

"I'll take you up on that. But I still insist on taking the girls today when Parker returns."

"Only if you promise to go back to the B and B and work. They can keep themselves entertained with the whiteboard."

"Is that your final offer?" she asked. Sounded like she was getting the better end of the deal.

"My final offer for today," he said.

That clarified nothing except what she dared to hope.

If all of this was negotiable, so was a continued relationship with him.

CHAPTER TWELVE

SIXTEEN FEET MIGHT as well have been a thousand.

Nash stared at the ground below. He had no intention of falling, but no one ever did. Maybe that's why he was already feeling the pain of falling for Jess, even though he'd yet to hit the ground.

He didn't have the luxury of imagining the possibility of injury right now. Getting the shingles battened down before the sky fell in on the mama and her newborn below was the priority.

"You still awake up there, Dad?" Parker called out.

Nash snapped out of it and looked down at his ranch hand, who was holding the bottom of the ladder steady. Parker had started climbing up himself to patch the roof, but Nash wouldn't let him. Hence Nash's new nickname: *Dad*.

Sure beat the one Vern called him every once in a while: *Mr. Grumpy Pants*. Well deserved, if he were being honest. But those pants only fit when he was hungry. Now that he thought about it, his stomach was starting to growl a bit.

Once he got his footing, Nash used screws instead of nails to secure the shingles to the horizontal joints. He needed to replace all the nails with screws at some point, but he'd have to save that for another day. This patch was good enough to get them through the rainstorm.

Parker tightened his grip on the ladder as Nash descended.

"I don't know about you, *son*, but I've worked up an appetite. Let's rustle up something to eat."

They made the trek back to the kitchen, where a sparsely stocked refrigerator and freezer stared back at them. Nash realized there was something perhaps even more important he needed to take care of before the rain set in: groceries.

"How do shrimp tacos sound?" Nash asked. They could head out to eat, then swing by the store on their way back.

Parker looked over Nash's shoulder and into the same abyss. "Will they magically appear?"

"In a way, they will. You just gotta know where to look. Let's go out."

"Shrimp Lake, here we come! I'll grab the nets. You carry the ice chest," Parker said.

Nash closed the refrigerator door. "I was thinking something a little closer and easier."

"Who's going to hold down the fort?"

That was the million-dollar question. Back in the day, he had a handful of people to rely on. The number had dwindled over the years. That was about to change. By focusing on cattle again, and eventually hiring more hands, he could turn everything around. Maybe even find time to go to a local rodeo or two, just to watch.

Feelings of selfishness, or perhaps stubbornness, about denying his horse-obsessed daughter the joys of the rodeo had begun to creep in. He'd just have to make sure Roxanne wasn't on the ticket. He'd still have to put his foot down about competing. Couldn't have the twins' names appearing anywhere. But perhaps Kat could do the drills at the ranch, just for fun.

Then again, where was the fun in that?

In any event, he needed Parker's help. And even this Gus person's, he reluctantly admitted.

"We won't be gone that long," he said. They'd taken care of most chores and checked on all the animals. The new mommy and her baby were safe and settled in.

Nash put on a fresh flannel shirt, and the two cowboys donned their respective Stetsons. This was one of the few times they'd done anything together that wasn't ranch related.

The ride to Ribeye Roy's was quiet, even though they had plenty to talk about. Once inside, the waitress seated them at a table for two in a dark corner. Would have been the perfect setting to stare into Jess's warm hazel eyes. Instead, Parker's cool blue ones were looking back.

"I'm glad we have a chance to sit down and talk," his ranch hand said.

"Me, too."

"We need to get some things out in the open.

And I'm not talking about any more heifers. I was giving some thought as to how we can make the ranch more efficient and profitable, aside from adding more cattle. You have, what, thirty-five?"

Nash was impressed that Parker was thinking of their future. They'd never really discussed it. Back in his father's and grandfather's days, they had about two hundred head. But something was holding him back.

Must be the weight of responsibility.

"Thirty-six. You forgot about our newest addition."

Parker smiled. "Not a chance I could forget about that little guy. How lucrative was your barrel racing business?"

Nash felt his stomach seize at the mere mention of it.

"Not as lucrative as my dad and grandad's cattle ranch. Why would you ask?"

"Hailey tells me you used to be one of the most sought-after teachers in the world."

"She's prone to exaggeration. You should know that by now," Nash said.

"She teases. Like someone else I know, whom I happen to be looking at right now. But she doesn't exaggerate."

Nash had to think about it, but he made a valid point.

"How much land do you have? About a thousand acres?" Parker asked.

"Eleven hundred, counting the house."

Parker looked to the ceiling as if contemplating the possibilities. This should be interesting.

"So, you could possibly have five hundred head of cattle with the anticipated forage supply."

"I'd pare it down to about three hundred fifty, max. Allot fifty percent for future forage, and about fifteen percent for wildlife," Nash explained.

"You thinking dairy or beef?"

To be honest, he had trouble thinking about his cattle in those terms. "Can't I do both?"

Parker looked at him. "I don't know. You tell me. What do you envision?"

"I'd like to be able to provide milk to some folks around here, like Vern does with the eggs."

"Whoa! Let's not be too ambitious," Parker said, feeling around his pocket and retrieving a pen, then stealing Nash's napkin.

It took a moment for Nash to realize his ranch hand was being sarcastic.

"So, for that scenario, your profit would be…" He jotted something down and held up the napkin. "Less than zero."

All of a sudden, Nash felt quite silly. Not that he ever needed the type of fancy math skills that Parker had developed as a former business consultant in Chicago. But if that big-city boy could learn ranching, then there was hope for Nash.

"Look. I'm not saying this to make you feel any sort of way," Parker said. "I'm just playing devil's advocate. Let me see your family's ledgers from as far back as you have. And any financial statements that you can line up with the activities at the time, whether it be cattle ranching or teaching. I'll put together some numbers."

"I'll leave out the ledgers from my teaching years. If I ever get the itch, I'll let you know and you can work your magic."

Nash didn't want to admit that the itch had grown and was now just beneath his skin. But there was no use going down a dead-end road. He didn't have a head for numbers, but he knew he wouldn't turn a big enough profit anytime soon. The girls would be grown up with families of their own by the time that happened. Not to mention the way it would make Kat feel in the meantime, having to watch him teach others.

"An itch can be a good thing, you know," Parker said. "You could focus on the horses and barrel racing. I could focus on the cattle. I have to admit, coming back and seeing that newborn calf was a rush I hadn't expected. Kind of wish I hadn't missed it."

"Most doctors advise against scratching itches. If you don't, they'll usually go away on their own. Cattle ranching only," he said. He looked Parker straight in the eye to let him know that the barrel racing training was off-limits.

Not that he hadn't been entertaining the idea. But the more he and Jess discussed their lifestyles, and the reminders of the past and how expensive and time-consuming the sport could be, the clearer the obstacles came into view. Too many barrels to circle, too little time.

Judging from Parker's expression, he got the message. Where were those fish tacos anyway? He was starving.

"Understood," Parker finally said. "I still need to see all the ledgers. Trust that I know what I'm doing."

Not that he didn't appreciate what his ranch hand was trying to do. But Nash had been at this a lot longer than Parker, and focusing on more than one goal wasn't as easy as it might look on paper.

"You got a rush about the calf because you're gonna be a daddy yourself someday soon," Nash said in an attempt to steer this conversation into another direction.

He'd never seen Parker smile that big. "I bet you're right."

"It's been known to happen."

Parker's expression turned serious. "There's one other thing I noticed that I wanted to point out. Jess."

"She's hard not to notice."

"I can tell you feel that way. Question is, what are you gonna do about it?"

So it began. The *feelings* discussion. And to think he almost got away with dodging it. The man gave up riches to win over the love of his life. Nash wasn't going to get out of this dark corner without giving the guy something to chew on.

He didn't need a professional forecaster to tell

him that there was at least a 50 percent chance she was going to leave and never return, and a 100 percent chance that he had to stay. Wanted to stay. This time, he was emotionally prepared.

Or was he?

Parker raised his brows as if seriously expecting an answer. The guy was relentless. That's what had made him so successful in business, and why Nash could rest assured he'd succeed in ranching. He also had a way of making people think anything was possible. It was a gift. And it was working on Nash.

"We need to pick up some cheese and hamburger meat, among other things, at the market on the way back to the ranch."

"That's a bit off topic," Parker said.

"I promised Jess a Juicy Lucy. I'm cooking dinner for her tomorrow night. Hailey offered to babysit. Maybe even have a slumber party. Just waiting on confirmation. That is, if you're okay with that."

Parker nodded slowly. "If it makes my wife happy, then I'm all for it. But this isn't about her happiness. I think I see where you're going with this plan."

Unfortunately, the place Nash was likely going was the hard ground below. Definitely more of a *when* than an *if*. Too late to stop the fall, and no way to assure a soft landing. Hopefully, that was enough of a *feelings* share for his ranch hand. Which reminded him...

"Do we have any metal sheet scraps left from the roof repair?"

"I think so. Why?" Parker asked.

"Just making sure we had some left in case of any emergency."

Like patching the inevitable hole in my heart.

AS IF THE day couldn't get any stranger, Vern was exiting the B and B just as Jess and the girls were making their way up the steps. Cody trailed behind him, familiar toolbox in hand.

"Did someone need a knight in shining armor?" Jess asked.

What she really wanted to ask was, shouldn't Vern be resting his back?

Cody shook his head. "Vern here is as stubborn as any bull I've ever been on. He located a working motor for your sewing machine and wanted to surprise you, even though he should be on the sofa with a heating pad instead."

"Surprise!" Vern said. "It's working again. Your machine, that is. My back is a work in progress. I'll get the motor I ordered in another day or two and then you'll have a spare to take with ya."

She set the whiteboard down and gave him a gentle hug. "You're the best."

Jess watched as they walked to the truck and played tug-of-war with the toolbox until Vern finally relinquished and allowed Cody to place it in the truck bed. Then something else caught her eye. Dorothy, standing alone in the parlor. Admiring Becca's sewing machine.

Jess barely recognized her outside of the group.

Come to think of it, though, she often saw other DEBBs together without Dorothy.

"Girls, wait at the bottom of the stairs for a minute please. Kat, you take this." Jess handed the board to the twin.

As the girls started heading toward the stairs, Jess held Taylor back.

"Will you do me a huge favor, my dear? Let's not talk about barrel racing around Kat," she said, softly enough that the twins couldn't overhear.

"How come?"

"Because it might make her feel bad since her daddy can't let her compete in rodeos right now."

"Why not?"

"Because he has a big ranch to run. You can still talk about horses," Jess offered. Telling young equestrians not to talk about horses wasn't remotely doable, after all. It would be like Jess getting together with Dorothy and not talking about sewing.

Taylor looked at her feet. "I'll try."

"That's all I ask."

Almost. Jess did have one more question. "Nash tells me you had a big breakthrough in the training. I'd love to hear all about it, and your thoughts on him as a coach."

The little girl's expression brightened. "Nash is great. I like him a lot."

Not as much information as she was hoping to hear, but it definitely cheered her up to know that Taylor was happy and thriving in the arena. That was what this whole trip was about, after all.

Jess smiled and nodded. "Wait for me over there with the twins. This will only take a sec."

Once she made sure the girls were waiting, as requested, Jess approached her sewing soulmate.

"I'm sure Becca wouldn't mind you using that if you need to mend anything. The one in my room is fixed," Jess said.

Dorothy tore her gaze away from the machine and smiled. "I haven't stopped thinking about your workshop. You really inspired me to get back into it. Pull out my old Singer."

A certain sadness passed over the woman's face. Jess couldn't pinpoint it.

"Is anything wrong?" she asked.

"Everything's fine. I'd like it to be *more* than fine, for a change. That's all."

Now, *that* Jess could relate to.

"What would make it more than fine for you?" Jess asked.

"To be at home more, yet stay productive."

Jess's first thought was that it must be nice to have such choices. She didn't have any. She *had* to work to make ends meet. Yet, she understood the fear of being idle, as well. The fear of feeling as though she wasn't needed in any measurable way. She'd experienced that a bit as a domestic engineer and stay-at-home mom herself.

"You could always do what I do. It's surprising how many people don't even know the basics, and you're well beyond that."

Dorothy nodded. "I was thinking of doing it more as a hobby, but I like that idea."

"I'm happy to go into more detail with you, if you want to talk later."

Again, the woman nodded. Only this time, she didn't add anything to the conversation.

Jess hated leaving her like this. Alone and seemingly sad. But Jess was destined to plunge into those same feelings if she lost her clients because she didn't deliver.

Once Jess and her crew got to the room, the girls claimed their spots and started entertaining themselves. Kat and Taylor hovered over the whiteboard, whispering and taking turns drawing and erasing. Lizzy kept busy grooming her new flower pen, lovingly straightening out the petals.

It didn't take long for Jess to accept that this suggestion of Nash's to bring back the whiteboard was brilliant. She was able to pattern and trim out the pieces for a Western shirt, leaving only one of its kind to go. Plus the crop top. The girls' chatter couldn't even break her focus. But something else sure did: the cry of tortured dot paper.

Lizzy had located the roll and was poised to take that pretty little pen to it.

No! Jess had barely enough left to pattern the rest of the items for Montana. She sprang up from the chair and gently reclaimed her property. "Let's get you something else to draw on, okay? This is for my job, and it's all I have left."

Lizzy looked a little sad and confused. No doubt Nash had difficulty telling either of the twins no.

Jess could go downstairs and scavenge for some loose paper. Then she remembered the box of retired pattern pieces she always kept with her. Sometimes, she'd rob body parts from the stash while putting together another garment. But that rarely happened, so she wouldn't miss a piece.

She took the lid off the box and offered up the bounty, which made Lizzy smile. "Take your pick of shapes. You could draw some flowers on one and give it to your daddy."

At that, Lizzy lit up again.

Taylor and Kat weren't paying any attention, but she had a suggestion for them, as well. "Kat, how about you and Taylor draw some horses on the board for Nash? He's working really hard today, and I know that would make him smile."

Her cell phone dinged, so she stepped away. A message from Mrs. Dudley.

Sorry it took so long for me to get back with you. I love what you've suggested so far. Especially the chiffon and velvet trims. If it turns out as pretty as it sounds, I'll mention it in my Dudley's Delightful Duds section.

Jess's breath hitched. This was huge. But that wasn't all. A second message from Mrs. Dudley followed on that one's heels.

Your design is also in the running to be featured on my blog. I select three per month. If you're interested, I'll need the completed suit when I see you in Montana.

Interested? Are you kidding?

Except, where would she find the velvet to replace the fabric she'd used for Kat's shirt? *Don't panic.* There had to be a store in or around Billings. At least those details could be added after most of the construction was done. But still, that would be cutting it close. She was leaving for Montana in a little over a week. Once there, she'd intended to focus on Taylor exclusively for a change.

Yet, the news couldn't have been better. Even the pending rainstorm had its perks. She'd have Taylor in the morning, then drop her off at Hailey's at high noon, per the woman's request. Jess would have every reason to stay inside the B and B that afternoon, where she could sew up a storm of her own.

It was an entirely different storm she was currently grappling with: the one brewing within her. Nash's voice, combined with the memory of their kiss, made her thoughts zigzag. Add to that the fact that they'd be making Juicy Lucys tonight. Without the girls around. How she'd managed to focus at all since that kiss had been nothing short of miraculous.

The phone rang this time. *Nash.* It was as if he'd read her thoughts.

"How are all my girls doing over there?" he asked.

Funny, but she'd made a similar slip within her own thinking.

"Everyone is having a good time. I was able to make some progress on my own work, so thanks for insisting."

"Glad to hear it. Parker and I are grabbing something to eat, and we'll be back at the house soon. We can swing by and pick up the girls."

That would be easiest for her. But she wanted to spend at least a few minutes with Hailey and make sure Taylor was comfortable with the idea of being left there with the twins tomorrow night. Besides, her hands were beginning to cramp. She needed to give them a brief break from sewing.

"That's a nice offer, but I'll drop the twins off in a while. I'm taking the girls to Sunrise Stables. I wanted to meet Hailey in person. Text me when you're home."

"You'll love her," Nash said.

From everything Jess had heard, she had little doubt about it. With the plan in place, she set down the phone.

"Lizzy and Kat. Let's finish the artwork for your daddy, then we'll all head over to Miss Hailey's."

She walked over to Kat and Taylor first, but they quickly wiped away whatever they'd been drawing.

"Why did you do that?" Jess asked.

At first, they both shrugged. Then Taylor said, "We didn't like it."

"Yeah. We didn't like it," Kat concurred.

She wasn't sure what to make of the alliance

those two were forming. Hopefully, they weren't talking about barrel racing. Not after Jess had asked Taylor not to. She had overheard Kat mention her horse, Sugar Pie, so that was probably it.

Nash was in a difficult position. She understood that now. Yet, it put her in a difficult, if not impossible, one with Taylor.

Then there was Lizzy, who must be feeling more and more excluded. Having only one child, and being an only child herself, Jess felt inadequate as far as navigating sibling bonds.

So much for those parenting skills she'd been convinced she had moments ago.

"We can't give your daddy a blank board, Kat. How about we think up a joke, and he'll have to figure out the punch line?"

"I don't know any jokes," Kat said.

Jess gave it some thought. "How about this one. Why can't your head be twelve inches long?"

The girls looked at each other and shrugged.

"Because then it would be a foot." Jess retrieved a measuring tape from her sewing box and laid it out. "See. These are the inch marks, and twelve of these equal a foot."

That earned a modest giggle.

"I like it," Taylor said.

"Do you think your daddy will guess the answer, Kat?"

"Prob'ly not. He's not very good with math. Sometimes he asks me to help him count things."

At that, Jess had to snort. *From the mouths of babes...*

"Then I think it's the perfect joke. I'll write it down." Jess sat cross-legged on the ground. Taylor handed her the board, and Kat passed her the marker.

"I'm three feet tall and five and a half inches, and Kat is only five inches," Lizzy called out.

"I'm more than five inches," Kat responded.

It was all Jess could do to not break out laughing as she finished writing the setup on the board.

"There. I can't wait to see what he says." Jess popped the cap back on the marker and scooted on her behind to where Lizzy had resumed drawing. It was nothing short of amazing that the flower pen had any ink left in it. She had created so many daisies.

"That's gorgeous! Your daddy is gonna love it."

Upon closer inspection, she recognized the pattern paper that Lizzy had selected. The little girl must have dug to the bottom of the box to find the largest piece: a wedding gown skirt with train. More specifically, Jess's "dream" gown. Much more opulent than anything else she'd created or sewn. It was designed with a long church aisle in mind. But her once-in-a-lifetime event had happened at the justice of the peace to save money. The dress would have been way too much for the courthouse.

Now the pattern piece was covered with flowers, with all the important markings buried beneath the landscaping. Jess saw it as a not-so-subtle sign that it was time to stop entertaining the possibility of a future built on a solid foundation that couldn't tear beneath her.

Unless it was a sign that somehow it could.

CHAPTER THIRTEEN

NASH HAD TOLD Jess that she'd love Hailey. Now she understood why.

The cowgirl ran outside to greet them as they drove up. She gave all the girls a hug first but saved the longest one for Jess without introducing herself. Not that an introduction was necessary. Jess felt as though she already knew her.

"I appreciate you letting us come over," Jess said as Hailey led them to the barn, without saying why.

When Hailey slid open the barn door, no explanation was needed. The place was a wonderland. The girls ran over to a goat pen. The three little seasoned equestrians avoided the ponies altogether.

"Anything for Nash's gal," Hailey said, adding a sly smile.

Jess blinked. "He told you about that?"

"Nash? Are you kidding? I heard it from Parker, who heard it from Vanessa's little boy, PJ. Not that Nash isn't an open book in many ways. He just has a few footnotes that he keeps to himself."

Her brain felt as scrambled as those eggs in the

migas recipe. "You may have to repeat all that more slowly."

Hailey's cell phone rang. She looked at the screen, held up one finger and answered it.

While Hailey was steeped in conversation, Jess surveyed the girls. So far, so good. Taylor and Kat weren't joined at the hip.

Jess tried to piece together what Hailey was implying about Nash and the footnotes, as well as the chain of gossip. Seemed like everyone's lives here were intertwined, either by family or marriage or friendship. Perhaps she should assume that everyone knew her nickname by now. That way, she wouldn't get caught off guard again.

Hailey ended the call and slipped her phone into the back pocket of her jeans. "That was Parker. He and Nash finished eating and are waiting on the check. You should take one of my goat yoga classes while you're here. Or, better yet, I could show you some moves now since you have a little time."

"That sounds…interesting."

"It's catching on slowly. People come here to play with the silly critters more than exercise with them, though," Hailey said.

Taylor walked over with the twins on her heels. "Mom, can we ride Hailey's horses?"

Jess hadn't intended to make this a long afternoon, but that sounded a little better than goat yoga. Plus, having the girls occupied would give her an opportunity to get to know Hailey a little better.

"It's up to our hostess," Jess said.

"Horses are what we're about here. Everyone, follow me," Hailey said.

As if they didn't hear the "follow me" part, the girls ran toward the stables, leaving the grown-ups in their dust.

"The horses need some exercise anyway since I don't have any trail rides booked for tomorrow, even though the rain isn't supposed to move through until the evening. Unless you'd like to go on one."

"I've heard your rides have an interesting story behind them," Jess said, without committing. She was interested, but she needed to keep sewing.

"They sure do. My tour guides are much better at it than I am. You would totally fall in love with the young man I hired."

Hailey managed to reroute the girls toward the tack room, where she contemplated which equipment they'd need. "Lizzy, you're familiar with Blaze, so you ride him."

Lizzy nodded her approval.

"And Kat likes Whiskey, don't you?" Hailey asked.

The little girl nodded enthusiastically, giving Hailey permission to pull the appropriate tack for that horse and rider, as well.

"Of course, I don't mean she likes *that* kind of whiskey," Hailey whispered to Jess, who got the joke.

Hailey looked at Taylor. "Let's put you on Charmed. I'd say No Regrets, but he still has issues with boulders. Hence the giant fake rocks spaced out in the arena."

Jess had noticed them but assumed it was some sort of weird landscaping design. Now it made sense.

Hailey and Jess put the tack on the horses, then took a seat on a nearby bench and watched as the girls went through some random warm-up drills, stopping and chatting every once in a while. It was fun watching the three of them. Part of her wanted to saddle up and join in. But having this opportunity to talk with Hailey alone had its perks.

"Tell me about this tour guide gentleman you think I'd fall in love with," Jess said.

Hailey grinned. "Well, he claims to be six feet tall, but he's definitely shorter. When it comes to personality, though, he's got tons of it. Lots of energy."

At least the description ruled out Nash. Not that he'd have time to assist with trail rides. He was a good six foot two, and his energy level seemed fairly moderate to her.

"Interesting way to sell it, if that's what you're doing," Jess said.

"Not at all. Besides, you're Nash's gal. I just wanted to add a little mystery and tempt you to take me up on my offer if you ever have some free time. No pressure, and no charge," Hailey said.

Although she couldn't accept the offer, there was something *Nash's gal* wanted from Hailey. Footnotes.

"Speaking of mysteries, I heard a rumor that it wasn't Roxanne who actually broke Nash's heart." A bold question, but Hailey had opened the door.

"Same here. I asked him outright one day if it was true. All he said was, 'I don't have any confessions to make at this time.' Kinda sounded like a confession to me, but I can't be sure of it."

"He used to confess a lot to me, but it was always things like, 'I have a confession… I like American cheese for my Juicy Lucy and not that sharp cheddar stuff,'" Jess said.

Hailey laughed, but all of a sudden, it wasn't funny. Jess put her elbows on her knees and cradled her face. Maybe she didn't want to know if there was another woman besides Roxanne.

"Hey, you okay?" Hailey asked, snapping Jess back to the present.

Jess looked up and nodded. "Yeah. Just thinking about what you said about Nash."

"The man is definitely sporting some deep wounds, which is why I don't poke around too much. All I know is that he pours all his love and attention into those girls. He deserves to have a good woman in his life."

"If you say so." Jess stared at Hailey, hoping for some deeper insight. Instead, Hailey looked straight ahead at the girls.

Jess was about to cradle her face in her palms again, when Hailey shouted, "Way to go, Kat!"

Jess snapped her attention to the scene playing out in front of them. Taylor must have shown Kat some moves and explained them in detail considering Kat's mock performance around three of the boulders. Not the perfect cloverleaf proportions and distance, but unmistakable.

A knot formed in her gut. Make that a boulder. Her cell phone dinged, forcing her to look away from the nightmare playing out before her and read the text from Nash.

We're home. Missing my girls, but y'all take your time at Hailey's.

Jess only wished they could. But she'd stayed way too long.

As she approached the fence, the girls stopped. Taylor looked guilty, as she should. Wouldn't even look Jess in the eye. Yet, she gave her mom a side hug as they were walking to the truck, which rendered Jess helpless against confronting the barrel racing topic.

Then there was the fact that Kat looked so... *happy*. Genuinely, and for the first time since they had met. Jess's heart was torn between respecting Nash's situation and trying to help a little girl's newfound dream come true.

Even though she needed to start wrapping up their trip, this was now a loose thread. Jess hated those. Yet, this was one she knew better than to yank.

This one she would have to cut.

"WHO IS THAT, and what have you done with my daughter?" Nash asked, pointing to Kat.

He wasn't sure how Jess managed it, but his normally quiet, reserved twin was all smiles and energy. He couldn't help but feel uplifted.

Jess froze. "What do you mean?"

"I've never seen her so happy, that's all."

Did Jess not notice the transformation? Or had his joking-around skills atrophied? Not that he needed to resurrect their joke-swap shtick. Not with the clock winding down to her departure from Destiny Springs. Eight more days, if his math was correct.

Jess started to say something, but Taylor jumped between them and offered him a pinkie handshake, which tickled his heart.

The three girls huddled and whispered something, then looked at the adults and giggled before running down the hall to the twins' room.

"I'm glad they've been getting along so well. I hope they weren't too much of a handful," he said.

"Not at all." Jess eased onto the love seat and patted the cushion next to her. He took a seat next to her and tried to keep as much distance as possible. Didn't need a repeat of the photo booth incident with the girls nearby. Which reminded him…

"Whatever happened to those photos we took? Wouldn't want those falling into the wrong hands." He nodded in the direction of the hallway.

Jess looked down at her own hands and laughed. "I'm afraid they already did."

Nash squinted. "So that's what the whispering and giggling was all about."

"I'm afraid so. The good news is, little girls generally move on pretty quickly from one thing to the next. I know. I used to be one," Jess said.

Nash only wished that were true about his daughters.

"The bad news is, the twins inherited my difficulty in letting things go. At least they got their mom's looks."

Jess looked away.

Oops. Maybe not the best thing he could have said to a woman who had become more than a friend.

"About Roxanne..." Jess said.

Nash held his breath and waited for the inevitable questions about the relationship.

"I was always a bit jealous of her," she continued.

"Why?" He was genuinely perplexed. Roxanne had to work for every trophy she got, whereas barrel racing had come naturally for Jess.

Same went for their appearance, if that's what she meant. Sure, Roxanne turned plenty of heads, but she put a lot of effort into it, what with all the fancy clothes and hair and makeup. Whereas Jess was the most natural beauty he'd ever seen. She'd turned heads back then, too—and his had been no exception. In fact, he had trouble taking his eyes off her now.

He couldn't say he understood any of this. When Jess didn't offer up an explanation, he had to ask, even if it meant opening an old wound. Then again, he was all but convinced that it never fully healed. Just like the heart that was practically beating out of his chest right now.

"Is that why you stopped coming to lessons?" he asked.

She pulled in her elbows tight against her rib cage, as if she were trying to disappear.

"You could have at least said goodbye. Or returned my call. I was devastated when you didn't." That was putting it mildly, but she needed to know.

"I figured you'd barely notice my not being there. Roxanne was able to corral you personally, but also professionally. Even on my time. Honestly, I felt shut out."

By me.

That was an unexpected gut punch. Not that there was any other kind, but this one was delivered with a twist. It wasn't jealousy that had ultimately driven her away. It was how he'd treated her, as if she wasn't as important as Roxanne, which couldn't have been further from the truth.

"Was I putting up one of those walls you've mentioned?"

Jess shook her head. "Not at all. That actually would have made leaving easier."

"I'm so sorry, Jess. Roxanne was very assertive about what she wanted, and I obviously didn't handle it the right way." Another understatement. He'd had the bad judgment to marry her, after dating for two years. It wasn't that she was a bad person. She simply wasn't a "for better or for worse" one.

"It wasn't that. I quit because... I had a crush on you." Jess shrank back into the cushion and looked down again.

Once the words set it, it felt as though a million tiny zaps of electricity flooded his body. As if he could feel every blood cell coursing through his veins.

"You must be good at keeping secrets. I had no idea." Because, if he had, his whole life would look a lot different today. He'd had a serious crush on her. Of course, he'd kept his own feelings a secret, as well, so who was he to judge?

"Really? I thought it was fairly obvious," she said.

Perhaps it had been, and it had been his mistake for not realizing it.

"I figured you thought of me as a teacher and friend and Juicy Lucy buddy."

"I did. I thought of you as all those things, too."

Yet, instead of treating him like a teacher and a friend, she did what all the women who claimed to love him ended up doing: left without saying goodbye.

His mom had been the first, but he had long since forgiven her. She was so sick. She'd promised him she would never leave him, and by the following morning, she had.

Nash gulped back the painful memory and tried to focus on this new revelation. Only one thing could cut the tension between them now, and it wasn't a confession. Rather, it was something she'd least expect.

He took a deep breath. "Wanna hear a roof joke?"

The look on her face could have only been described as incredulous. Couldn't blame her after she'd just bared her soul.

"O-kay," she said hesitantly.

Nash smiled and bit his lip. "Good. The first one's on the house."

JESS WAITED FOR the punch line. And waited. It wasn't until he started laughing that she realized he'd already delivered it.

The first one's on the house? Even though the joke was awful, in her opinion, there was nothing better than seeing him laugh again. He didn't return the sentiment about the crush, which she wasn't expecting him to. But that wall he'd constructed had crumbled even more, allowing her to see the friend she once knew so well. Besides, he deserved to know the truth about why she couldn't face him.

"Nice try, my friend, but you still owe me that Juicy Lucy," she said.

"What? That was a joke."

"Barely. Regardless, I'm still ahead."

"I'm not so sure about that. But I *am* sure you dropped the ball just now. Did you forget how the game worked? We have to come back within a certain amount of time," Nash said.

"I remember. I thought you'd decided not to play along anymore, so I didn't come prepared.

But since you're game, here's one. What do you call a sleeping bull?"

Nash thought about it. "I give up."

"A bulldozer."

He let out a painful-sounding howl.

"Oh, no! I wish I could unhear that." He dropped his head back against a cushion and just as quickly sat up and rubbed his hands together as if summoning a genie from an invisible bottle.

"What did one boat say to the other?" he asked.

Jess was determined to get this one. As she thought about it, Nash hummed the theme to *Jeopardy!*

"Stop it! I'm trying to concentrate," she said, swatting at his arm. But she couldn't come up with the answer.

After a few moments, he leaned in and whispered, "How about a little *row*-mance."

Jess gulped. Hard. She recognized the punch line now. She also recognized the seriousness of the moment. And how close they were sitting.

And how Nash had yet to lean back.

Shrieks and giggles from down the hall were enough to make their spines stiffen. They pooled to their separate sides of the love seat, which still left them quite close.

They seemed to be on the same page about the risk of crossing the friendship line again anywhere near the girls. At least until they could figure out a few more things, such as...

"What did the boats say when one was anchored

to a single port, and the other was destined for many?" she asked.

He turned serious, as if he understood exactly what she was saying, then reached over and squeezed her arm. But he didn't have an answer, either.

The girls reappeared. Lizzy first, followed by Taylor and Kat, who were practically joined at the hip.

Jess stood, then Nash.

"Girls, say your goodbyes to Taylor and Jess."

The twins gave Jess a hug, and her heart felt as though it might melt right down to the soles of her feet and spill across the floor.

The girls released their grip. Taylor hooked pinkie fingers with Nash, then let go and headed out the door.

Nash walked Jess to the door, but paused. Neither seemed to know quite what to say.

"Thanks again for the jokes. And for offering to make Juicy Lucys tomorrow. It'll be a nice thing for us to share before I have to leave Destiny Springs."

The last words hung in the air between them, as more of a "definitely" rather than a "maybe."

"It's worth it to see you laugh again," he said.

A bittersweetness stuck in her throat as she attempted to swallow. *So this is how closure tastes.* She'd never really had it before. It was always too easy to abandon an uncomfortable situation and avoid confrontation altogether.

Taylor was already in the truck, and Jess was halfway down the stairs when Nash called out.

"Hey, Jess, one more thing."

She was almost afraid to ask. The pause felt like an eternity before he finally spoke.

"I had a crush on you, too."

CHAPTER FOURTEEN

I HAD A crush on you, too?

What was she supposed to do with that information?

Jess had been expecting a joke. Not a confession that would change the whole way she looked at their past. It was like how Lizzy had drawn daisies all over Jess's dream wedding dress pattern, altering those memories forever.

Not to mention, how it opened the door to the possibility of a future with Nash, even though all the other obstacles still blocked a viable path.

Jess was somehow able to focus enough to use the morning as originally planned and get the second Western shirt done for the rodeo moms, along with patterning the crop top.

She'd hoped to have some free time to talk with Taylor, especially since she wouldn't see her tonight or in the morning. Maybe even find out more about that mystery insight that helped with her breakthrough. But the morning had already come and gone.

So many mysteries, so little time.

Maybe tonight, on their dinner date, she could extract at least a hint from him.

Date. She hadn't really thought of it in the traditional sense of the word. Until now. It was supposed to be two friends, making Juicy Lucys for old times' sake.

For now, she needed to get the two of them moving. Dropping off Taylor at noon would give Jess plenty of time to come back and put a dent in the Dudley job. That one required the most focus, so the free afternoon would be invaluable.

Jess stood and stretched, then walked over to Taylor and motioned for her to remove her headphones for a second.

"Ready for your slumber party?" Jess asked.

Taylor nodded enthusiastically, which was a good thing. Taylor was completely on board with it.

The two of them got ready and landed at Sunrise Stables right on time, where an older woman with a long silver braid was tacking up the horse Jess recognized as Charmed.

"You must be Jess and Taylor. I'm Sylvie," the woman said as they approached. Sylvie was old enough to be a grandma but looked to be much more fit than Jess felt.

Hailey wasn't anywhere in sight. However, the short-but-energetic young man that she'd teased Jess about was there. It all made sense now.

Max ran over to greet her, but instead of a proper hello he launched into a story.

"A zillion years ago, Hailey's grandma and her

boyfriend rode the trails we're gonna ride on. He gave her a bracelet, and they ended up loping."

Jess raised a brow and looked to the woman.

"Taylor and Jess aren't going on the ride, Max," Sylvie said as sweetly as possible.

The little boy looked crestfallen.

"The noon couple canceled at the last minute," Sylvie said, which explained why four horses were tacked and no one else was around.

Max perked up and pointed at a truck coming down the long drive. "Maybe that's them!"

Jess shielded her eyes from the sun. But the closer the truck got, the more familiar the vehicle and driver were to her. And the passengers. Nash was dropping off his girls for the slumber party. At high noon, as well.

What a coincidence.

Jess redirected her attention to the immediate issue at land. Sylvie had cast a sympathetic look toward Jess, which matched what she felt in her own heart. The little boy obviously loved his job and was looking forward to the ride.

"I would have guessed the horses would walk or trot instead of loping, but y'all are the experts," Jess said, encouraging Max to finish his story. It was the least she could do.

"They eloped," the woman clarified.

"Yep. Loped," Max confirmed.

"Ah! Okay, that makes more sense," Jess said.

Hailey emerged from the barn and headed their way as Nash and the twins were getting out of the truck. She came over and gave Jess and Taylor a big hug first, then Nash and the twins had their turn.

"I'm glad everyone is on time. I need all the girls' help with perfecting the new moves I'll be offering in my goat yoga class," Hailey said. "Jess, you're free to join. You, too, Nash. Or maybe you two could fill in for the couple that canceled. My horses need the exercise now because that rainstorm is supposed to last twenty-four hours."

Nash moved to Jess's side and whispered, "What do you think?"

She whispered back. "I think I need to get back to a big sewing project. Then, I have some very important plans for the evening."

"A woman who has her priorities straight. Gotta love that," Nash said, then cleared his throat and answered Hailey and Sylvie. "I'll go on the ride, then I'll help work your other horses when we get back."

The thought of the calf birth, and Nash's reliance on Parker, immediately sprang to mind. If Parker called with another emergency, Nash wouldn't be available.

"How long is the ride?" Jess asked.

Sylvie and Hailey looked at each other, with Hailey nodding to the older woman for decision approval.

"This can be a short one. How about one hour? Fifteen minutes on the trail, thirty minutes lunch, then back home. Can't let Hailey's amazing grilled cheese sandwiches go to waste."

Jess wanted to say that perhaps the girls could

eat the sandwiches, since they were staying behind to help with goat yoga. But she knew exactly what was going on here. Furthermore, she didn't mind it. One more hour wouldn't make a huge difference in her sewing progress.

"Okay. I'll go, too," Jess said.

"You sure?" Nash asked.

Jess nodded.

"Max, come inside with me and get the snacks for Sylvie," Hailey said.

The precious little boy did as he was told and followed Hailey's lead. Jess found herself admiring his adorable cowboy outfit. She would love to embellish the jean pockets for him. Silver studs in the shape of bulls. Or, perhaps purple to match his sparkly riding helmet.

Yeah. In my spare time.

"Which horse do I have the honor of riding today?" Jess asked.

"How about Gabby? She's a sweetheart," Sylvie said, pointing to the nearest horse. "Nash, you take Blaze."

Max reappeared, carrying a couple of thermal bags. Sylvie tucked the bags in Charmed's gear and helped Max mount Star, then she and Jess and Nash followed suit. With Sylvie in the lead, Max in the middle, followed by Jess and Nash, respectively, they headed out the back gate and across the grassy field.

Jess soaked in the warmth of the sun as the bluegrass turned to meadows dressed in colorful wild-flowers.

"Has Lizzy ever drawn a landscape like this?" Jess asked Nash.

"She's been all about daisies. I'm trying to get her to expand her horizons. Try something new."

Right away, Jess's mind went to Kat and how badly *she* wanted to "try something new." In fact, she'd been thinking about the financial aspect of barrel racing being one of the issues Nash had brought up. Jess had been looking for sponsorships for Taylor. There could be one out there for Kat, too, in case that possibility hadn't occurred to him.

Of course, there was still the time issue, but maybe by the time Kat was ready to compete, he'd have more help with the ranch. Until then, there were the area rodeos. Or, just barrel racing on the ranch for fun and exercise.

But such a conversation should be done in private.

They meandered along to the sound of hooves and an occasional elk bugling somewhere in the distance, until Max broke the silence to continue his story.

"I forgot to tell you the parents wouldn't let Miss Hailey's grandma get married, so her boyfriend couldn't get her a ring, and so he made a bracelet out of their horses' hair instead," Max said in one galloping sentence, which clearly winded him.

"That's a fascinating story, Max," Jess managed to say.

"The kicker is, it's true. And there's more. Hailey inherited the engagement bracelet, which she gave to my boyfriend, Vern, so that he could propose to me. Let's stop and have our snack, and I'll tell you more," Sylvie said.

Nash helped Max spread a blanket on the ground while Sylvie and Jess secured the horses. That's when Jess noticed the bracelet that Sylvie was wearing.

"Is that the one?" Jess asked, pointing to Sylvie's wrist.

The woman twisted the bracelet around delicately, as if it might easily come undone.

"Yes, it is. Funny thing about it, I used to make these out of hair from my horse's tails when I was a little girl. Gave one to all my friends."

"Friendship bracelets? Taylor and her buddies love to make those, too, but theirs are from a kit. She would absolutely adore these."

"I'll write down the steps when we get back to Hailey's. Then perhaps you can show her how to do it. Same concept as the kits, I imagine."

They all got situated on the blanket. Max took the liberty of handing out sandwiches and chips and drinks.

"Vern tells me you're a professional seamstress," Sylvie said.

Professional? Jess had taken a huge bite of her grilled cheese sandwich and swallowed it in one gulp. "I'm trying to be."

In fact, she should be deep into the Dudley project at the moment, rather than being on this trail ride. She could work a couple of hours when she got back from the ride, though.

"I sewed all my kids' clothes and my husband's. I miss it," Sylvie said.

"It's like riding a bike. You can jump back in at any time," Jess said.

Sylvie looked out over the landscape. "I may do that someday."

"I can ride a bike, but I like riding horses better," Max said.

"You can do both," Nash offered.

Max seemed to think about it, then scrunched his brow. "How?"

He was so cute, Jess nearly choked on a chip she'd just popped into her mouth. It took a moment for her to realize that he thought Nash was proposing the impossible.

"Not at the same time, of course," Nash clarified. "You'd probably fall off one or the other. Or both."

"That would hurt," Max said.

"Falling usually does," Nash said, only this time he was looking directly at Jess.

"You'd only have to try it once to end up not wanting to do either ever again. If you survived to tell about it. So whatever you do, don't try it," Jess added, in case Nash had inadvertently put a bad idea in the little boy's head.

Seemingly satisfied with the explanation, Max took another big bite of his sandwich.

Meanwhile, Nash seemed to have an idea of his

own. He leaned in and whispered quietly enough that only Jess could hear, "What if the potential gain outweighs the possible pain? Wouldn't it be worth a try?"

"Love is that way, too," Sylvie said, as if knowingly picking up the thread. "Your heart gets all skinned up, and you swear you'll never try again. For widows, it's even worse. Our lives come completely apart at the seams, don't they? Feels impossible to mend."

Sylvie was right about that. Such a thing created a hole in the fabric of one's life unlike anything else.

"You should put a Band-Aid on it," Max said.

If only it were that easy.

"You could do that, until a charming fella comes along and heals it altogether. No better feeling than that," Sylvie said.

"I'm never gonna fall in love," Max said. "Yuck!"

All three adults exchanged knowing glances.

"I think you'll find that you don't have a lot of control over certain things, Max. I didn't plan to fall in love again. Then I met Vern. Can happen to you, too." Sylvie took a long moment to look at Jess, then looked to Nash, who was clearly suppressing a smile. She wasn't doing much better.

Max shook his head vigorously. Could he be any more precious? Jess could relate to the defiance. His face looked the way she felt inside most days. Trying so hard not to fall for Nash again but feeling completely helpless against it.

I had a crush on you, too...

"No, it won't," Max insisted.

Sylvie laughed. "I didn't mean you, sweetie."

"Are you and Miss Jess getting married?" Max asked, causing Nash to nearly choke on his sandwich.

"What makes you think we might?"

"'Cause I heard Mommy say that Miss Jess is Nash's gal."

"It's just a cute nickname," Jess assured him. "Apparently everyone has one. Except for Nash."

"Not true," Sylvie said. "According to Vern, Nash can be a little unpleasant when he gets hungry. In fact, Vern calls him 'Mr. Grumpy Pants' when that happens. Isn't that right, Nash?"

The poor guy turned a diluted shade of crimson.

Max dropped backward on the blanket and started giggling. Jess had to laugh, as well. She'd experienced that side of Nash before and always thought it was rather cute and harmless. Nothing a Juicy Lucy couldn't fix. Or, hopefully, grilled cheese.

Nash took his time chewing and swallowing a bite, then slowly wiped his mouth with a napkin.

"I can confirm," was all he said, and he did so with a smile.

The trail ride back to Sunrise Stables was quiet, but the noise in Jess's mind was louder than ever.

Hailey and the girls were waiting when they returned. While Hailey had Nash's attention, the girls took Jess by the hand and pulled her several feet away from the others.

"What's this about?" she asked.

"We think you should wear your new skirt tonight for your date," Lizzy said.

"But we're making Juicy Lucys. They're pretty messy."

"Daddy has an apron," Kat offered.

She looked over to Nash to see if he'd noticed she'd been kidnapped. How was she going to explain this conversation?

Then again, maybe she could negotiate a conversation trade. He'll tell her what Taylor had revealed, and she'll tell him about how his twins were future matchmakers. As if they both hadn't already figured that out.

"I'll think about it," Jess said, which was enough for the girls to release her arms and run over to Nash.

Jess followed behind as quickly as she could. If they were bold enough to give her wardrobe suggestions, no telling what advice they'd give him. But the only thing they seemed to be exchanging were hugs.

"I've gotta get back to the ranch," he said as Jess approached. "I'll see you tonight. Pick you up at seven?"

"I'll come to you," she said, if only to disabuse all the curious onlookers of what their evening was sounding like more and more: a date.

Surprisingly, Nash didn't argue. He tipped his hat to all, and Jess watched as he drove away.

Hailey handed the thermal bags to Max and filled the void that Nash had left behind.

The little boy ran to the house as if he'd finished rounding the third barrel at the world championships.

"Smart kid," Jess said.

"He's a sweetheart. Just like his parents. He's lucky to have the two of them. Becca was doing a wonderful job of raising him alone, but little boys need a daddy. So do little girls."

"What? I didn't realize she had been a single parent."

"Oh, yes. Secret baby. Cody found out less than a year ago that Max was his son. Now, he's making up for lost time by being the best daddy ever."

"That would be quite a secret for a guy to learn about. And for a woman to keep."

"Just goes to show that love really can overcome huge obstacles."

Sylvie reappeared before Jess could make a counterargument.

"Here are the instructions for the bracelet. Let me know how it goes. I'm going to finish untacking these lovely horses." Sylvie walked away, leaving Jess and Hailey where they left off.

"Thank you for hosting the slumber party," Jess said instead.

"Thank *you* for letting us. Parker and I can't wait to have a home full of children," Hailey countered.

"Wrangling those three might make you change your mind."

But as soon as Jess said it, she realized she'd lied. Wrangling those three was nothing but rewarding. In fact, she hadn't even left Hailey's and she already missed the girls. All of them. How was it going to feel when she had to leave for Montana and say goodbye to the twins?

Seemed Nash wasn't the only one in an increasingly difficult situation.

THAT CHORE BOARD of Nash's had turned into an Etch A Sketch in his absence. This time, it read:

1. Pull ledgers.
Workin' on it. Got sidetracked.
2. Pick out something clean to wear for your date.
No brainer.

Nash grabbed a towel and wiped the board, once again.

Clean clothes, yes, but there was no point getting too spiffed up. Juicy Lucys could be quite messy to make, and even messier to eat. The girls had been whispering and giggling and hinting around that they could tell he and Jess liked each other. Yet, the writing was on the wall, where it couldn't be erased. Jess and Taylor were leaving soon. He could put a big fat period at the end of that line item.

If anything good could come from them leaving, it would be that the matchmakers in this town would shift their focus to someone else.

Parker busted through the back door just as Nash was wiping away the last remnants of his handwriting.

"Why did you do that?" he asked.

"I could ask you the same thing. I can't let my girls see this."

"I didn't mention a dog this time."

"But you did mention a date. They're already a little too giggly about seeing us hugging. And kissing. Don't ask."

"Don't really have to. But could your girls even read that word?"

"Taylor's eight, so she probably could."

As soon as the response slipped from his lips, he realized his gaffe. He already thought of Taylor as a daughter. Couldn't deny it.

Parker squinted. "I think I see."

"Think again. This is not a *date* date. It's—" Nash stopped short. He wasn't quite sure what it was.

"Dinner?" Parker asked.

"Exactly."

"If you're done with me here, I have a date with my lovely wife. And *your* girls."

"You're sounding like an old married couple. Y'all are still in the honeymoon phase."

"And we're going to stay there forever, which is why we're ready to move forward with adopting a little boy we met."

"Are you serious?"

"As a heifer giving birth to her calf. We talked about an infant, and we will someday. But this little fella captured our heart, and he's up for immediate adoption. Just need to make some arrangements."

Nash felt as though his chin needed to be fork-lifted off the floor. Things were happening so fast.

"That's terrific!" Nash said. And he meant it. Still, he had a million questions. Such as, how could an adoption happen so fast? No doubt, Parker and Hailey would make wonderful parents, but wasn't an enormous amount of vetting and paperwork and legal mumbo jumbo involved?

Then again, there wasn't any vetting for regular couples to have little ones of their own. If there had been, Roxanne's lack of maternal instinct might have been flagged.

"I know what you're thinking. That I won't be available to help around the ranch as much. But I assure you that isn't the case. Remember that ranch hand I mentioned? I'll bring him by after the rainstorm moves through."

No use arguing. Parker had clearly made up his mind. Nash honestly hadn't thought about how Parker and Hailey's eventual adoption would impact his own situation. Still, he wouldn't change anything.

"Bring him by whenever you wish," Nash said.

With that, Parker tipped his Stetson and exited out the back door.

Dinner. *Right.* He didn't fool Parker, or himself.

Nash remembered his parting words from yesterday. *I had a crush on you, too.* Not that he could forget. That big, fat period he'd mentally put at the end of the writing on the wall was looking like a question mark. There was only one way to figure out which it was, and that was to be alone with her. Only then could he begin the process of letting her go.

Or convincing her to stay.

CHAPTER FIFTEEN

"You must be at the wrong house," Nash said.

If Jess wasn't already standing on his porch, wearing a knockout long skirt and boots and holding a brown bag, he would have told her not to come.

Not because it looked like an anvil was about to be dropped on the entirety of the town and he didn't want her to be out in this kind of weather, although that was true. Rather, once again, he was having visions of her being a permanent fixture in his life. Only thing missing tonight was the girls to make the vision complete.

Seeing her all dressed up, he wished he'd put on something nicer than an old-but-clean pair of jeans and a well-worn flannel shirt.

"Since I'm already here, perhaps you could invite me in," she said.

"Please." He ushered her inside with a wave of his hand and closed the door behind her. Thankfully, he'd had the wherewithal to throw some wood on the fire at the last minute.

Jess set the brown bag by the door. "These are some drawings for you from the girls."

"Really? How sweet. I'll look at 'em when they get back," he said, as tempted as he was to look at them now.

Jess removed her coat and put it on a hook.

He could have stood there all night and admired her. Instead, he turned on his heels and motioned her to follow him to the kitchen.

"I thought we'd jump right into dinner while the den warms up. I'm starved. How about you?" he asked.

"Same."

Nash grabbed an apron that had been freshly washed and folded.

"Here. Even though I'm doing the cooking, you might need this. Wouldn't want to get hamburger grease on that pretty skirt of yours."

He hadn't meant to be so forward, but it practically begged to be complimented. She always looked pretty, but this skirt took it to a whole other level.

She paused for a moment as she held the apron, then smiled as if he'd given her a gift as she tied it around her waist.

"*We're* doing the cooking, so I'll take you up on it. Lizzy picked out the skirt for me at Kavanaugh's. She wanted me to buy it because she thought you'd like it. How cute is that?"

It did look like something Lizzy would gravitate toward.

"I should've had her pick out my outfit, too. I'm afraid I'm not very fancy."

Jess bit her lip and smiled.

"What?" he asked.

Her smile spread. "I'm just glad you decided not to wear your grumpy pants tonight."

"Mr. Grumpy Pants promises not to crash our party if we feed him soon, so let's get started. You fix the patties, I'll add the cheese."

"Because I can't be trusted to use American instead of cheddar?"

He neither confirmed nor denied. Truth be told, her Juicy Lucys had always tasted better than his, in spite of her cheese choice. Although it took some time for him to pinpoint why, it seemed to have to do with how thick she made the patties, the amount of salt and pepper she used and how she forced a bit of a well in the center, which made them cook evenly.

He retrieved the cheeses from the refrigerator. Both American and cheddar.

"I thought we'd try combining them. Once slicé of each, per burger. Who knows? Maybe they'll be even better this way."

Jess raised her brows and nodded. "Interesting concept. That said, you're the chef de cuisine. I'm a mere sous-chef tonight. It's your reputation on the line."

Nash smiled. "I'll take my chances."

Together, they went through the steps. Jess added a big pinch of salt to the ground beef, separated and rolled it into four equal balls and shaped them into flat patties.

"I hope the girls are okay," she said.

Nash added one slice of each cheese and closed them in between two patties each, sealing the edges.

"They're in excellent hands. With both Parker and Hailey there, they'll be one big happy family."

She added the perfect well in the center of each set, then salted and peppered the tops while he sprinkled the bottom of the heated skillet with a pinch more of salt.

"Bigger than you think. Hailey told me Parker was venturing out to pick up some guy named Gus and bring him back to Sunrise Stables."

That was odd. How well did Parker even know the guy? Then again, his ranch hand's plan was probably to coach Gus on the answers he should give Nash for the informal interview. For some reason, Parker was obsessed with having this particular person help with the herding.

Nash couldn't say he blamed Parker. He'd probably teased the guy a little too much on his lack of skills.

With the burgers officially prepped, it was time to start cooking.

"You time. I'll flip. They're pretty thick, so five minutes a side," he said.

"Three. Respectfully," she countered.

"You sure? The cheese might not melt enough. Especially with two slices, one being cheddar."

"Excellent point. We should account for that. Let's check 'em at four. We don't want a repeat of the hash browns incident. *Ahem*."

Nash squeezed his eyes closed and half laughed. "Good to know my angels can't keep a secret."

"Maybe you should have made them pinkie shake on it."

He gulped. He knew she'd witnessed it between him and Taylor, but since she hadn't asked, he hadn't offered. Unless Taylor had decided to tell her mom everything, which would take him off the hook because Jess really needed to know.

They cooked the burgers in silence for their agreed upon four minutes per side. Once done, Nash cut into one of the patty combos. It couldn't have turned out more perfect.

"Now, this is an example of good teamwork," he said.

She pulled two plates from the cabinet and set up the buns and condiments. Then they put together what he would consider the best Juicy Lucys he'd ever tasted. They didn't even bother to sit down at the table before digging in. Instead, they leaned against the counter.

"So you noticed my pinkie shake with Taylor," he said as Jess bit into the cheesy center of her burger.

She finished chewing and wiped her mouth and chin.

"Did it have to do with the whole breakthrough thing?" she asked.

He nodded and took a bite of burger, as well, if only to give himself a few moments to come up with a response.

"I'll tell you anything you want to know, as long as she tells you first," he said.

"It has to do with her dad," Jess said.

"Then she did tell you."

"Nope. But I got you to reveal something."

Nash shook his head, wagged his finger at her and smiled.

"I can't say I'm surprised," Jess said. "She and I have a hard time talking about him."

Nash's heart ached for both of them. He wanted to say it would get easier, but his situation seemed to have only gotten worse with time. Pretty soon, the twins would want to know more about their mother, and he didn't have a clue what he was going to say. In the meantime, he was determined to put off the inevitable for as long as possible.

"I have a question for you," he said.

"Go ahead," she said, taking another bite. It was almost as if neither of them had eaten in days.

"Has Kat brought up the subject of barrel racing?" he asked, hoping it didn't sound too accusatory.

Jess washed down the bite with some ice water. Then some more, before taking a deep breath. "She had some general questions on that first day. At the time, I suggested she talk with you and that maybe you could show her some moves. Then you asked me not to encourage her, and she and I haven't talked about it since."

Her soft stare and slow blink convinced him she was telling the truth.

"Thanks. I appreciate that."

"Maybe someday you'll be in a position to let her learn," Jess said.

He'd dared to entertain that possibility lately because of the similarities Kat had with Taylor as far as riding, which Hailey had pointed out. As a teacher—former teacher—he also had an eye for talent.

"You may be right. But *someday* is a little too far away right now."

Jess nodded. Another period of silence followed as they finished eating, but it was nice. He remembered them well, those long stretches of quiet where they were together but didn't have to say a word.

Nash moved to the next step of their ritual and put on a pot of coffee. Once the coffee maker stopped burping, they each grabbed a cup and retreated to the den.

The rain had slowed to a sleepy pulse, which made him wonder if they'd dodged the worst of it. In any event, he would insist on driving her back to the B and B. He could deliver her truck in the morning and ask Becca or Cody to give him a lift back to Buck Stops. With a little luck, Jess would offer to drive him back instead.

Nash privately smiled at how he'd inadvertently come up with a possible way to spend a little more time with her.

The den had warmed to a perfect temperature. They settled in on the love seat once again. Except this time, it felt different. Maybe because everything was different. Even though they'd sat in this proximity dozens of times before, he'd never felt so close to anyone. He would have been fine to spend the rest of the evening simply enjoying being with her.

"My turn to ask you a question," she said. "Are there any other secrets I should know about?"

Just one. The fact that Roxanne had not only left him once, which Jess already knew, but that she had done it twice.

"If I share it with you, then it won't be a secret anymore, will it?"

She shrugged. "I can't make you tell me anything. Obviously. But be warned—I already know something about you that no one else in this town knows."

"No one else? I highly doubt that." He liked her confidence, though.

Jess put her finger on his chest, directly over his heart and paused.

"There's a tiny hole, right there," she finally said.

Nash gulped. That was a whole other subject. A whole other story that he wouldn't begin to know how to explain. He'd been born with a small hole in his heart. Atrial septal defect, the doctors had called it, although it wasn't diagnosed until after his mother died.

Shortness of breath. Heart palpitations. Easily written off as stress. Any five-year-old might display such symptoms under the circumstances of losing a parent. But when his legs swelled up, his father took him to the doctor.

Nash was convinced that losing his mom had created the hole, even though the doctors insisted it was there at birth. Supposedly, it closed on its own. That much he believed. The tests all proved that was the case. But Nash would never be convinced that it hadn't been ripped back open.

Maybe it had never shown up on a transesophageal echocardiography, but he'd felt it. Until this very moment, he'd blamed Roxanne for that. Blamed her for leaving him and the girls. The whole thing even launched a rumor in Destiny Springs about there being another woman who'd broken his heart. Which he denied. But they'd known something that even he didn't know. It was so clear now.

Jess had been the one to put it there.

"How did you know?" Nash asked.

Jess couldn't even begin to describe his expression. So serious. It was almost as if she'd hurt his feelings by pointing it out. A tiny hole in a shirt wasn't anything to be ashamed of. It was going to eventually happen with a cotton flannel work shirt.

"Don't worry. I won't tell anyone. Besides, I can barely see it. I wouldn't worry that anyone else has noticed. Nothing I couldn't mend in a few minutes. Do you have a needle and some blue thread?" she asked.

He blinked hard, then looked down and examined the place she'd pointed out. He tugged at a frayed edge of the hole, then let out a nervous laugh.

"I have a hole in my shirt. Right here." He pointed at it and laughed as if someone was tickling him.

Weird.

"I'm glad you can accept it," she said.

Nash leaned back on the pillows, looked to the ceiling and laughed a little more.

"You already know that Roxanne abandoned us. Walked out on me and the girls when they were less than two weeks old."

Jess's breath caught in her throat. Less than two weeks? She, quite literally, did abandon her babies. Nash was stating it so matter-of-factly. Then again, some people laughed out of nervousness or fear or even grief. Perhaps that's what was happening.

In one way, she was relieved that he'd decided not to reveal what Taylor had confided in him. If he had, she might have been forced to mention the whole barrel racing event at Hailey's. After everything Nash had done to help her daughter, that wasn't the way for the little girl to repay him, even though Taylor was too young to fully grasp the depth of Nash's predicament.

"I'm so sorry," she said.

"It gets better. She came back around again when they were barely past toddlerhood, wanting another chance. The engine hadn't even had time to cool on her Jeep before she up and left again."

Wow.

"Is that why you don't go to events anymore? Kat said she'd only seen part of one."

He nodded. "Some years ago, I heard through the grapevine that Roxanne was talking about *her* girls and wanting to see them. As far as I'm concerned, she forfeited her place in their lives."

"Totally understandable."

"No matter. I lost my love for the sport before that," he said.

So it *was* Roxanne who broke his heart. Not someone else. That Destiny Springs rumor wasn't true. But the worst part was, he hadn't moved past it. She'd had to compete with Roxanne ten years ago. Maybe she still was.

"Thank you for confiding in me." She extended the pinkie of her right hand. "I won't tell anyone."

He hooked his pinkie with hers. "I appreciate that. While we're at it, promise you won't leave Destiny Springs without saying goodbye."

"If you'll promise not to put up any more walls," she said.

"Then promise the twins and I will see you and Taylor again at some point in the future, after y'all leave for Montana," he said.

"It's a deal."

At that, they squeezed each other's pinkies so hard she thought they might break. Furthermore, she felt the power of it.

Nash finally softened his grip and released. He picked up his coffee and took a sip. Even though the confession about Roxanne must have been difficult, there was a lightness about him now. Getting something that heavy off his chest must have felt good. Kind of like her confession about her crush.

They sipped their coffee in silence. The fireplace could have used another log, but she had to get going anyway.

"The rain stopped. I'd better get back and get some sleep." Then get up early and sew.

"I'll drive you," he said.

"That's not necessary. I'm a big girl. I've driven in worse weather than this."

"I know. But it's a convenient excuse to see you again tomorrow."

It was true; she didn't need to be taken care of in that way. She'd been taking care of herself for years. But the chivalry was beyond sweet. And, if she were being honest, she was looking forward to more time with him after he'd let her in a little more.

"Then I insist on mending that hole, as payment," she said, pointing once again to the tear in his flannel shirt.

He glanced down at the thing again and then back up. "You're the only one who could."

Jess rolled her eyes. She could think of at least two other people who were good with a needle and thread: Dorothy and Sylvie.

"You're giving me way too much credit, but I appreciate the vote of confidence."

They looked at each other for the longest time before leaning in for a gentle, extended kiss that felt perfectly natural and expected. This time, she kept her eyes open, and he did, too, softening any suspicion she'd just had about him not being over Roxanne.

She searched for any holes in that wall that he'd constructed. Only to realize that he was no longer hiding behind one.

CHAPTER SIXTEEN

NASH FELT LIKE a nervous groom, waiting for his bride to walk down the aisle.

Except the "bride" in this scenario was supposedly a seasoned ranch hand, the venue was his greenhouse and the aisle was lined with yet-to-bloom potted gerbera daisies.

They were coming along. Probably needed about two more months, if Nash didn't mess things up. This was his first attempt at raising florals.

Otherwise, he would have taken a daisy with him and presented it to Jess when he dropped off her truck at the B and B, which didn't go entirely as planned. Vern had made a late run with the eggs and insisted on giving Nash a lift back to his place.

Just as well. Nash used the extra time to locate all the ledgers. Parker had texted that he and Gus were heading his way. Since Vern managed to get him back to Buck Stops first, Nash decided to check on the progress of this future surprise for Lizzy, since she and Kat were still at Hailey's and probably eating Pop-Tarts about now.

He looked around at the other aisles. Plenty of

open space, but until he got some more help around here, he wasn't inclined to develop it. Maybe Gus had a green thumb and could take on extra duties.

In fact, Nash was getting a little excited about the possibilities.

The door to the greenhouse opened, and Parker strutted in. Alone. As he watched his "best man" walk down the aisle, a certain fear struck him.

"Did Gus get cold feet?" Nash asked, trying to mask his disappointment.

"Not at all. But I didn't want him to get 'em wet, so I left him in the house."

"Gus isn't one of your city buddies in wing tips, is he?" Nash asked, although at this point he couldn't imagine what else it could be. A seasoned ranch hand wouldn't mind getting his boots a little muddy.

All of a sudden, this felt like a huge waste of time. No matter how highly Parker thought of this stranger, Nash would have to stand firm if he wasn't a good fit. No help was better than bad help.

Same went for relationships, for that matter. Being alone was better than being with the wrong person. He may have a bad relationship track record, but at least his intuition and judgment were usually spot-on when it came to the ranch.

"No comment on the shoes. I'll let you make your own judgment about that," Parker said.

Not helpful.

"Okay. Let's see what you've gotten me into."

Once they reached the house, Parker went straight

inside after wiping his boots. Nash took a little extra time while contemplating how to put an end to all this nonsense without hurting Gus's pride.

Even that might have to wait, because once he stepped inside, he was staring down a different kind of problem. Looking up at him was the most adorable Australian shepherd he'd ever seen.

"What's going on? Where's Gus?" Nash asked.

Parker looked down to the dog. "Gus, beg for the job."

The dog took the cue and sat on its hind legs.

Nash tried to make sense of it. Was this some kind of joke?

"You said Gus was an experienced ranch hand."

"I said he was an experienced cattle herder. Worked at the Tanner ranch for ten years. Old man Tanner said you're welcome to call him for a reference."

Nash knew of the place. Buck Stops was a dot on the map compared to them.

"They replaced him with a younger dog since they've added more cattle. And they put Gus up for adoption. They let me bring him home and introduce him to the family to make sure it was a good fit for everyone involved."

So much for Nash's grand plan of giving Gus even more responsibilities. He rubbed his eyes and blinked a few times.

"What's with not getting his paws dirty?" he asked.

"Oh, he'll have no problem with that. I just didn't

want him to track mud back through your clean house."

That begged the question…

"Do Lizzy and Kat know about *you know who*?" Nash asked, nodding sideways toward the dog.

Parker shook his head. "Gus spent the night in the stables with the horses. We want to introduce him to Hailey's cat, Sergeant, when there aren't three other little terrors running around. The poor kitty went into hiding last night and hasn't come out."

The dog seemed to study Nash's every expression, as if Nash was the one being interviewed instead of the other way around.

"What do you think? Does he get the job? We can round up any cattle and move 'em to higher ground. Hailey wants to keep the girls a little longer. She'll bring 'em back this evening."

Nash wanted his little ones back more than anything. It was always tough being away from them for even one night. The more he thought about it, the more he realized that Gus was the perfect solution to the dog problem. The girls could have one around to play with sometimes, but Nash wouldn't have to take care of him.

"Okay. Don't say anything to the girls or let them see this adorable little guy until I have a chance to talk to them."

"The not-saying part I can do. The not-seeing part might be a little tricky. I'll need to take him back to the house for an hour because I'm leading half of a workshop over at the B and B. I'll be back here to finish up any chores after. I have a feeling my topic isn't going to draw a big crowd, so I might be talking to an empty room. Unless Jess makes an appearance like she promised when I took the girls off her hands, which she's certainly not obligated to do."

"If Jess said she'll do something, she will. She's amazing that way," Nash said.

Judging from Parker's stoic expression and the absence of a clever comeback, the guy was taking the statement too seriously.

Nash looked at the pup, who cocked his head as if still waiting on an official offer. Hopefully, Nash wouldn't regret what he was about to say next.

"Gus can stay here with me."

"Said like a man in love."

Nash squinted. "Gus is good lookin', but he isn't my type. And don't leave without taking that box."

"I wasn't talking about Gus." Parker tipped his hat and headed toward the front door this time, collecting the ledgers on his way out.

That's when Nash noticed the brown bag Jess had brought over. Drawings that the girls had done, did she say? How could he have forgotten about those?

He took the sack to the twins' bedroom, set it on the edge of Kat's bed and looked around. Even with all the stuffed animals and dolls and Breyer horses, the room should have felt larger without them in it. Instead, it felt smaller. Emptier. Colder. Is this how it would feel in twelve or so years, when they left the nest? If so, how did parents stand it?

Although he wanted to wait until they got home, his curiosity got the best of him. A quick peek wouldn't hurt.

He pulled out and unfolded the enormous piece of paper first. Oddly shaped and filled with daisies in all different sizes.

Next, he turned over their whiteboard, except there wasn't a drawing on it. Only a question.

Why can't your head be twelve inches long?

Nash had to laugh. "Because then it would be a foot."

Of course he'd pretend not to know the answer for Kat's sake. Except, this probably wasn't her joke. Definitely wasn't her handwriting. But something else caught his eye. Faint, layered loops in the background. As if whatever had been drawn didn't get fully erased.

He turned on the overhead light and tilted the board for a closer look. They'd started to draw one thing, then something over it. The darker marks could have been the leaves of one of Lizzy's giant flowers. Or...*a lazy daisy*. Those also had six petals.

He compared Lizzy's artwork that she'd drawn for him. Many of those had six petals, but not all. He retrieved his cell phone and pulled up the photo he'd snapped of her drawing the other day on his board. Those daisies had too many petals to count.

The slightly darker, semi-erased marker on the

girls' board appeared to only have three loops, which wouldn't qualify as any kind of flower he'd ever seen. Now he wished he had forgotten about the brown sack, because this was enough to raise some serious doubts he thought he'd never have to raise with Jess.

The handwriting was hers. And one of the drawings beneath it was a cloverleaf.

Dear Ms. McCoy—I can't stop thinking about all those fun details you're including on the suit. I would love for Meghan to wear it to a celebration dinner in Montana. I want to feature it this month instead of next. Meghan's in the morning slack. I can collect the garment then and there. Yours truly, Mrs. Carol Anne Dudley.

Jess literally gasped. She looked up and around, wanting to share the good news with Taylor. In fact, throughout the morning, she'd kept looking around for her. She'd even saved her a seat at breakfast in the barn.

But Taylor hadn't been there, since Hailey had kidnapped all the girls yesterday and was still holding them hostage. Taylor was such an integral thread in her life, it felt as though she would fall completely apart without her.

Then another kind of reality sank in. She hadn't made any actual progress on Mrs. Dudley's outfit, aside from patterning and daydreaming. And she'd used her last scrap of black velvet for the number on Kat's shirt.

Jess glanced at the clock, which reminded her of the workshop that Parker was leading. The one she'd promised to drop in on, only she was late. She slipped her boots on, combed through her hair and brushed her teeth.

By the time she got downstairs, the parlor was packed with DEBBs. She considered slowly turning around and going back upstairs. Except she'd caught Dorothy's eye. The woman patted the empty seat next to her on one of the sofas.

Another surprise: Vanessa was standing next to Parker. Jess was hoping she'd get to see her again.

"I'll fill you in on what you missed later," Dorothy whispered as Jess squeezed into the small space.

Jess turned her attention to Parker. The cowboy looked as comfortable in front of a crowd as Nash did in jeans.

"Now for the part you've all been waiting for," he said. "Accounting software for your home."

That earned a few chuckles from the audience.

"Does anyone currently use any software, either for home budgeting or business? Or both?" he asked.

Jess was the only one to raise a hand.

"Good! Then I'll let you take over from here, Ms. McCoy," Parker said, then pretended to walk away.

Unfortunately, she wasn't prepared to speak on such an important topic. As with her sewing, her budgeting and software skills had been self-taught out of pure necessity. But if he was okay with that—

"He's teasing, Jess," Vanessa said, grabbing Parker's arm and pulling him back to his post.

Jess exhaled. Yep. That woman was an angel, for sure.

"Vanessa is right, as usual. But since my cousin didn't let me get away with it, I'm going to hand the workshop over to her instead. After a quick wrap-up."

At that, Jess perked up. She'd been thinking about what Vanessa had suggested about her hiring someone to help with the garments. Hopefully, she'd delve into that concept more. If so, all the anxiety of taking the time to come down here would be worth it.

"Instead of putting the room to sleep, I'll post a link on my website where you can download a free trial to a couple of my preferred accounting software programs," Parker said. "With that, I'll let my cousin Vanessa take over from here and share her part of the workshop on work-life balance for the 'sandwich' generation. We'll both hang around for a little while afterward to answer any questions that you're too embarrassed to ask in front of your friends."

Again, that earned him a few chuckles and plenty of smiles.

"My cousin is a tough act to follow, but I'll try." Vanessa looked down at some notes, then looked back up. "I met someone here in Destiny Springs the other day. I won't name names, but I saw myself in her."

Vanessa had been scanning the room, but her gaze settled on Jess long enough to suggest the woman was talking about her.

"I also know that at least one of you is caring for a spouse because of major health issues while holding the whole sandwich together on your own," Vanessa continued. "We don't have much time left, but I want to give you a few pointers and resources on not only balancing our responsibilities to others, but also our responsibilities to ourselves and our own future goals and dreams."

Dorothy shifted and wiggled as if Jess was sitting too close. They were all sandwiched in, which seem to be the food reference of the day. Jess glanced at her sewing soulmate just as the woman dabbed away a tear, and she realized she was sitting next to the main ingredient in Vanessa's last scenario.

Her sewing soulmate had mentioned being interested in getting back into the craft and doing that from home. At the time, Jess assumed it was because she wanted a productive hobby. Now she realized it went much deeper.

In fact, Jess looked around at all the women and men in the room. She'd assumed they all had spousal support—emotional or financial, or both—and that this was nothing more than a fun retreat they gathered for each year. She'd been wrong.

"This isn't a phenomenon that only affects women.

Many men are juggling home life and work on their own, too—like at least one local cowboy I know. He could use a partner in his life. Preferably someone who can do accounting spreadsheets, because I'm afraid he's a lost cause in that area," Parker added.

Again, that earned a laugh from some of the DEBBs. Parker didn't even have to say Nash's name, although his identity wouldn't be obvious to the others. Except Jess. And she'd bet the cowboy knew it.

Was the whole town in cahoots?

That was the least of her concerns at that moment. Jess squeezed her eyes closed. Whatever Vanessa had started explaining turned into white noise, although she recognized much of it from their private talk. There was no way she could finish the Dudley project without some help. And there were two working sewing machines in the house.

What if...?

Jess began to see the possibilities. Her mind suddenly felt as though she'd been sleeping like a champ, when in reality, she'd been lucky to get in four hours a night.

The sound of Parker and Vanessa's voices wrapping up the meeting, and the rustling of DEBBs starting to leave, reeled Jess back into the moment. And back to Dorothy, who thankfully looked somewhat uplifted.

"What did you think of all that? I found it helpful but a bit overwhelming. Vanessa and Parker made it sound so easy to have a home business, but I wouldn't know where to start." Dorothy's eyes were now dry but tinged in red. She slipped something into the pocket of her sweater. Looked like a tissue.

"I know Vanessa talked about having to go it alone, but what if you didn't have to?" Jess asked.

Dorothy seemed confused. No surprise. Jess wasn't too clear herself on what she was about to propose, but it seemed like a possible solution for both of them.

It also might be a good way to test the waters for what she was contemplating. A work from home situation…in an actual home instead of an apartment. Maybe with a sewing studio, or just an empty corner she could call her own.

"You mentioned wanting to sew again. I'm desperately behind on a project with a tight deadline. I could pay you a standard hourly rate, if Becca is okay with us continuing to use her sewing machine."

Dorothy sat up straighter, and her expression lightened. "Honestly, I'd do it for free. It would take my mind off certain things. I have a sewing machine at home, as well, if it still runs."

Jess wanted to say that this couldn't wait until they returned home from their workshops, but this deadline was her fault and her problem. Not Dorothy's.

"There is no way I'd let you work for free. Your time is precious, and it might take away from your experience here."

Dorothy fidgeted with her nails. "Well, I've missed

out on a lot already. The DEBBs were so sweet to have the retreat here this year so that I could go back and forth to my house."

"You live in Destiny Springs?"

"About fifteen minutes outside of the town, in an even smaller one."

That explained why Jess didn't always see her. It also confirmed what she suspected about Dorothy's situation. In fact, maybe being around these men and women, who appeared to be happier and less burdened by life's senseless tragedies, reminded Dorothy of easier times. Just like it was doing with Jess.

Still, the choice was Dorothy's.

"Give it some thought. I stand to gain a lot from the completion of this project, so free labor is off the table."

"Okay. If you insist. Can't say I couldn't use the extra money," Dorothy said.

The woman didn't ask for further details, and Jess was happy to omit that the outfit would be featured on a prominent blog. Yet, even though it was Jess's design, she wouldn't be the one to assemble it. This could backfire. The woman could do a less-than-stellar job, in which Jess would take the fall.

All Jess knew for certain was that she couldn't finish the garment without spending every available waking moment on it. She wasn't about to shortchange the twins or further alienate her own daughter.

Or see less of Nash. Not if she absolutely didn't have to.

"Terrific! I have it all patterned out, and I'll provide you with the fabric and notions. All I'm missing is the black velvet for some trim, but I'll come up with something," Jess said.

Even though Jess was taking a huge chance, she felt lighter already. But there was something else. She hadn't heard much of the workshop, but she did hear Parker's and Vanessa's indirect message to her about a certain local cowboy they knew needing a partner in his life.

For the first time, Jess believed that so many people couldn't be wrong. That maybe she had been wrong about certain things, like feeling confined by planting roots. And about Taylor not needing a stable father figure because Jess should be able to handle both roles.

Most of all, maybe she'd been wrong to think that this relationship wasn't meant to be. She felt safe with Nash in a way that she hadn't for years.

It was time to trust that feeling again.

CHAPTER SEVENTEEN

FOR THE FIRST time ever, the twins burst through the front door and halted without giving their daddy a hug.

Nash didn't want it any other way.

Even though he hadn't seen his girls since yesterday afternoon and had been suffering serious hug withdrawals, the look on both of their faces was priceless.

Kat stood, slack-jawed. Lizzy started crying happy tears.

Gus knew exactly what to do to comfort her. He ran over with his backside wagging furiously, giving her slobbery doggy kisses.

"Before you get too excited, he doesn't belong to us. He's Parker and Hailey's. But he's going to be a Buck Stops employee, so we'll get to play with him every day."

Parker followed behind and leaned on the door frame. "And I'm open to letting him spend the night every once in a while, if it's okay with your daddy."

The twins obviously didn't hear a word that either had to say. They were too busy hugging the happy little fella.

Nash nodded for Parker to join him. His ranch hand came inside and closed the door behind him.

"Hope I didn't overstep my bounds by suggesting a slumber party," Parker said.

"No worries, as long as it gets me out of having to adopt one myself," Nash said.

"My evil plan has been exposed. Plus, it might be good for the girls to have a distraction while you make some important life decisions." Parker flashed a large envelope. "These are the preliminary suggestions I promised, based on annual summaries for each year. I wanted you to mull everything over before I spend many hours in the weeds, pulling together specifics and a working budget. You had quite a business going back in the day. I'm impressed."

"I'm not as bad with numbers as people think," Nash said.

"I've found that most people are better than they think. Numbers are like relationships," Parker said.

Nash looked at him sideways.

"You have to work at them sometimes. But when everything adds up, it's a beautiful thing," Parker said.

"And when it doesn't?" Nash didn't mean to sound so cynical. In fact, he'd almost forgotten how some things in his life—and, admittedly, his relationship with Jess—didn't add up as easily as he wanted them to.

"That often means you didn't try hard enough," Parker said, relinquishing the envelope.

Nash pulled out the binder-clipped stack of paper and glanced at the summation.

- Primary source of income: teaching (barrel racing).
- Secondary source of income: cattle (dairy and/or beef production).
- Optional income stream: growing crops (farmers markets, or branching out).

Nash looked Parker square in the eye. "Pretty sure I asked you to leave barrel racing out of the equation. Or did I dream that?"

"No. I concur that happened."

"And you agreed, as I recall."

"I said I understood."

"Same difference. I know you're doing this as a favor, and I appreciate it. But please try again." At that, Nash placed the envelope on the hall table between them, folded his arms and prepared for a witty comeback.

His ranch hand obviously sensed Nash wasn't in the mood.

"I'm going to check on our momma and her baby," Parker said in a calm but cooler tone than before. The cowboy then turned on his heels and left.

Nash closed his eyes and rubbed his temples. His mind returned to another situation where his request had been ignored. His thoughts kept going round and round those faint loops he'd noticed on the whiteboard. Running in circle eights and clover-leafs and daisy petals until he couldn't tell which was which. Maybe there was a way to get some clarification.

When he opened his eyes, his girls were standing there with Gus. Watching. Time to pull himself up by his bootstraps and paste a smile on his face. Maybe even get some clarification.

"Girls, I brought the drawings home that you did with Jess. Remember? They're in your room, and I can't wait to see them."

They looked at him for a long minute before they remembered, which eased his guilt over forgetting.

"Can Gus come with us?" Lizzy asked.

"Absolutely!"

The twins each took a hand and practically dragged him down the hall. Gus followed, his entire back end wagging so hard he could have knocked a hole in the wall.

Lizzy unfolded hers first. "They're daisies. Miss Jess let me draw on some of her special paper."

"Those are the most beautiful flowers I've ever seen," Nash said.

Lizzy produced a pen with a flower on the end. "She bought me this to draw with."

"That was awfully nice of her."

"And I picked out a skirt for her. It's really pretty," Lizzy added.

Now *that* he hadn't forgotten.

"Did you get a pen, too, Kat?"

"She got a bracelet like Taylor's," Lizzy said.

"Let me see," Nash said. Kat held it up. Horse-shoes, intertwined.

"That's beautiful. And did you draw something for me, too?"

"Miss Jess drew a joke for you instead 'cause I can't draw," Kat said. She reached into the sack, pulled out the board and handed it to him.

"I wouldn't say that. Your stick ponies are amazing. Can you help me read this?" he asked.

As Kat pointed to each word, Nash took the lead in sounding them out for her. "Why can't your head be twelve inches long?"

He then pretended to think about it. "Gosh. I don't know."

"'Cause twelve inches is a foot!" Lizzy called out.

"That was my joke. You ruined it!" Kat yelled.

The earth could have stopped rotating. Kat had never pushed back that hard against Lizzy. Unless it had to do with cupcakes versus sugar pies. And even then...

Nash's hope of getting any insight into the faint markings on the board was superseded by the need to put a stop to this argument and calm the waters.

He stood and offered one hand to Kat and one to Lizzy. "C'mon ladies. Cupcake and Sugar Pie miss you. We need to stretch their legs, but we're gonna walk. Not ride."

Hand in hand, they went to the stables, Gus trotting happily beside them. The arena was reasonably dry, but he didn't want to risk any injuries to the horses or the girls. He'd exercise them himself later. Or have Parker do it, if the guy was even speaking to him. He hadn't meant to come across as ungrateful, but what Parker had proposed would create more problems than it would solve.

Together, they put the halters and lead ropes on their horses. Once done, Nash claimed his teaching spot on the fence and observed.

"Be careful. It's muddy in places," he called out.

It had become only a minor point that the barrels were out there. One more session with Taylor, and they'd go back into storage, even though he'd considered getting rid of them completely. But he'd gotten reattached to them over the past few days, at least enough to hold on to them for a while.

Lizzy went through her usual walking drill around the perimeter of the arena. Gus followed her and Cupcake instead of Kat. Lizzy seemed to relish every moment of it.

Kat, on the other hand, deviated from her usual drill and took Sugar Pie around the barrels. Right turn around the first, left turn around the second. Another left turn around the third.

His stomach seized. No way that was accidental. He jumped off his perch and joined them in the arena.

"Where did you learn to do that?" he asked Kat.

She stopped and looked down. "I don't know. I saw Taylor do it."

That was believable. She had caught a glimpse of Taylor going through the drills. Once. Maybe he didn't know a lot about six-year-old girls. And he was pretty sure he wasn't biased in believing that Kat was smarter than the average kid. But he was certain it took more exposure and practice than that to pick up that much detail.

"Miss Jess let us all barrel race at Miss Hailey's around rocks at her house while they watched," Lizzy said.

What?

"Is that true?" he asked Kat.

The little girl nodded. Poor thing looked terrified, which wasn't his goal.

"Did you have fun?" he asked, to let her know he wasn't upset. Not at her.

She lit up a bit and nodded harder.

He pulled out his phone and dialed Hailey, but she didn't answer. Then again, he hadn't talked to her about not encouraging Kat. This one was on Jess. She'd said she wanted to stop by tonight. Had a surprise for all of them.

Hopefully, she'd also have an explanation. Trying to make a relationship like theirs add up, even in the best-case scenario, might not be easy. He would have been willing to try. But if honesty and transparency weren't there...

Maybe he wasn't good at math, as Lizzy and Kat always joked about. But he could add a cloverleaf drawing and bracelet and competition shirt together just fine.

And it equaled a breach of trust.

CUPCAKES AND SUGAR PIES. Didn't get much sweeter than that.

Jess balanced the grocery sacks, filled with all the necessary ingredients for the girls' favorite desserts, on her hip and knocked on the front door of Nash's house.

She wasn't sure how a relationship between them was going to work, but she wanted to try. What he'd said on the trail ride, about the potential gain outweighing the possible pain, convinced her that he felt the same way.

That wasn't all. She had Becca's permission to fix pancakes with fresh strawberries and blueberries and raspberries and chocolate-maple syrup and whipped cream for Taylor tomorrow morning in the B and B kitchen. Just the two of them.

It was a small thing that she should have done for her daughter a long time ago, and more often.

At first, she'd felt guilty about not bringing her daughter, but Jess wanted tonight to be one-on-two time with the twins, making cupcakes and sugar pies in the kitchen. The main course being some one-on-one discussion with Nash in the den while the girls decorated the treats. Becca had stepped in to help by inviting Taylor to "movie night," with her own little family.

The sun had already begun to set, and smoke was rising from the chimney. It was the only movement against a backdrop that otherwise looked like an Albert Bierstadt painting, except for a few cattle stirring in the distance.

When Nash opened the door, she felt a certain chill, even though she could see and hear the fireplace crackling from where she stood.

"C'mon in," he said, barely looking at her before walking away and leaving the door open behind him.

Someone's a little grumpy. Looked like she'd arrived in the nick of time with sustenance.

Jess took a deep breath, crossed the threshold and struggled to push the door closed with her knee.

"Miss Jess!" The girls ran over to greet her, along with an unfamiliar face: an Australian shepherd.

"And who's this?" Jess asked as she struggled not to topple over.

"Gus, and he's our new dog! But he really belongs to Miss Hailey and Mr. Parker," Lizzy said.

Jess looked to Nash for clarification while still struggling with the groceries. He had to realize her immediate predicament.

"Sorry. Let me take those off your hands," he said, rushing over to relieve her of the two paper bags but without making any further eye contact.

"Thanks." *I think.*

"Gus is the ranch's newest employee. Cattle herder. I offered to keep him tonight for Parker and Hailey. He doesn't get along with the cat." He paused to look at the girls. "But he's not technically ours. Okay?"

Lizzy's chin dropped, but she quickly recovered once the pup went over and snuggled with her. Animals were so perceptive that way. People, not so much. Jess could use a snuggle from Nash right now. Didn't have to be a full-on hug or kiss.

"Those go in the kitchen," she said. "I come bearing food."

"Actually, we just ate," he said. Nothing else. No curiosity. No *thanks anyway.*

She clearly wasn't welcome here. And she didn't have a clue as to why. She halfway expected him to hand the sacks back to her.

Instead, he carried them to the kitchen. Jess stayed behind and tried to make some sense of his cold reaction. If they hadn't already eaten, she would have assumed he was wearing his grumpy pants. Except they didn't look the least bit cute on him tonight. Instead, he was decked out from head to toe in attitude.

She got the same knot in her stomach as she did less than two weeks ago, when she knocked on his door after so many years. When she'd hugged him and he barely hugged her back.

Not that she had blamed him. The difference now was that he knew she was stopping by tonight. They shared more than a history of training sessions and bad jokes and Juicy Lucys. They shared hugs, secrets, a pinkie promise. Kisses. And, most important, hope for a future together.

Jess summoned her courage and joined them in the kitchen.

"I bet Gus could use a walk. Take him around the house a couple of times. No farther," Nash said to the girls.

Lizzy collected the leash, and together the twins managed to attach it to his collar. Nash checked to make sure it was secure, then opened the door and watched them exit, leaving it cracked open for their return.

"I wanted a chance to talk with you, alone," he said.

What could have been that moment of privacy she'd hoped for tonight was something she now dreaded. The person looking back at her wasn't Nash. It wasn't even Mr. Grumpy Pants. She didn't know who it was.

"I guess my coming over to bake cupcakes and sugar pies with the girls wasn't the best idea," she said, even though the thought of that being the reason for his sour mood was ridiculous.

Nash exhaled and looked down at his feet. "This doesn't have anything to do with desserts. It was nice of you to think of the girls."

"Then what does it have to do with?"

"Lazy daisies and a cloverleaf," he said.

"I'm confused."

"You don't remember?"

"Of course. The lazy daisy was our version of the six-barrel drill," she said. The cloverleaf was self-explanatory.

"Did you show Kat either one of those?"

Jess's mind was a blur. No one knew about their lazy daisy drill except her and Nash. And Taylor. But there was one possible explanation.

"A lazy daisy is also an embroidery technique. Hence the name. I showed Lizzy how to draw one."

"On their board?"

No. Taylor and Kat were drawing on that.

"On a piece of pattern paper," she said. Her stomach tightened.

Nash nodded and didn't blink.

"I'll come right out and say it. She's been coached by someone, Jess. It's unmistakable. Was it you? All I'm asking is for you to be honest with me."

She knew exactly what he was asking now, and nothing about that question was simple. Jess replayed the past week in her mind. How Nash had helped Taylor in the arena. How the two had formed a bond. How her little girl was happy again.

The simple answer to Nash's question would be *yes*. The honest answer would be that Taylor had been instructing Kat beyond what she'd witnessed at Hailey's, as Jess suspected. Yet she hadn't done enough to prevent it. And maybe part of her—that little girl she used to be who fell in love with barrel racing and was encouraged to pursue it—didn't want to.

She wanted to ask him if he'd cared that it had made *his* little girl happy. But that issue wasn't simple, either.

"Sounds to me like you have the only answer you need." That was as much of a confession as she would offer. At least, until he made one of his own. "Now I need an honest answer from you."

Nash blinked. She took a deep breath and asked

a form of the question she should have asked ten years ago when she should have confronted a fear but ran away from it. "Are you still in love with Roxanne?"

"What? Of course not! How could you even think that, after what I told you?"

"Because I don't think this is about whether Kat was coached by me or anyone else. I know you'd let her pursue this in a heartbeat. You'd find a way around the time and money constraints. Because, guess what, I did. Except Roxanne is still in your life. And she's calling the shots."

Nash shook his head in denial. "You're wrong. I've gone to great lengths to make sure she isn't. And doesn't."

"I know you have. You've created a safe home for the girls. You protect them from the big bad world, like any good father would and should do. Your daughter wants to try barrel racing, but she's afraid to talk to you about it. Just like Taylor seems to be afraid to tell me what you two discussed."

Nash nodded in concession. "You deserve to know. She wanted to be the one to tell you, but maybe she's not quite ready. I'd tell you now, but she trusted me with her secret. I hope you can understand."

"I sure do," she said. *And I trusted you with my heart. Difference is, you're breaking it.*

She understood other things in that moment. She still wanted to explore the world, and the rodeo was a big part of that. He still wanted to hide from it.

She believed in doing whatever a parent had to do to help make their child's dreams come true, even if it meant facing demons. He did not.

That was what she'd tried to do by coming here in the first place and by asking for his help. And that's what she ended up getting.

In a way, he'd been right on that trail ride, because all the pain she was feeling right now was ultimately worth the gains she'd made for Taylor. But there was one thing she did want to take responsibility for.

"I take the blame for letting this get personal between us," she said. After all, she was the one who had admitted to having a crush in the first place. If she could take all of it back, she would.

Nash unfolded his arms and straightened. "I share the blame for that."

A softer look crossed his eyes. For a moment, she thought he was going to take it back. Say he didn't regret it for a minute and then embrace her so hard she couldn't run away. Tell her that they would find a way through this. Instead, he stuffed his hands in his pockets and looked away.

Just as well. There was nothing remotely appealing about hugging a wall.

"All that said, I want to make sure Taylor is good for Montana. If you're still okay with one more session, first thing in the morning tomorrow," he said.

There they were. Back to being friends. Not even that, really. A former teacher and his student. That was what it should have been all along.

"I'll pay you for your time."

"That's not—"

The girls busted through the door, all smiles. Jess willed herself not to cry.

"Gus is fun, Daddy! Can we adopt him?" Lizzy asked.

Nash's entire demeanor transformed. The wall came crashing down for his girls. That smile of his busted through it.

"I have an idea. Since Gus is older, let's see if he will adopt both of you. He can take y'all on walks instead. Who wants to try on the leash first?" he asked.

When Nash reached for them, they let go of Gus and tried to run. But they didn't get far. He scooped them up, one in each arm. Gus started barking as if trying to protect the twins, which made them giggle even more.

Jess rubbed her arms. It was too cold in here for those who didn't belong. Too cramped. She stepped out of the kitchen, most likely unnoticed. She pulled a pen and slip of paper from her purse, along with two butterscotch candies, and jotted down a note.

Lizzy and Kat—I had to leave, but I'll take a rain check on baking. In the meantime, here are a couple of sweets for two of the sweetest gals on this earth.

Jess slipped the pen back inside her purse, exited through the front door and locked it behind her.

Sure, they didn't have the skills yet to read the letter, but Nash did. She hoped he would convey the sentiment.

She needed to focus on her own world now. The one that embraced her. She and Taylor were all each other had when they came to Destiny Springs. And all they'd have when they left, even though it hadn't felt that way for a while. Nash broke his promise not to put up a wall, but in a way she was grateful.

She was about to break one, too.

CHAPTER EIGHTEEN

NASH NEARLY CHOKED on a sip of coffee as he looked out the back window. A woman was sitting on the fence, facing the arena.

Jess?

She'd slipped out last night while he was playing with the girls and Gus, which was a bit unsettling. Sure, they'd had a confrontation, but nothing was resolved to his satisfaction. They had nearly a week to see if it could be.

At least Jess had left a note and candy for the girls, saying she had to leave. But he figured she'd be back this morning with Taylor since she hadn't proposed a later day. He simply hadn't expected them so early.

He set down the cup and called out to Parker. He'd only caught glimpses of his ranch hand this morning. "Watch the girls for a few, please?"

"Yes, sir," Parker called back.

The formality was annoying. Nash shouldn't have acted so ungrateful about the proposal, but his ranch hand had driven him to it. They'd have to hash it out and talk about their *feelings* another time, however.

Nash put on his Stetson and headed outside. As he approached, he realized it wasn't Jess after all.

Relief swept over him, because he wasn't sure what he would have said to her. She'd broken his trust. Yet, his own daughter had been secretive, too. After a couple of talks, he'd thought—hoped—Kat understood his situation, even though a child that age shouldn't have to.

Turned out, he was the one who hadn't understood how important this was to her, and his role in denying her. In a twisted-logic way, Jess was right about Roxanne calling the shots. And Kat was paying the price.

Then again, so was he. He'd given up something he loved. Make that two things: teaching and Jess.

"What are you doing here?" he asked.

Hailey half smiled. "I thought you could use a friend this morning, since you're running all the others off."

Nash didn't have to ask. No doubt his ranch hand had told his wife what had happened.

"Parker's a professional. He'll get over it. He's inside playing with Gus, in case you didn't know," Nash said.

"I know. I don't have the heart to watch, so I thought I'd come check on you."

"Why is it hard to watch Gus?" Nash asked.

"Because Parker is convinced that he isn't cut out to be a daddy. Can't get Gus and Sergeant to coexist peacefully. I told him to give it some time. We'll figure out something, together. At least, that's the way it *should* work."

Nash needed to figure out something, as well. How to run off the person who might be the only friend he had left. Not permanently, however. He simply didn't want Hailey to be there when Jess and Taylor arrived.

He turned on his heels and headed to the stalls to check on the horses, except something was different. Mischief's stall was empty.

The air escaped his lungs. He ran over to make sure he wasn't imagining it. The gate wasn't opened. The horse couldn't have gotten out.

Hailey came up behind him. "Becca called me this morning. Said Jess and Taylor checked out before dawn."

The blade of abandonment was swift. Nash froze. Everything around him seemed to do the same. He felt beyond sick. Pressing his hand into his stomach didn't begin to tame it.

In Jess's note to the girls, she'd mentioned she had to leave. But it didn't sound like goodbye. She'd even mentioned a rain check for baking, albeit without a proposed time or day.

"I'm sorry," Hailey said.

Nash straightened his back but couldn't look at her. He proceeded to feed the other horses through the pain while Hailey maintained a respectful distance.

"Sorry for what? Jess got what she came here

for," he said when it was clear that Hailey wasn't taking a hint and leaving.

"And what was that?" Hailey asked.

"To get my help with Taylor. I thought we had one last session. I must have misunderstood. No big deal."

"I really thought you two had something good going on," Hailey said.

"So did I." He didn't mean to say it out loud, but he was hurting too much to hold it in.

"Let's go sit on the fence. Watch the sunrise." She took his hand and led him to his old teaching spot.

As they sat there in silence, Nash stared at the way the sun started glinting off the barrels, and thought about how he should have said no to Jess in the first place and avoided reopening that hole in his heart. He could feel it now, as sure as he felt the wooden railing beneath his seat and the frigid air in his lungs. No doctor or fancy tests would ever be able to convince him otherwise.

"You were saying," Hailey said.

Nash breathed in and exhaled slowly. "Jess was training Kat to barrel race against my explicit directions. I confronted her about it. I know you saw it happening, so don't deny it."

"I saw Kat rounding the boulders like she would the barrels. Taylor was doing it, too. Jess put a stop to it."

"She admitted she'd trained her, Hailey."

"Jess said that?"

Not in so many words, and he'd memorized all of them from last night.

"She didn't deny it," he said.

For once, Hailey didn't have a response, which always struck fear in him. That meant her brain had shifted into overdrive. This time was no exception. Except, there wasn't much she could say. Not if she wanted to remain his friend, of which the numbers had dwindled. If she was a good one, she wouldn't take Jess's side in this.

"I…" She took a deep breath and started to say something, then paused.

He gripped the railing beneath him.

"I admitted to Parker the other day that I knocked his favorite coffee mug off the kitchen counter and broke it. But it was Sergeant."

Nash looked at her sideways. "Okay. I won't tell your hubby. He isn't speaking to me anyway. Cats tend to do that sort of thing. He'll get used to it."

"That's true. But I didn't want Parker to be mad at Sergeant. I'd rather he be mad at me."

"You're strange."

"Says the man who ran off the love of his life. Have you talked to Kat about what happened?"

"I'm gonna get whiplash if you keep changing the subject," he said.

"I'm staying on point. You'll see if you answer the question."

"No. I haven't spoken with her."

"I'll tell you what I bet happened. Taylor has been the one teaching Kat."

The thought had briefly crossed his mind, but then Jess took the blame. Kind of.

"If you're right, and I'm not saying you are, why wouldn't Jess say so?" Nash asked.

"Gosh, I don't know. Maybe because she didn't want you to be mad at Kat. Or Taylor. Like I didn't want Parker to be mad at Sergeant, so I took the fall for the kitty. And I'd do it a million times over 'cause he's my baby."

If Hailey was right, and she usually was, that would mean that he and Jess were both protecting Taylor. Furthermore, they both wanted what they thought was best for Kat. Except he was the only one who *wasn't* trying to make that happen.

Nash blew out a long breath. "You really believe that's what happened?"

"Like you said yourself, I was there. I saw what Jess saw. Talent and drive. The pure excitement on Kat's face as she raced around the boulders. I never realized she even had dimples when she smiles that big."

Kat has dimples?

"I put up walls," he confessed. "Is that something you can see, too?"

"Are you kidding? You could quit your day job and start a construction company. You'd make a fortune. Should I ask my hubby to put together some numbers for that?"

"Absolutely. Anything to get Kat involved in barrel racing. Or whatever sport she wants."

Hailey simply stared.

"What?" he asked.

"Oh, just wondering why you didn't think about that sooner."

Nash blew out a long breath. "I haven't stopped thinking about it lately. I wanted to avoid crossing paths with Roxanne, at all costs. Turned out, that decision has cost a lot more than I bargained for. Jess thinks that's why I'm against Kat getting involved in the rodeo. She even asked me if I was still in love with Roxanne."

"You're not in love with that woman. Jess is smart enough to know that."

"I know. I'm not in love with Roxanne. I'm in love with Jess. Is she smart enough to know that, as well?"

Instead of waiting for an answer, Nash jumped from the fence and hightailed it to the house. He turned around long enough to shout, "Tack up Sugar Pie, if you don't mind."

"Yes, your highness."

Nash shook his head, grateful he hadn't run her off. Then again, that woman would never let something like a wall get in her way.

Once inside the house, he followed Lizzy's and Kat's shrieks and Gus's bark and Parker's laughter to the den.

Nash gave Lizzy a wink but didn't make eye contact with his ranch hand quite yet. First, he had a very important bridge to build.

He knelt to Kat's level and searched for those dimples she supposedly had. Not even a trace. One thing was for sure: he wasn't letting this little girl out of his sight until she revealed them to him.

"I want to watch you and Sugar Pie run around the barrels," he said.

"Really?" she asked.

"Only if you want to."

Kat nodded so hard, he was afraid her pretty little head would come right off.

He looked to Parker. "You and Lizzy stay here and play with Gus. It's important that the pup get used to hanging around here more often."

Thankfully, the comment went right over Lizzy's head, because he didn't want to get her too excited until he had a chance to talk to Parker and Hailey about a possible solution to all their problems. Perhaps they could share custody if the dog and cat couldn't stop fighting. Or Nash could adopt him outright, and the Donnellys could have unlimited visitation.

"What did Hailey tell you?" Parker called out.

Nash paused in his steps without turning around. "Everything I needed to hear."

By the time he and Kat reached the arena, Hailey had tacked up Sugar Pie. She handed Kat a pink riding helmet, and together, she and Nash gave the little girl a leg up. Nash led her to the starting point.

"I want you to trot through this first. Start with whichever barrel you want. I'll call out instructions if you get turned around."

He and Hailey took their respective places, once again, on the fence. He intentionally didn't call out for her first round. Wanted to see how much she'd learned. Turned out, she didn't need any direction to get through the basic pattern.

"Are you seeing what I'm seeing?" Hailey asked.

"Everything except those dimples of hers that you'd mentioned."

Hailey smiled. "I have a feeling you'll be seeing a lot of those from now on."

Now, *that* made him smile. So did the idea of teaching again, now that he'd stopped resisting the urge to scratch that itch. He also realized what a friend he had in Parker, even though the guy didn't listen. Then again, Nash wasn't finished talking.

There was another itch begging to be scratched. To have a life with Jess. She was…*everything*. Friend, joke swapper, Juicy Lucy buddy. In other words, the perfect woman for him. Always had been. The icing on the cupcake and the sugar on the sugar pie was that Jess was exactly the kind of mom the girls needed. Yes, she'd broken their promise not to leave without saying goodbye. But he'd broken his first by putting up a wall.

There was only one way to possibly fix everything: a road trip. Him, the girls and a horse named Sugar Pie.

AVOIDING CONFRONTATION MAY have worked for Jess in the past, but it was backfiring royally now.

Taylor was sad again, and any chance Jess might have had with Nash was in the rearview mirror.

Another horrible consequence: she'd abandoned the twins.

Just like their mom had done.

Hopefully, Nash would read them the note and they'd know that she cared, as small of a gesture as it had been.

Jess had also abandoned her responsibilities when it came to her sewing. Dorothy had handed over what she said was the completed Dudley project, which would have been next to impossible to execute in such a short amount of time. Jess hadn't summoned the courage to open the box that her sewing soulmate had placed it in. Might as well have been a casket for Jess's career. But by getting to Montana earlier than planned, she would have time to fix any problems once they got settled into their hotel.

A diner's lights were on, up ahead. Might be a good time and place to stop and get something to eat, since Taylor was wide awake.

They were still a couple hundred miles from Billings, having stopped halfway at a friend's dude ranch outside of Wyoming to exercise Mischief. The family was even kind enough to put out barrels and let Taylor practice, which only underscored how horribly Jess had messed up by leaving. Her daughter seemed to have slipped back into slow beginnings and slower finishes.

Jess wouldn't have stopped at all, but their room in Billings wasn't going to be ready until later anyway. And the morning had arrived, even though the sun had yet to make its announcement.

They had their choice of booths. Taylor led them to the one with the best view of their trailer through the glass. Her little eyes didn't veer from it.

The waitress was promptly at their side.

"What can I get for you ladies?"

"Coffee for me, please. What would you like, Taylor?"

"I'm not hungry."

"I'm starved." Jess scanned the menu and found what she was looking for. "I'll have pancakes. Tall stack. Do you have strawberries and blueberries and raspberries and chocolate-maple syrup and whipped cream?"

That got Taylor's attention. She cast a hopeful look to the waitress, who was mouthing the list to herself and processing it.

"Ohh-kay. I can do strawberries, blackberries, blueberries, and I can bring you some chocolate syrup and maple syrup, but you'll have to mix 'em yourself."

"I think we can manage. How about whipped cream? And milk and orange juice for her," Jess said.

It took a minute, but the waitress caught up with jotting the order down on a pad. She promptly returned with the beverages, along with the silverware and an extra plate.

At least Taylor hadn't returned to gazing out the window. She wasn't looking at her mom, either. The diner was quiet, their food was being prepared and Jess had a captive audience. It was now or never. She took a deep breath.

"I messed up, Taylor. I owe you a huge apology."

That earned some eye contact.

"We shouldn't have left without telling Lizzy and Kat and Nash goodbye," Jess continued.

Taylor looked down again, this time at her friendship bracelets. It tore at Jess's heart that, once again, she'd so brutally yanked her away from her newest friends, as swiftly and impulsively as one of those threads. Although this time felt like the cruelest of all.

It also gave Jess a brilliant idea.

They sat in silence until the waitress brought the pancakes, with the fixings on the side. "Let me know if you need anything else. I'll swing back around in a little while and check on you."

"Wait! Do you mind keeping an eye on our food for a few minutes? We need to run out to the trailer."

"Happy to," the woman said.

"C'mon," Jess said as Taylor reluctantly eased out of the booth. She took her daughter's hand and led the way to the trailer.

Jess opened the truck cab and retrieved her notions box. She pulled out her scissors, a square of suede she'd been hauling around for a while and a needle and thread. With those in hand, she walked around to the side of the trailer and consulted Mischief.

"Forgive me for what I'm about to do, but I need your help," Jess whispered to Mischief. She walked farther down, reached through a slat, and snipped some of the hair from his tail. Once she felt she had enough, they went back inside.

Jess served up the biggest smile as they both eased back into the booth.

"Can you help me assemble these pancakes? You always do such a good job," Jess said, tucking the notions and horse hair away for now.

Taylor took the lead, and Jess followed. Together, they put quite a dent in the feast, which gave Jess time to summon her thoughts, and courage.

"I want to tell you something, but I need for it to be just between us. For now, at least. Can we pinkie promise on it?" Jess asked.

Taylor took a good long time contemplating it, but finally nodded.

"I miss Nash. A lot. In fact, I love him. I'd like to drive back to Destiny Springs after the rodeo. But that would mean missing the one in Nevada. I'll make it up to you," Jess said.

Taylor sat up straighter. "Can I see Lizzy and Kat again?"

"Absolutely! Y'all became good friends?"

Taylor deflated a little. "The best. But…"

"You can tell me anything, sweetie."

"Kat was asking a million questions about barrel racing, and you said I wasn't supposed to talk about it, but she said her daddy wouldn't talk to her about it, so…"

You coached her.

"You wanted to be a good friend, which you were. You still are. Since y'all are such good friends, we can't go back to Destiny Springs empty-handed. But I'll need your help, because you're a lot better at this than I am."

Jess pushed their plates to the side and cleared a spot on the table. She wasn't sure how the management would feel about her placing unwashed horse tail hair on the dining table, but she'd offer to clean it up. And leave the waitress a very good tip.

She spread out several napkins and placed the notions between them, along with Sylvie's written instructions. Together, they started making friendship bracelets while taking periodic breaks to check on Mischief.

The first couple Jess made were a mess. Taylor's were much prettier. They could always make more in Montana. What they were accomplishing now was perfect.

Once they'd finished five, Taylor spread them out on the table. The early sunrise coming through the window illuminated the beauty of what they'd created together.

"Which one do you like best?" Taylor asked.

Jess had a favorite, all right. She pointed to the last one Taylor had made. It was going to look perfect next to those friendship bracelets that her daughter loved so much.

Taylor picked it up and double-checked the ties to

make sure they were stitched on tight, then reached over and draped it across her mom's wrist.

Jess's breath hitched. This couldn't be happening.

"A friendship bracelet? For me?" she asked.

Taylor secured the tie. "Of course. You're my friend."

It was all Jess could do to hold back her tears. Meanwhile, Taylor inspected the others they'd created together.

"Which one do you think your daddy would have liked?" Jess dared to ask. "We'll take it when we visit him at the cemetery."

Whether it was the right thing to say in the moment, or completely wrong, Jess knew that Lance had been Taylor's friend, too. Maybe even her best friend.

Taylor sat up straighter and selected the bracelet with the thickest weave, then picked it up.

"This one," she said.

Jess nodded. "I agree. I think we've earned a hot chocolate for the road. What do you think?" Not that either of them needed more sugar, but the diner was beginning to fill up and they'd best head out anyway.

Taylor nodded, looked directly at her and smiled.

Jess waved at the waitress.

"More pancakes?" the woman asked.

It was a reasonable question. Between the two of them, they'd cleaned the plate.

"Can we get two hot chocolates to go? And the check, whenever you're ready."

"Extra marshmallows please," Taylor added.

"That's the only way to drink it." The waitress finished tallying the damage, tore it from the pad, and placed it on the table.

Jess took possession of the scissors while her daughter collected the thread and remaining strands of horsehair. Taylor picked out one of the bracelets that Jess had made and wrapped it around her own wrist while struggling with the tie.

Jess reached over to help.

"Thanks, Mommy. I really like this one."

The waitress returned with their hot chocolate in the biggest insulated to-go cups Jess had ever seen.

"Hope these fit in your drink holder. Needed plenty of room for those marshmallows."

Taylor pulled the top off hers, peered inside and took a long sip. When she came up for air, she had the biggest grin. Along with a white marshmallow mustache.

"Hmm, looks like my friend is being silly," Jess said.

"Nash taught me this after he showed me how to pinkie shake," Taylor said.

That. She'd all but forgotten.

"Do you think Daddy would be proud of me?" Taylor asked.

The question took Jess aback.

"Of course. He was your biggest fan." She wanted

to add *next to me*, but this wasn't about her. Maybe it never had been.

"Mr. Nash told me that Daddy would want me to have fun, even though he isn't here to have fun with me."

Jess took several moments to process the fact that this was what Taylor had revealed to Nash. The thing that he'd left her daughter to reveal. Furthermore, he was right to do so. This moment was so special. Furthermore, she and Taylor didn't even need a pinkie promise for it to be revealed. They had something even stronger: a mother-daughter friendship.

"Mr. Nash was exactly right. So let's go have lots of fun in Billings. Then we'll go back through Destiny Springs so you can see your friends and have even more."

With that, all of Jess's grand plans unraveled, along with her confidence. What if the fact that they'd both broken their promises to each other didn't level the playing field, much less raze that wall of his?

All she knew was that she had to try. If nothing else, she wanted to repair any damage she'd done to the twins, even if it required a full-on confrontation with their daddy.

She realized that sometimes the most logical plans and patterns benefitted from alterations and could even end up with a more perfect fit. With any luck, he would realize that, too. She'd found her perfect fit in Destiny Springs. With Nash.

If it wasn't too late.

CHAPTER NINETEEN

"THERE YOU ARE, Parker. We need to talk," Nash said.

Parker had hightailed it out of the house and to the calving barn the moment Nash walked back into the house with Kat. Even Gus had trouble keep up with the guy.

His ranch hand stopped petting the calf, rose from his squatting position and brushed off his hands. "I'm all ears."

"First, I owe you an apology," Nash said.

"For what?"

"For being so hard on you for not listening. And for putting up a wall. At least, that's what I do, according to Hailey. And Jess. I put one up with you. I know your heart is in the right spot. By contrast, my heart's been all over the place lately."

Parker straightened his cowboy hat, widened his stance and folded his arms.

"That's one lousy apology, Nash. I can't accept it."

Huh? It felt as though he'd spilled his deepest thoughts and feelings and they were both neck-deep in it.

"And why's that?" Nash asked.

"Because I *did* listen to you in putting together the proposal."

"Um. No, you didn't. With all due respect, you're as stubborn as your grandfather."

"That's quite a compliment. Hopefully, I'm as wise. Although Vern is more eloquent."

Why did Nash feel as though he were losing this argument, even though he was the only one making sense?

Parker continued. "I stand by my proposal. I listened, but more to what you *didn't* say. Your lack of enthusiasm for cattle ranching. The smile that you failed miserably to suppress when you talked about coaching Taylor. The footnotes in your ledgers."

"I wrote footnotes?"

"Yeah. Read more like a diary. Most of the comments were about Jess."

Nash closed his eyes. It started coming back to him. He had written notes about the progress of the students. Thankfully, nothing personal. Or had he?

"I even know how you sneak out to the greenhouse," Parker continued. "Which is why I suggested adding some crops. We could start small. Cucumbers, tomatoes, eggplant. Maybe even participate in the farmers market. Expand from there. You have a lot of land that could be put to use if you don't go the full-on cattle ranch route."

"You've been spying on me?" Nash tried to joke.

The fact that Parker had nailed it so precisely based on what Nash *hadn't* said was a little unsettling. Nash had read the proposal, in its entirety, last night when he couldn't sleep. It managed to keep his mind from wondering why Jess had snuck out of the house. And, ultimately, out of his life once again.

Now he knew why. He'd never let her in. Not completely. Only for certain moments, and he shut her out as quickly.

"You're hard to miss, so I suppose I spied on you accidentally. As far as walls go, those don't deter me. I can see right through them. It's my superpower. You just need to have a little trust," Parker said.

Nash shifted his stance. "I disagree with one thing."

"Oh, yeah?"

"You're as eloquent as Vern, if not more so. I'm glad you didn't listen to my words, because I accept your business proposal. Perhaps with a few modifications. And I trust you to look after the ranch while the girls and I go to Montana for a few days. Gus can even sleep at my house. Just move anything he might be tempted to destroy."

Ambitious and impulsive, perhaps. Yet, the other three heifers weren't due for another week or two, and the new momma and baby were doing fine. No storms were on the horizon. Except for one, and that was only if he didn't try to fix this situation with Jess right away.

Parker was all smiles, which was somewhat comforting. Except confidence wouldn't be enough to get him through some of the issues he might encounter.

"Before you get too excited, I want reinforcements in place," Nash said.

"Since I knew you'd eventually come to your senses and go with my proposal, I've already put out some feelers. Grandpa's ranch hand Trent offered to be on call in case I need help, and Cody made a standing offer to pitch in. Then there's Gus. Free labor all around."

"Which brings me around to my proposal. Since Gus and Sergeant seem to have irreconcilable differences, how about he stays here with me and the girls at night, or whenever he needs to? That way, he'll have two families who care for him. Two homes. And you'll get to see him all day because, yes, I want to hire him," Nash said.

Parker dropped his head. Was the guy about to cry?

"You win. Your proposal is better than mine," his ranch hand said.

"I don't know about that. I didn't type it up and put it on fancy paper like you did. But I appreciate the vote of confidence."

Parker extended his hand, but Nash pulled him in for a solid cowboy hug instead.

"I'll let Gus take over from here. I have something to add to the chore board. Do you mind watching the girls outside for about ten minutes, if I send 'em your way?" Nash asked.

"It would be my pleasure."

Once alone in the house, Nash grabbed the marker, jotted a clear directive on the board, then snapped the cap back on and admired his artwork. Only one word.

YES.

Yes to letting Kat learn about barrel racing and seeing where that leads. *Yes* to getting a dog that they could share with the Donnellys. *Yes* to teaching again, although this time he'd focus on the students who were most important...and not get distracted.

Nash hopped online and submitted a late entry for Kat in Billings. If they kicked back for any reason, he still had connections over there. He'd pull some strings. Kat was a rookie, but it was an open rodeo. She wouldn't even advance beyond slack, but that was fine. Kat wasn't ready to compete. Not by a long shot. Neither was Sugar Pie. Although the horse was sound, she needed instruction. Plenty of time to perfect that.

However, time felt as though it was running out when it came to winning Jess back, and that meant convincing her that his wall-constructing days were over. He never wanted to give her any reason to run away, ever again.

He did have one more idea that might help win her over.

The girls busted through the door right at the ten-minute mark. He pulled out all the ingredients that Jess had left behind.

"Ladies, I need your help. We're gonna make

cupcakes and sugar pies to take on the road tomorrow. We'll need enough to leave some for Parker, and to share with Jess and Taylor when we get to Montana."

It took the girls a few minutes to realize the magnitude of what he was saying. Lizzy was especially excited.

"We're going to Montana *and* we get to make cupcakes?" Lizzy asked.

"And decorate them with daisies if you want to," he added.

"Yesss!" Lizzy practically jumped out of her skin.

"We get to watch Taylor in the rodeo?" Kat asked.

It wasn't lost on him that she didn't care anything about the desserts in this moment.

"We sure do. We'll also get to watch you, if you want to go around the barrels. Nothing faster than a trot. That's my only rule."

Kat looked at him in disbelief. Then her smile grew so big that he caught a glimpse of those dimples before she wrapped her arms around his neck.

"I guess that's a yes," he managed to say. That made two *yeses* he'd collected so far.

He had one more very important, life-changing one to go.

JESS ALWAYS LOVED the morning slack times. So much fun to watch the talent within the overflow of contestants, but without the noisy crowds that the performances drew.

Today, however, she had a different reason for being there.

The bleachers were quite stark, so she had her pick of the seats. She went to the top for the best view. Taylor was in the warm-up pen, as were the other contestants, so Jess was on her own.

All of her rodeo mom projects had been completed and delivered to their respective hotel rooms except for the one she was holding. The box containing the Dudley project.

She'd finally mustered the courage to peek inside in case she needed to make any last-minute modifications. What she found was a beautifully executed two-piece yellow-and-black tweed suit, with pale yellow satin lining, black chiffon cuffs and black velvet trim. No wonky stitching. No uneven hems. No loose threads. Dorothy had exceeded Jess's expectations. Hopefully, she'd exceed Mrs. Dudley's, as well.

The wait, it seemed, was over. Although they'd never met in person, Jess recognized the woman from her blog. Jess set the box down, then stood and waved.

The woman waved back and navigated the myriad steps to join her.

After they introduced themselves and were situated, Jess got down to business and handed her the box.

"Feels like Christmas," Mrs. Dudley said with a huge smile as she ran her palms over the lid.

Jess bit her lip, grateful that there wasn't a lump

of coal inside the box. If the garment hadn't been up to par, Jess would have taken full ownership of it anyway. She also proudly refused to learn her lesson about not being honest about everything. Her unwillingness to throw Taylor under the bus had backfired, but she'd do it all over again to protect her daughter from any blame Jess should ultimately shoulder. Same applied to her sewing soulmate.

The competition started in the arena, and they both watched the first barrel racer. Wasn't either of their girls.

"The time of 24.184 seconds going to Angie Cartwright, Dallas, Texas," the announcer said over the loudspeaker.

Second competitor, same story. It was neither of their girls.

Being seasoned at this, they both knew they had about thirty seconds to chat before the next one's turn.

Mrs. Dudley opened the box. When she pulled out the jacket, she audibly gasped. Same with the skirt.

She pulled out a folded piece of paper and flipped it over, where someone had written Jess's name on the front. Jess hadn't even noticed it inside the box. Must have been buried at the bottom.

"Looks like this is for you, dear," Mrs. Dudley said.

Jess opened the note.

Thanks for letting me help. I hope I did your heart justice. Thankfully, I was able to rob some black velvet from my room-themed gift bathrobe to add the accents you wanted. Hope that's okay!

It was way more than okay. If Dorothy were there, Jess would assure her that she'd gone above and beyond what was expected. As soon as she and Taylor got back to Destiny Springs, Jess would request the Velvet Room, if available, and she'd send that complimentary robe to Dorothy.

"That will be a time of 20.132 seconds for Sophie Pendleton, Flagstaff, Arizona," the speaker announced.

The next rider took her position at the gate.

"Oh! That's Meghan!" Mrs. Dudley said. Jess squeezed her arm, hoping for the best while secretly rooting for her own daughter.

"Time of 19.520 seconds to Meghan Dudley, Albuquerque, New Mexico," the announcer said.

The best time so far. This was the first run, though. Still a chance for Taylor to beat it.

Mrs. Dudley returned her attention to the suit, examining the yellow satin lining. "I love this! Makes it so expensive-looking. And these chiffon cuffs are precious! I'm not a seamstress, but it must have been tricky to get these so perfect."

Jess nodded. *Yes, it must have been.*

They glanced up in time to see the next rider, who looked to be one of the youngest ones, based on her size. She didn't appear completely confident in her seat.

"Isn't that the cutest thing you've ever seen?" Mrs. Dudley asked.

"Adorable." Especially the way the little girl trotted around the barrels instead of running. Upon a closer look, the pink shirt with the black piping looked awfully familiar. As did the horse. And the girl herself.

When Jess finally figured out why, her breath caught in her throat. *It can't be.* The crowd, which had grown in size, went wild as the little cowgirl took it home with a determined trot.

"We have a time of 49.538 seconds going to Katherine Buchanan, Destiny Springs, Wyoming," said the announcer.

That did it. Jess couldn't have stopped the waterworks if she'd wanted. She searched the stands for Nash and Lizzy through the blur of tears but didn't see them. They were probably with Kat behind the scenes, smothering her with hugs and kisses.

"Well, what have we here?" Mrs. Dudley asked as she turned the jacket inside out.

Jess wiped away the moisture from her eyes and cheeks with the back of her hand. She'd all but forgotten the woman was there, looking at the garment that could possibly launch the next phase of Jess's career.

"Looks like a tiny yellow heart," the woman said.

Or a mistake. Jess leaned in closer. Definitely a little heart, embroidered into the inside front panel in dark yellow thread that complimented the lighter yellow lining. A hidden treasure. That wasn't in her design specifications to Dorothy. The woman must have added it as her special touch.

Yet, didn't Dorothy write that she hoped she'd done Jess's heart justice?

Jess remembered clearly now. She'd fallen asleep on the pattern paper, and her mascara had left a mark in the shape of a heart. Dorothy must have thought it was intentional and added her interpretation of what the mark meant.

"That's exactly what it is," Jess said. "Western wear with heart."

Mrs. Dudley looked at her square in the eye. "That would make a wonderful company name. Not that your name alone isn't lovely, but a proper one would look good on a garment label, too. Just thinking out loud."

"Mrs. Dudley—"

"Please, call me Carol Anne."

Jess smiled. "That is a brilliant suggestion, Carol Anne. I'll have to clear it with my associate, Dorothy Lawrence, but I'd love to use it. For now, for this project, I want Dorothy to get full credit for executing this garment so beautifully. I'll give her your contact information for the blog, if that's okay."

"Are you sure, dear? Isn't it your design?"

"Very sure. My design was nothing more than a vision in my head, and lines and curves and notches on pieces of dot paper. Dorothy breathed life into it."

"Well, either way I'm thrilled. I can't wait for

Meghan to try this on. Better go check on her now, if you'll excuse me."

"Of course!" Jess had some checking on to do herself. She'd yet to see Nash or Lizzy, but her peripheral vision had been working overtime.

Taylor hadn't had her turn yet, either, and Jess wasn't about to miss it.

She stood and did a visual sweep of the bleachers as another racer took her turn. That's when she noticed three familiar people standing at the bottom. One big one. Two little ones. Looking up.

At me.

Her heart was beating out of her chest, but it was tamed by Nash's smile. One odd thing, however. His arms were crossed. The twins, by contrast, were wiggling and giggling and waving. She headed down the steps as fast as her feet would take her.

They had the same idea and headed up the stairs. At the halfway point, she found herself eye level with the crush of her dreams.

"I'm not going to let you run away again, Ms. McCoy. Not until you know how sorry I am for shutting you out. And not until you mend this. You're the only one who can." Nash placed his hand over his heart. Over that tiny hole in his threadbare flannel shirt.

"You said it wasn't necessary."

"I was wrong."

The breeze blew his hair ever so slightly over his eyes, but he didn't blink. Neither could she.

"Daddy! It's Taylor!" Lizzy screamed, breaking the trance.

Jess peeked around Nash in time to see Taylor glance up at the stands and wave.

"Everyone sit," Nash demanded.

They all clamored for the closest seats, and just in time. They seemed to hold a collective breath as Taylor made a strong start, then circled the barrels and took it home in record time.

"That was 17.316 seconds! Let's hear it for Taylor Simms, Rock Springs, Wyoming," the announcer said.

Jess jumped up from her seat. They all did. It was Taylor's personal best, and she was in the lead so far. Barring any mistakes on the second run, the little girl could win the top prize tonight.

And barring any mistakes on her own part, Jess could, too.

CHAPTER TWENTY

WHAT ARE YOU thinking about out there, Taylor? Jess was dying to know.

Whatever it was had put a fire beneath the little girl as she rounded the first barrel, then the second, then...

Jess held her breath and didn't dare blink. She did take a quick glance at the man sitting beside her, along with his two adorable daughters, if only to assure herself that this wasn't a dream.

Jess's guy. That would be a good nickname for Nash, because she was going to insist that he retire his grumpy pants. The new nickname would complement the long list of keepers: friend, teacher, Juicy Lucy maker, joke swapper...

Back in the day when he was all of those, Nash had asked her what thoughts went through her head during a competition. She remembered that answer so clearly, because it always resulted in a win.

I imagine the thing I want most is waiting at the finish line. The faster I get there, the sooner it's mine.

She didn't even have to hear the time to know

that Taylor had won. Didn't need to hear the roar of the crowd, or the loud-and-proud "Bravo!" from *her guy*. Jess knew.

The whole crowd knew.

"C'mon, ladies. Let's go back there to see her," Nash said.

They shimmied past a family and rushed down the steps. Lizzy and Kat launched into a run.

"Slow down, girls! Stay where we can see you," Nash called out, but they kept going.

He turned to Jess. "Nobody listens to me."

"Did you say something?"

Nash pulled her in and gave her a huge lip smack on the side of her head.

The twins turned around, ran back and circled around her and Nash.

"Looks like you spoke too soon," Jess said.

Lizzy took the lead. "I should be a barrel racer, too."

Nash dropped his chin in a gesture that looked like defeat.

Jess put her arm around his waist and rested her head on his shoulder. "You've got this."

The girls spotted Taylor, who was having her and Mischief's picture taken by people on their cell phones. Lizzy unapologetically photobombed the whole thing, while Kat had the discipline to stay out of the frame.

Nash and Jess stopped even farther away, but close enough to breathe it all in.

But there was something that needed to be said, in the spirit of total transparency.

"You probably already know. But in case you don't, Roxanne is here tonight. Somewhere."

Nash didn't even miss a beat when he looked at Jess and said, "Roxanne who?"

"It's okay. She's part of your past."

Nash kissed the tip of her nose, then moved down to claim a quick kiss on the lips.

"You're right. My past. *Not* my future. Or even my present. I didn't even think to consider whether she'd be here tonight."

Jess knew he was telling the truth. He hadn't looked around even once.

Nash continued. "I can't protect the girls from everything for the rest of their lives. We'll face other obstacles. Plenty of 'em."

"But we can face them together," she added. *And never run away.*

"Don't tell Taylor this, but she wasn't the main reason we came all the way to Billings," Nash said.

"Oh, I know. You realized that barrel racing is what Kat is destined to do and what will make her happy. You get bonus points for making it happen," Jess said.

"There's that, too. But my trip here is more about what you and I are destined to do."

A thrill raced up Jess's spine. "And what's that?"

Nash looked at her with those soft brown eyes. "Make cupcakes and sugar pies. What else? You told the girls you'd take a rain check. I'm holding you to it."

"I know. I also left without saying goodbye." Jess knew she was stating the obvious, but if they were destined to move forward, they needed to put everything out in the open.

Nash took a deep breath and blew it out. "I don't blame you, Jess."

He looked at her now, the softness of his eyes warming her back up.

"I have trouble embracing confrontation, but if you're willing to embrace what I'm about to tell you, that's all that matters." He pulled her in. "I'm going to start teaching again, but I need a partner. In love and in life, and in everything that entails."

Was that a marriage proposal? Kind of sounded like one. It could also be a business proposal. Or maybe both.

"I'll let you know if I think of anyone," she said, adding a smile. Not quite a joke, but she needed to be sure.

"I have someone in mind, but I'm afraid that if I say her name out loud, one of Destiny Springs's most popular rumors will be put to rest. That won't leave folks much to talk about," he said.

"Which rumor? There are so many," she said.

"The one about Roxanne not being the one to break my heart and drive me away from teaching. That there was another woman."

Jess's breath hitched. "I heard that rumor. If you'll tell me her name, I promise to never repeat it."

"I'm pretty sure people will figure it out. For now, let's call her Nash's gal."

He winked.

She melted.

"Be honest. You have more than one gal, don't you?" Jess asked.

As expected, Nash pulled back and pinched his eyebrows together. She nodded toward the twins.

"Ahh, yes. You're right about that. And my little barrel racer might soon become The One to Watch," he said.

Jess's competitive spirit nudged her to respond.

"I'm afraid you may be right. But she'd have Taylor to thank for that." Realizing what she'd just done, Jess clapped her hands over her mouth.

Nash pulled her even closer. "It's okay. I know she coached Kat."

"How did you find out?" Jess asked.

"Hailey sold me on the theory. You just confirmed it."

Jess shook her head. Although Nash and Hailey weren't siblings, they could pass as fraternal twins much of the time.

"I hope you won't be mad at Taylor," she said.

"That isn't possible. As long as she hasn't revealed our secret weapon without clearing it with me first."

"She told me about how you convinced her that her daddy wanted her to have fun."

"There is that."

"You mean there's something else she hasn't told me?"

"Apparently," he said.

Jess squinted. "I do wonder what she was thinking about today, and what she envisioned was waiting at the finish line."

At that, Nash cocked his head. "So she *did* tell you what we discussed."

There it was. Another accusation. Jess matched his gesture for effect. "No. Why would you think that?"

"Because that's what I told her to think about to get her over the hump. To imagine that what she wanted most was waiting for her at the finish line and—"

"The faster she gets there, the sooner it would be hers. You're really gonna take credit for my secret formula?" Jess asked.

Nash pulled away, put his hands on his hips and huffed. She matched his body language. They had a stare-off for a good fifteen seconds, until he caved. He dropped his chin, then covered his face with both hands and shook his head.

"You did tell me that, didn't you?" he said.

"Um, yeah. I'm afraid so," she said.

"I guess that means you ultimately get credit for helping her."

Jess looked to Taylor, who was waving at them. Make that, waving at Nash. Maybe Jess deserved credit in a roundabout way, but she had no intention of taking any of it.

Once the little girl finally looked away, Jess presented her pinkie finger to Nash. "I won't tell her about it if you don't."

Instead of hooking his pinkie onto hers, he straightened out her hands and kissed the top of her ring finger instead.

"I'd rather we make a promise to each other in a more permanent way."

Jess gulped. Was this really about to happen? She didn't get a romantic proposal the first time, from Lance. Nor did they get a proper wedding, complete with bridesmaids and organ music and lots of flowers. Not that she needed any of those things to be happy with someone. But she had given up her career to build a home—one that ended up being built on shifting sand.

This time, it would be on solid ground, and in a town that she'd fallen in love with as deeply as she had with Nash. Now, the thought of having a home was…*freeing*.

But she was getting ahead of herself. They weren't at the finish line quite yet.

"Is there something you want to ask?" She offered up her most dreamy look. Might as well give him an encouraging nudge because the suspense was killing her.

He shifted his stance and looked to the ground. Instead of kneeling, he crossed his arms and said, "As a matter of fact, I do."

"I'm listening," she said.

The poor guy looked terrified.

"What did the cowgirl say to the rancher when he asked her to marry him?"

So much for the romantic proposal, although it was super adorable. As was his nervousness. She knew the answer to this one, but she simply smiled instead. She wasn't going to make it that easy for him, although she was determined to get everything she wanted.

Hopefully, Lizzy would be willing to give the bottom half of her wedding dress pattern back—the piece that the little girl had drawn all over—if only temporarily. Even though Jess hadn't officially accepted, she already had the perfect spot for their nuptials in mind. She also intended to have the original wedding dress of her dreams, because it would fit in beautifully there.

With one very important modification.

Okay, so his setup for the proposal didn't get the punch line response he'd hoped for. She hadn't said no, either. Nash still had one thing left in his bag of tricks.

"While you're thinking about that, do you mind corralling the girls? Looks like they're wrapping things up in the ring. I need to run to the truck," he said, then sprinted away before she asked any questions.

He reached to the floorboard of the back seat of the cab. Fortunately, neither twin had stomped on the box. Taking it slow and easy, he carried it back to the pen area where he'd left all his gals, dodging enthusiastic little barrel racers and their friends and family along the way.

No doubt Jess would be expecting a much smaller box with something less fragile inside, but that was next on his list. For now, this should be a sweet surprise.

As he approached, he noticed how the girls seemed to be hanging on Jess's every word. He didn't know what they were talking about, but they turned silent as soon as he approached. They also smiled in unison, so whatever it was had to be good.

He pivoted the box so that the flap was facing them, then opened it.

"Our cupcakes and sugar pies!" Lizzy called out.

"Yes. But these are special. I decorated these after you ladies went to bed." Nash reached into the box and retrieved the one he'd decorated with Taylor in mind. It had a lopsided icing barrel drawn on top. For Kat, he'd executed a squiggly number eight. For Lizzy, he retrieved the one with her favorite flower. Or, at least a reasonable facsimile.

"It's a lazy daisy, like you taught me to draw with six petals," Lizzy said to Jess.

"It's also a barrel racing drill," Nash said. "Maybe Taylor and Jess can show Kat how to do it."

The little girls looked at each other, then back at Nash with huge smiles.

"Are we splitting that one?" Jess asked about one that had nothing more than a smear of vanilla icing.

"Nope. That's mine. This one is yours." He pushed

aside a piece of tissue paper that had separated one of the cupcakes from the others. He'd piled this one with flowers of all shapes and sizes and colors, taking inspiration from all of Lizzy's drawings. What it lacked in floral beauty, it made up for in height.

Jess lifted it out of the box and cradled it as if it was topped with a cluster of diamonds.

"Hopefully it will taste better than it looks," he said.

She smiled. "What do you mean? It's beautiful! But I'll let you know," she said, taking a huge bite out of the thing. Nash took a bite of his cupcake, as well. And another. Before he was halfway through, the girls had already demolished theirs and had started on the sugar pies.

While the twins were distracted, he turned his full attention to Jess. There was something he needed from her.

"I'm still waiting for an answer," Nash said, launching into the *Jeopardy!* tune. Not that a marriage proposal was a joking matter, but he'd never been so nervous in his life. The longer she took to answer, the worse it got.

Jess finished her last bite of cupcake, wiped her hands on a napkin and motioned for him to follow. They stopped far enough away from the girls that they wouldn't be able to hear. All of a sudden, a sharp pain shot through his heart at the possibility that she intended to let him down easy.

She faced him and took both of his hands in hers. "What was that question again?"

Nash cocked his head. Even though he'd concluded that his original proposal wasn't the least bit romantic, it wasn't forgettable.

Yet, he recognized this as a second chance to get it exactly right. And he was going to take it. After all, he got another chance with their relationship. From now on, he vowed not to make the same mistakes. He'd probably make some new ones, but hopefully she'd be just as forgiving of those.

Nash gave her hands a gentle squeeze and looked into her eyes. *Those eyes.* He took a cue from Parker and listened to what she wasn't saying. Sure enough, he got the answer he wanted. The only thing left to do was take it home. He cleared his throat.

"Will you be my gal, forever?" he asked.

She opened her mouth to answer, but he was faster.

"No…wait. Let me start over. Will you marry me, Jessica McCoy? Because I love you. I always have and always will."

"I love you, too. My answer is yes. There never would have been any other."

Nash didn't care who saw what he was about to do next. He leaned in and kissed her. After a moment that probably lasted only a few seconds but would stay with him forever, she pulled away and licked her lips. "Wow. That was really sweet."

"In more ways than one." It wasn't merely a cliché. The moment was sweet, as was the residual taste of the cupcakes between them. Then he noticed something else. How could he have missed it?

Easy. He'd been lost in her eyes.

Should I tell her? He couldn't hide his grin.

"What?" she asked.

"Oh, nothing. I've just never kissed a woman with a mustache before."

Her eyes widened. She wiped at her upper lip. "Why didn't you tell me?"

"Because I'd rather you see me smiling instead of crying if you'd said no." It wasn't a complete lie. He'd been too caught up in and nervous about the proposal to notice the icing.

"You thought that was a possibility?" she asked.

"The fact that you're standing here at all makes me believe that anything is possible." With his thumb, he wiped the last remnants of icing from above her upper lip.

"You still have one, too," she said, doing the same for him. "When should we tell the girls?

Nash looked at them and exhaled. As perfect as this all seemed, they had a lot of things to figure out. Jess needed to know what she was getting into. Full transparency.

"How do you feel about semi-adopting a boy?"

Jess's eyes widened. "Um, I haven't given it any thought, although I love the thought of having a boy. I'm not familiar with semi-adoption. Is that like fostering? Can we wait until after the honeymoon to decide?"

Nash put on his most serious expression and shook his head. "I'm afraid not. In fact, I've already committed to letting Gus live at our house as long as necessary. Maybe forever."

Jess squinted and looked at him sideways. "Parker's dog?"

Nash nodded.

"As long as you don't let him sleep between us," she said.

Nash pulled her closer. "Not a chance. What I really wanted to ask was, are you willing to embrace being the wife of a cattle-ranching, barrel-racing teacher who grows crops in his greenhouse and sells them at the local farmers market?"

"Only if you're willing to embrace a rodeo mom who is the CEO of her own company."

Her own company? Nash closed his eyes and tried to remember if she'd told him about that, even though such information would be hard to forget. His mind drew a blank.

"Don't look so nervous," she continued. "I have a sewing soulmate who wants, and needs, the work. You can thank Parker and Vanessa for putting that idea in her head, and the idea of thinking about having a home business with employees in mine. It would free me up to do more of the actual designing and pattern making, which are my favorite parts of the process anyway. Oh, and marketing, starting with Kavanaugh's. I'll have more flexibility to take our girls to compete in rodeos if you can't get away."

"I'm good with anything you and the girls want

to pursue, as long as you promise to come back every time."

"If the door is open to me, I'll always come home."

Nash made a mental note to thank Parker and Vanessa. Oh, and Hailey and Vern and the rest of Destiny Springs for helping him realize that the walls he constructed at times didn't protect him. Rather, they kept out the love he wanted.

That much was clear. Otherwise, his brain felt scrambled even thinking about how to juggle their combined responsibilities, and shuffle two—maybe three—little girls to and from rodeos around the country. Also, he and Jess might be apart from each other at stretches.

For now, she was in his arms, and there was only one thing to do about it.

This time, their kiss lasted more than a few seconds. He was hoping to exceed Kat's barrel racing time of 49.538. Maybe set a new national record. And he would have, except it was interrupted by something even better than winning. And infinitely sweeter than icing. A trio of giggles only a few yards away. From the girls.

Our girls.

EPILOGUE

Two months later

"NICE FRIENDSHIP BRACELET," Parker said, pointing to Nash's wrist.

Nash pulled up his black tuxedo jacket sleeve, bent his elbow, held the horsehair jewelry eye level and rotated his hand like he was some sort of royal in a parade, waving at the crowd.

In reality, he was standing in his own arena, smack-dab in the middle of the three barrels that now had flowers painted all over them. His and Jess's closest friends and relatives were sitting patiently in uncomfortable-looking wooden foldout chairs that framed the imaginary dirt aisle.

"Thanks. My daughter Taylor made it for me."

Technically, his soon-to-be legally adopted daughter. Nash couldn't wait to get that process started, along with Jess adopting the twins.

Parker lifted his jacket sleeve, as well. "She made one for me, too."

His ranch hand raised his wrist so they could

both get a closer look, twisting the bracelet around to the opposite side to show off the suede tie details.

"Good. Saves me from having to make you one since you're my best friend and all," Nash said. He had to bite his lip to keep from laughing. From the corner of his eye, he could tell that his ranch hand was about to burst.

Today, Parker was more than a ranch hand, or even a best friend. He was the best man.

"That hurts. I was going to make one for you, but now…" Parker said.

At that, Nash snorted. Couldn't hold it in any longer. That's all it took to make Parker start shaking as he attempted to contain the laughter. The guy's eyes were even watering. After all, this was a serious occasion. And they had an audience.

Truth be told, that bracelet was one of the sweetest gifts Nash had ever received, and he was certain Parker felt the same way. The laughter was more out of nervousness. The wedding was supposed to start twenty minutes ago, and all sorts of awful scenarios were stampeding across his imagination.

He corralled such thoughts with a more reasonable one: Jess had been one busy gal lately.

Even though she was staying at the B and B, Nash had given her a key to *their* house. She'd already transformed the kitchen. The curtains and chair cushions were new, the cabinet was stocked with all sorts of cookware, and the scent of fresh-cut flowers greeted him every time he walked through the door.

Then, when Taylor picked up a sponsorship from a national boot company, Jess helped secure Kavanaugh's Clothing and Whatnot as a sponsor for Kat. All while selling Ethan on the idea of carrying children's clothing from her and Dorothy's new company—Western Wear with Heart.

And, of course, there were the rodeos: Taylor had been in two more competitions since Billings—and placed first both times.

It wore him out just thinking about all that Jess had been up to.

Nash had been busy, too, building a student roster that wouldn't pose a conflict of interest with his most important student of all...his own daughter. Thank goodness Lizzy got over the itch to compete. Instead, she'd been mastering the art of cupcake baking and decorating. She even made the wedding cupcakes for all their guests, with Georgina's help at the B and B.

Speaking of his go-getter, she entered the arena, running at full speed. The little bridesmaid was out of breath by the time she reached him.

"Is everything okay?" he asked.

"Yeah. We're almost ready. Miss Dorothy had to sew her in her dress." Lizzy bolted back toward the house before Nash could ask what that even meant. Wasn't going to attempt to explain anything to all the folks staring at him with questioning looks.

Instead, Nash crossed his hands in front of him and tried to resist the urge to rock back and forth on his heels.

Parker leaned in and whispered, "I feel like we should sing or tap dance or something."

Nash was about to say, "Maybe you could entertain 'em with one of your workshops," but the officiant finally appeared, saving him and his best friend from a bad joke.

"She's getting sewn into her dress, so…" Nash explained to the lady once she got situated.

The officiant nodded and smiled as if it were perfectly normal.

Maybe it was. He had no recollection of his wedding to Roxanne. For the life of him, he couldn't remember anything about the dress she wore, either.

Finally, the twins appeared on horseback. Both in matching pink satin pantsuits with faux fur cropped jackets and white cowgirl boots. They walked their horses around the cloverleaf, single file, with Kat in the lead and Lizzy following behind. Once done, Kat and Sugar Pie stood on Nash's side. Lizzy and Cupcake stood on Jess's, leaving room for the maid of honor, Nash assumed.

Next came Taylor, on foot, looking so grown-up in a long fitted pink satin dress and cropped faux fur jacket that matched the twins'. She was carrying a small bouquet of daisies, held together with a satin tie, her hands slightly shaking.

Is she cold? With the sun about to set, the temperature had started to drop. The twins looked comfortable.

Nash couldn't stand it any longer. He removed his tuxedo jacket, then stepped over and draped it across Taylor's shoulders before assuming his groom position again. That earned him some smiles and *awws* from the group.

Next down the makeshift aisle was PJ, keeper of the rings. Vanessa had been walking behind him but took a seat with the others. The little boy didn't seem to remember where he was told to stand but ultimately settled in the right place. Next to the best man.

"Earth Angel," Nash said, a little too loud.

"Pardon?" Parker asked.

"Your cousin. That's her nickname."

His best man snickered.

"Is that funny?" Nash asked.

"No. She is an angel. I was thinking about how that's going to throw all the good people of Destiny Springs off. Someone started a rumor that she's more of a *fallen* angel. Not in a bad way. She hasn't had an easy life is all. Maybe this nickname will shut that one down."

Speaking of rumors, Jess hadn't believed Nash that day at the farmers market when he'd claimed to be on a nickname basis with country music star Montgomery "Monty" Legend. But she would believe him as soon as she walked down the aisle and saw him, or at the reception later on.

They stood there for another good five minutes. Nash began softly humming the theme song to *Jeopardy!* as a stress reliever.

"Shhh," the officiant gently admonished.

Not that it was necessary. The whole world

seemed to turn quiet when Jess walked into the arena on her father's arm, while her mom looked on through teary eyes. No music, no talking. Not even any nickering from the horses. Only the sound of her dress *swooshing* with every step she took.

He didn't know a lot about wedding gowns, but weren't they usually white or ivory? Her skirt looked to be covered in some sort of pattern.

As soon as she joined Nash, he recognized the pattern as the drawing that Lizzy had done on that big piece of paper. Right down to the size and number of petals on each of the daisies, best he could tell. Except, the flowers were softer and more muted. The fabric they were printed on was a sheer layer that appeared to float over the white part underneath. How did she do that?

He was about to ask, but the officiant cleared her throat and began. The ceremony itself was a bit of a blur as he got lost in Jess's eyes and didn't come up for air until the "I do's." No telling what he agreed to, but that didn't matter. He was totally present for the most important part: the kiss.

A few camera flashes went off in his periphery, and all of a sudden, they were back in that photo booth. Only this time, he'd have the pictures framed. He was pretty sure that little Max hadn't taken a flattering one, but he held out hopes that Georgina had, since she was a wedding planner in addition to making herself indispensable at the B and B.

As they struck a few more poses for the cell cameras, Jess said, "Sorry I took so long. The special fabric I ordered didn't get delivered until this morning. I wanted this to be perfect."

He kissed the top of her hand. "It was already perfect the moment you said yes."

She wrapped her arms around his neck while smiling for the camera, then turned back to him.

"I respectfully disagree. It was perfect ten years ago. We simply didn't know it."

He couldn't argue with that.

"I almost ran down that aisle tonight," she said.

That gave him an idea.

"We could run down that aisle right now. Toward the finish line so we can start our lives together as fast as possible. I'll help carry the train. It'll be a good workout for my arms," he teased. That really was some dress. Abundantly beautiful, like the flowers that graced the fabric. Most of all, beautiful like her.

"No need to strain yourself. I have what I've always wanted most, even though it took ten years instead of sixteen seconds."

The camera flashes reduced to distant stars in his periphery.

Imagine the thing you want most is waiting at the finish line. The faster you get there, the sooner it's yours.

"Is that a confession?" he asked. Back when she first told him about her formula for winning, he hadn't asked what it was that she'd wanted most.

"I suppose it is."

He looked at each of their girls, who were becoming the focus of the wedding paparazzi. If Jess had revealed it a decade ago, they all wouldn't be standing here today. Like this.

Maybe it was his perfect mistake not to ask.

He still wasn't a math whiz. Probably never would be. But he could safely subtract "mistake" from that self-assessment, because what was right in front of him now was nothing short of…

Perfect.

* * * * *

Don't miss the next book in Susan Breeden's Destiny Springs, Wyoming miniseries, coming April 2025 from Harlequin Heartwarming